Hunter's Gambit

Kitsune-Ken, Book 1

Brandy Ackerley

BA

Inked Fox Press

Calgary, Alberta

Edited by Clare Marshall

Cover created by Starla Huchton at DesignedbyStarla.com

ISBN: 978-1-9995165-2-9

Joe, you are my sounding board and soulmate. Without you, this book may have still been published, but it and I would have been poorer for the loss.

Hunter's Gambit

Brandy Ackerley

Chapter 1

Kuzunoha struggled to smile. The lights were dimmed except for the ones near a temporary stage that had been set up beside the bar specifically for tonight's event. The tables had been shoved against the walls. Aside from a few benches, one of which Kuzunoha shared with her sister, the guest of honor, there was standing room only in the bar. A bead of sweat settled against her skin and she rubbed it away, harder than she needed to.

A few feet in front of their bench, standing at the podium, Tim Mason, their regent for the next five minutes, continued his speech. "Our little Himiko is all grown up. Her father worked hard to groom her for this role, knowing one day, she would have control of the family businesses again."

Kuzunoha stretched her tense neck to the left and took a sip of the white grape juice in her cup, grimacing. She'd been drinking wine for years, but tonight she wasn't allowed. She was the younger daughter, after all. If her elder sister was just attaining her majority, then she couldn't be old enough, even though their birthdays were only a month apart. As if they wouldn't notice that she'd been drinking for the last few years. But everything was tied to perception here.

For instance, Himiko hadn't been the only one their father had groomed to take over. Most didn't know that he had also trained his bastard daughter, Kuzunoha as well, knowing full well he'd never give her any say in the company. She'd been used her to whip Himiko into shape and then he'd left her with nothing. No job, no life outside her home.

What sort of monster wouldn't be happy that her sister had come into her majority?

Tim looked at her sister fondly, not even glancing at Kuzunoha. "He'd always hoped to sit at your side and help you through your first few years."

Tim bowed his head in deferential memory of his friend and everyone else followed suit. Kuzunoha refused to bow for him. For any other ancestor, yes, but he deserved nothing from her. Himiko hesitated and lowered her head, pinching Kuzunoha's leg. She gasped but kept her head up. Himiko glared out of the corner of her eye but stayed silent.

Kuzunoha would hear about it later. Her sister would be embarrassed by her lack of respect and what it meant about their family. But Himiko wouldn't do it in the open where anyone could listen. That would have been worse for their image.

"Still, I'll be here to help you hold the reins... not that you aren't already." A ripple of laughter followed.

From anyone else, that comment may have come with a sarcastic edge. Kuzunoha knew it was genuine. Tim had enjoyed working for her father and he'd been the perfect choice for the position. He was a good joint partner, but he didn't want to be the boss.

Compared to his easy smiles, Himiko's looked forced. She'd been ready to take over as soon as their father had died. Instead, she'd patiently worked alongside Tim for the past four years. The silk industry and glass works kept Hidan growing, even during recessions. It was the town's livelihood; everyone was waiting for the day the businesses fell back under Tanaka control.

But not hers. Her father had promised her that she wouldn't be left out, forgotten.

He'd lied.

Tim smiled widely at Himiko, his warm brown eyes wet with tears. When she stood up, Tim made a show of handing her the ledgers, the imprinted leather gleaming warmly, first from the silk mill and then from the glass factory.

There wasn't enough air in the room and what there was smelled of humidity, sweat, and oil. There were too many people; more than even a crowded morning in market. She needed air to clear her head but knew she couldn't leave. It would have been rude… too rude for even a bastard to get away with unpunished.

At the podium, Himiko, raised the ledgers over her head. Everyone applauded and a few whooped. Her short hair, a dark chocolate shade under the lamp lights, was black like Kuzunoha's own, and it hung around her face perfectly, just touching the bottom of her ears, a single tiny braid in the front offset the simple hairstyle. One length of the braid was bright red, dyed professionally a few days before, calling attention to her aristocratic cheekbones. Her clothes, a set of black pants and vest in the Sian Ku style, fitted her in such a way that suggested it had been designed with her sister's slim silhouette in mind. Simple, but powerful, like ink flowing across a page. Her black silk slippers, adorned with a few tastefully placed rubies, held authority without overwhelming opulence.

"Thank you, Tim." Her sister's clear voice rang over the room, quieting everyone in an instant. "I promise that I will do my best to lead our family business, this town, and the Tanaka family to even greater heights.

"Now, let's not waste any of this good food. With respect for both my father, may his rest continue unabated, and the family businesses returning to his heir, everyone's food and drinks will be covered for the evening!"

There was a brief silence, and then the applause deafened those within the Lucky Koi.

Himiko lowered the books, smiling winningly at the crowd. Kuzunoha downed her juice, wishing again that it had been alcoholic.

Some time later, after food had been eaten and a few toasts had been made, it was time for the next thing Kuzunoha dreaded; the social part of the evening. She hadn't been on her own for a full five minutes before the two fishermen had backed her into a corner. She'd met them once before, but she didn't know where. They apparently thought that this gave them special privileges to talk at her, rather than with her.

"Well, she'll be a fine woman to take over your daddy's businesses and I know that she'll watch over your family good," the brown-haired one said.

The man's lighter-haired brother nodded vigorously.

"Not only that, but it will be good to have her over again. It's been a long time since your pappy died, leaving the company floundering."

The smiles they kept sending her way seemed fake and greasy, especially since they refused to meet her gaze. They kept looking to their plates, filled with grilled fish on toast, or at the people around them. Anywhere but at her. She'd come to accept it. No one had ever much liked challenging her, meeting her eyes or talking with her, if they could avoid it. Even now, when they had come up to her, they stood as far from her as they politely could. That insult she could tolerate since, despite having washed recently and wearing their finest, they still smelled like old fish.

"I couldn't be happier for my sister, really." Kuzunoha just wanted the conversation to stop, but she couldn't yet. Protocol demanded that she keep them company for just a bit longer before she could make her escape. It had been grueling so far. One minute of useless niceties and then two of listening to them praise her sister and her father. She would have rather discussed how they went about catching fish each day. At least that topic would have only bored her to tears.

"There was one thing we wanted to know though, miss. Is your sister planning on marrying soon?"

Her smile froze as the other brother continued.

"Because, miss, we wouldn't want this sort of situation to happen again."

"I really don't keep track of my sister's plans, but no, I don't think there are any wedding plans."

"Well, me or my brother here would be more than willing to marry her," the elder one said.

"I'll let her know," Kuzunoha said, turning slightly. Rudeness be damned, she could not handle this conversation anymore.

"I could provide you with an hei…" the younger one began, hesitantly.

Before Kuzunoha could react, the man's brother dragged him away. "He didn't mean nothing, miss. You tell your sister now, please."

"That was brazen," a voice said from behind her.

Kuzunoha turned, seeing Himko's best friend, Isashi. She was sitting alone at one of the small tables, the private ones used for couples or those that preferred dark corners. Kuzunoha didn't know her well, but she knew the choice of table was a preference and not from a lack of options.

"All of them are like that," Kuzunoha said. "When did you get back, Isashi? I heard you were out of town earlier this week."

Isashi may have been the town's only eledar, but she was also one of only five hunters, people that protected them from the dangers of the outside world. Still, Kuzunoha wasn't as afraid of the outside world as many people were. The monsters were just that, monsters. Even though her father had been killed in a raid of the horrid little birdos, a goblin-type creature living nearby that wove bird skulls and feathers into their dress, she didn't fear them.

"Just arrived this morning," Isashi said, her green eyes flitting away from Kuzunoha's, looking behind her rather than at her. Common behavior for a hunter. You had to be good at taking in information quickly to survive. You weren't supposed to follow their gaze when they did that.

Isashi had been young when she had become an eledar. Because of it, she wasn't really human anymore. Her skin had a rough paper-like texture and its shade now mimicked the cool silver of birch bark, rather than the yellow or white skin tones that were more common in Hidan. Her hair hadn't changed when the rest of her had, but tonight she sat directly under one of the candelabras, and its natural red glowed crimson. It was tied in a simple ponytail. She was wearing a similar outfit to Himiko's, except that her vest was an evergreen shade and her pants were a dark brown.

Her appearance was striking, even if she would never be considered pretty.

Kuzunoha opened her mouth and slammed it shut again when Himiko appeared from the crowd behind her and sat down at the table. Her sister slid an orange-tinted ale in front of Isashi and placed a paler one in front of herself.

"I feel like I've been smiling forever. How was your trip?" Himiko asked.

"Short and bittersweet, as usual." Isashi smiled in appreciation as she sipped the ale. "The birdos managed to get their hands on a few of those giant bird eggs. They were trying to breed the ill-tempered creatures. We put a crimp in their plans."

Kuzunoha didn't want to have to deal with her sister until she got home. She tried to make a break for it, ducking her head and stepping backwards. If she'd been anyone else, people may have let her in and she would have faded into the background. Instead, they fanned around her, fish suddenly aware of a predator in their midst.

"Glad to hear, Isashi. I am just glad that your job left you unhurt. As for you, Kuzunoha, your lack of attention at the speech was noticed. The least you could have done was bow your head in public for Father. You haven't been drinking, have you? I told the staff not to give you any, but you never know when someone will take pity on you."

Kuzunoha gritted her teeth at the barrage of questions. "Not yet."

"Well, make sure you don't. We need to keep up appearances and both of us drinking will make the wrong one."

At this point, Kuzunoha could have repeated her words by route. She turned away and pushed through the crowd.

Her sister wouldn't have lied about telling the staff not to serve her alcohol, and she only had one friend who would be willing to get her a drink if she asked. Jack was the illegitimate son of the other noble family in town. Though not as well off as her own family, the Kerlow family was old money.

They'd helped to found the town and the abbey, while her own family had given many of the townsfolk honest work and decent pay.

The Kerlow's main source of revenue now was the docks. They controlled the ships, the docks, and all travel in and out of Hidan by water. It gave his family a lot of power in the village, even if their fortune had declined over the last few years. Their noble cousins lived closer to the capital but had found themselves spending their wealth faster than they could make it through just their vassals. Jack's father and brother were helping them regain their old power. Jack had avoided losing anything in the situation by taking over the illegal market in Hidan. His father didn't approve, but that had never bothered Jack. If anyone would help her get drunk, it would be him.

She let out a breath in annoyance. Of course, when she wanted him, he was nowhere to be found.

Then she smiled. If he'd left already, perhaps that meant she wouldn't be noticed if she slipped out. She wound her way through the crowd, reaching for the door, relieved that soon she'd be able to breathe again.

The door opened, catching her face-first. Kuzunoha tried to step back, but the crowd was unyielding. Someone jostled her. She fell, blinking back stars. Deckard didn't seem to notice as he finished pushing the door the rest of the way open. His eyes were only for his companion behind him.

"—worry. It will be busy, but we should be in time for the dinner. Oh! I'm sorry…"

His weight came down on her foot. Kuzunoha yanked it out from under him. Deckard nearly fell but grabbed the door handle in time to steady himself. Once he had his balance again, he looked down at her in confusion and apology, and then annoyance.

"Kuzunoha, what are you doing on the floor?" He extended a hand to her.

"Getting stepped on by a brutish oaf," she said, slapping his away, though it was her face that was still smarting. Her gaze caught on a tear in the lace shawl that had been her joy and as she stood, she saw a dirt streak on the back of her dress. She put a finger on the hole and batted at the grime. Her dress had been the one good thing about this miserable evening. Now it was ruined.

Her ankle hurt as she put weight on it. She must have slipped on it wrong. She refused to show any weakness. Not in her sister's presence, and gods damn it, not in Deckard's.

"Who is this, Deckard dear?"

The woman behind Deckard touched his shoulder as she spoke. Her skin was just a few shades lighter than her caramel-toned hair, which had been bound into innumerable tiny braids. Hundreds of colored beads clicked together as she moved. Her clothing was so garish and bright that it looked like she'd bought it from a Corvidae, if she wasn't one of the travelling folk already. While the woman wasn't beautiful, she did have a presence that drew the eye.

Deckard introduced her reluctantly. "Tieni, this is Kuzunoha. She's the youngest daughter of the Tanaka family." Nobody important, his description said. Just an arrogant bastard daughter of an arrogant noble.

She put weight on her injured foot and hissed. Deckard reached out a hand. She warmed at the contact and knocked his hand away, hating the way the heat stayed with her.

"I was just leaving," Kuzunoha said.

She stumbled past him, nursing her embarrassment instead of the twinge in her ankle.

Chapter 2

Kuzunoha sighed and walked into the alley. The blacksmith's shed was there, as was the bench that was her destination. She sat down, gasping at the pain that blossomed as soon as she sat down. Lifting it, she started to massage it, daintily. It didn't look that bad. Just a bit of swelling that her rubbing seemed to clear.

She listened to the silence of the night, broken once or twice by the door of the Lucky Koi opening and the general din rolling out. The noise assailed her senses. As the sound disappeared, a couple walked by the front of the alleyway.

The woman was Calla, one of the villagers even more well known for her wandering eye than Kuzunoha was. The boy on her arm was much more interesting: a stranger, young, with darker skin and hair than a Corvidae. His clothes, a dark shirt and jerkin with matching trousers, were old, but serviceable. Landsman outfit, rather than a sailor's digs.

Calla led the man drunkenly around the corner towards her house. Kuzunoha waited a moment before testing her leg. It seemed fine so she walked to the mouth of the alley. The Koi's doors opened again, filling the quiet night with noise once more and she hugged the shadows.

In the alley across from her, a man stepped out of the shadows. He gestured towards the men leaving the Koi.

Kuzunoha's eyes widened. These men were also strangers. Unlike Calla's boy, they looked rough, unshaven. Worse, they were wearing swords and one, a thin brute, was carrying a crossbow. She frowned. It was illegal to carry one in town unless you were a guard or a hunter. The man from the alley gestured again and all three walked past her spot. Kuzunoha slipped further into the darkness of the wall's shadow, watching as they pulled their weapons free. The man with the crossbow and another man stayed to the shadows, following the couple. The other two ducked around a far street.

The man with the crossbow glanced her way, and Kuzunoha gulped in relief when his gaze passed her by. She took a deep breath before peeking around the corner. If Calla were taking the stranger to her home, she would have led him down the second side street. The men were standing at its lip, leaning in. Hunting.

They were planning to ambush them.

She pulled back into the alley across from the Lucky Koi, feeling like the air was too thick to breathe. It would be stupid of her to get involved. These men were better armed than she was and skilled in the business of thuggery. She was one woman and she didn't kid herself. She was fair to middling with her dagger. It was small, meant for protection against an unarmored assailant, and hardly a real weapon. She was lucky she was carrying it today at all. Men grabbing her wasn't much of a problem, but sailors didn't always understand that no meant no.

The sheriff had been at the party. She glanced back at the Koi, wrinkling her nose. The last she'd seen him, he'd been drinking the thick ale like water in the midday heat. She'd be lucky if he was still conscious.

She peeked back around the corner. The men had disappeared into the street. Kuzunoha's hand went to her dagger.

Before she could talk herself out of it, Kuzunoha stalked out of the alley, glad the pain in her foot had disappeared. She took the second path in and ran silently down the thin side street that Calla and the thugs had avoided. Calla would have known that it would have been faster, but none of the strangers would. When she reached the boatswain's home, she crossed his yard, peeking around the home. Surprisingly, most of the lights were off in the homes and she wondered whether everyone was asleep or out at the party.

Calla's breathless laughter filled the street as they pulled apart and continued walking. It took her a few moments to locate the two thugs, well hidden in the darkness afforded by the faint flames sparking in the uneven streetlights. Even if Calla and her boy had been sober, they wouldn't see the men until the last moment.

As she watched, they came around the corner, their blades drawn. As they stepped into the light, their weapons shone revealing pits so uneven they looked toothed. Whoever these men were, they couldn't afford to do proper upkeep on their blades.

Calla's boy yanked her to his side when the woman didn't stop fast enough. His hand was already on his weapon. Maybe he wasn't as drunk as she'd thought. Kuzunoha slipped into the street, stealing forward while she drew her dagger.

"She's changed her mind," the man in front told Calla's stranger. He nodded at the stranger without taking his eyes off him. "Take him but don't bang him up any worse than we have to. She won't be pleased if he isn't in good condition when she gets him back."

The man at Calla's side drew two daggers. "I won't go easily."

Calla frowned at him and the other strangers. "Richie…are these men friends of yours?"

Richie ignored her as the two men dove in, intent to kill clear in their body language. He caught the blade of the first one with his own and stepped nimbly out of the way of the second attacker, who blundered into Calla, still sticking close to Richie's side. She shrieked and squeezed him as if only he could save her but hampering him even more. Amazingly, he continued fighting; a dervish with a short blade in each hand.

The third thug came moved behind them, hoping to catch the man unaware. Calla got in his way, shrieking loud enough that Kuzunoha's ears hurt. The thug tossed her to the side but Richie, with little more than a glance behind him, elbowed his attacker in the face. Kuzunoha blinked, realizing that she hadn't been needed at all. This man could handle himself in a battle and he was way more competent than she was.

"Screw it. She may have said alive, but I'll take him back dead if I have to." Kuzunoha heard the last man say as he stepped out of the shadows, aiming a loaded crossbow at the melee.

"Watch out," she called, breaking into a run.

The man shot his crossbow and then turned to her as he reloaded it. He didn't try to block her and raised the weapon as he finished loading it. Staring the barrel of the weapon down, he cranked the weapon. Her eyes widened, and she dodged to the left while moving her blade to defend herself. The bolt whizzed by. Kuzunoha dove toward him. Bile filled her throat as her blade slid between his ribs. Hot blood poured onto her hand and she thanked her ancestors that she hadn't eaten much at the party.

The man coughed, spittle burbling out of his mouth. He pushed her away and Kuzunoha fell back, leaving her weapon in his side.

He reached for her and she shivered, leaping forward to grab her knife again. It didn't come out when she tugged on it. She saw him draw his own knife and she panicked, twisting the blade and yanking as hard as she could. The knife made a popping sound as it slid out.

The man gasped and his mouth bubbled over with black blood. It was pouring from the open wound as well. She could smell his blood. It wasn't sickening and dead like the scent that infused the slaughterhouse. It smelled sweet and heady. A shiver ran down her spine and she shook her head. She couldn't think about it now.

The man's crossbow fell from his hands and she kicked it away, turning to see if Richie was still alive. One of the boy's opponents had fallen, but he was slowing down against the other two. Worse, he was favoring his side. She ran up, abandoning all pretense of stealth. Kuzunoha's arm tingled as her blade bounced off the man's armor. She grit her teeth and took a step back, locking her hand around the weapon's handle. She wouldn't lose it again.

The big man turned partially, keeping his eyes on his target and her. "What's a weak bird like you doing? You made a bad decision getting involved."

"It's never a bad decision to help someone," she snapped.

"We ain't trying to kill him," the man scoffed.

"Then what…?"

The man smiled. He was fast enough that she almost missed the blade coming for her belly. Kuzunoha leapt back, avoiding the blow. Stepping in close, she aimed her blade at his shoulder. The man hit her arm carelessly and her blade skittered away on the cobblestones.

"What? Don't you know how to actually fight?" he said with a grin. "Let me school you before you hurt yourself."

"No, let me," a voice said from behind him.

Her opponent stiffened, his eyes widening and he took a pained breath, coughing. Blood bubbled up around his lips and his eyes opened in panic as if he couldn't draw in a breath. She heard a sound faintly like a whistle and as he fell, she saw the stranger behind him, yanking two long, thoroughly soaked blades out of the man's back.

Kuzunoha looked and saw the others lying on the ground, pools of blood widening around them. The men were all dead and Calla was gone. She lifted her eyes back in time to see the stranger's eyes widen in surprise.

"Glory of Kristinel," the stranger said. "You're a woman."

Chapter 3

"Of course, I am," Kuzunoha said, wondering how he hadn't noticed before. "You looked like you needed help, Stranger. What was it Calla called you? Richie?"

"Beautiful... what are you…?" He swayed as if standing upright were too difficult. His head rolled to the side and he blinked at her, sheathing his daggers. "Sorry, I'm not used to women killing people for me."

Beautiful. Even in a dark street with blood around them, it was the first thing people noticed about her. Or perhaps it was because of the dismal surroundings that her appearance stood out. Either way, it annoyed her. She was more than just beautiful.

"It isn't something I make a habit of." She paused, the scent of blood, piss, and feces hitting her like the scent of just the first hadn't. She felt sick and covered her mouth. "Were you injured?"

He nodded, swaying again. "I think I'm going to fall down..."

Kuzunoha grabbed him before he could hit the cobblestones. She shuddered when her hand touched warm, sticky blood dripping from his abdomen. The crossbow bolt was stuck deep, a little over half the shaft just above her hand.

"I'll find the healer and bring—" She paused, looking back towards the Lucky Koi. Would Deckard have left yet? She thought she'd heard his companion's voice while she sat on the bench. She cursed herself for not paying more attention.

The stranger drew a deep, coughing breath. "Don't leave. Take me with you. I can walk."

"Not with a bolt in your side," she told him. If Calla had stayed…she rolled her eyes. Calla didn't have enough sense sober to help. They'd been lucky if she even remembered him the next day.

"Then take it out. I can make it."

Kuzunoha weighed her options. She couldn't carry him, but she didn't want to leave him. Her hand hovered over the bolt.

"This is going to hurt. I'm sorry." She took off the lace scarf and untied one of her silk belts. She used the lace to tie her dress closed again and folded the thick cloth. She would need something to stop him from bleeding out.

He nodded, hissing when her finger touched the bolt. "Gently, if you can. I don't like it... that rough."

She gave a gasping laugh without any real humor and yanked the bolt out.

He choked on his screams, writhing while Kuzunoha held the thick ribbon of fabric against his side, trying to staunch the flow of blood. After what felt like an eternity, he quivered, his breathing deep and irregular. His hand was a bloodless white, gripping the hilts of his daggers.

Kuzunoha's heart thudded as she pulled away her scarf. His wound was sticky and covered with blood. The hole began filling again. Too deep to stanch. She took off the layer of lace and tied it around him as tightly as she could. Her dress was loose, and she quickly used the inner ties to make sure it stayed closed. It would have to do until she could get him to Deckard's.

"Stranger?" His eyes were wide but unseeing. She patted him on the cheek. "Stranger, wake up. I'm going to need your help here. I'm not strong enough to carry you the whole way."

He blinked. It took his eyes too long to focus on her. "Kristinel," he gasped. "Where are we going?"

It was the second time he'd said the name. Dimly she wondered who the woman was. Kristinel was such an uncommon sounding name.

"I'm taking you to our healer."

"I don't suppose he's *almaed*, is he?"

"Almaed?" she asked, helping him up. He groaned.

"I can't remember the word," he muttered to himself, "What do you call them here... magical healers?

"Oh, you mean a blessed," she said. "Deckard is amazing, but he is not blessed."

The blessed were healers who didn't need to use herbs or medicine.

They couldn't be taught or made. It was something you were born with, that manifested when you or someone you knew had been hurt. It was said that they could heal anything short of death. She'd never seen one, and most likely she never would.

"A man can but dream," he said through clenched teeth. "How far?"

"It isn't," She told him. It was better that he not know.

By the end of the first block, she could feel the sweat running off him in sheets. At least, she hoped it was sweat. She glanced at her belts. They seemed to still be holding, but he was shaking so hard that she couldn't help but worry. Should she have left the bolt in? Left him to get help faster?

"I need something to keep my mind distracted," he said, biting each word, forcing them out through clenched teeth. She almost laughed. Clearly, she needed one as well.

"We haven't been introduced," she said after a moment. "I'm Kuzunoha."

He grunted. "My name's Richard."

"Richard? A fine name that. Strong." It certainly suited him better than 'Richie' did.

Richard frowned and tried to poke her. "You're not following the rules, pretty lady."

"Rules?"

"I told you my name, and you were supposed to tell me yours."

She had, but she didn't blame him for having trouble concentrating. They'd passed another block and if this game would keep him distracted from his pain, she would play along. She sent a quick prayer to the gods that Deckard was home already. Richard wouldn't survive the walk back and may not survive even if she left him on Deckard's doorstep and ran herself.

"It's Kuzunoha."

"And what's a Kunohi when it's at home?" Richard said.

She giggled at his mispronunciation but stifled it before it could get away from her. If she started laughing here, she was sure she wasn't going to stop.

"Not Kunohi. Ku-zu-no-ha." She said it slowly. "It's my name, an old name from Sian Ku."

He blinked at her a few times as if he was about to pass out. They had another half block to go. He had to stay conscious.

"Come on, Hero. Say it with me," she cajoled.

He growled at her, a faint light of anger in his eyes.

"I'm not a hero," he bit out.

"Villain then. Let's say it together now. Ku-zu-no-ha."

They spent the rest of the trip repeating her name and he tried to get it right. It felt like no time had passed when she found herself banging hard on Deckard's door. She almost cried when she heard the familiar fizz of a spark and saw candlelight flicker to life inside.

"Cardinte… won't go into that light…" Richard mumbled. The door opened.

"Kuzu... what in blazes..." Deckard said, staring at them both.

She gritted her teeth. She'd given Deckard permission to use the nickname when they'd been dating, in defiance to her father. She hadn't thought then what it would be like to have him use it now, years and choices down the road. Richard's head rolled her direction.

"Kuzu. I can say that. Why didn't you just say that?"

"He's hurt. I had to help."

Kuzunoha hoped that Richard wouldn't remember the nickname. She could teach him how to say it correctly later, when he wasn't bleeding to death. Deckard took Richard out of her hands and carried him to his healing room. She'd forgotten how strong he was. She shivered and stepped inside, closing the door. With Richard's body heat gone, she could feel his blood cooling on her. She felt dizzy and grabbed for the wall. She blinked, steadying herself.

"You weren't injured, were you?" Deckard asked her as he set Richard down on his healing table. She shook her head. He turned back to Richard immediately. "How are you?"

"I's gots shot," Richard mumbled, gesturing towards his torso. "I's starting to feel betters now."

"What you're feeling is the warmth of the fire," Deckard corrected him, looking at the wound. "He was shot with what?"

"A crossbow. Men attacked him on the street and–"

He cut her off. "A what? Where's the bolt?"

Deckard leaned down, squinting at the wound. Kuzunoha leapt away from the wall to light the wall sconces. Something to do other than worry.

"I yanked it out."

Deckard swore. She flinched, nearly dropping the candle. Her heart pounded and she risked a glance. He was looking at the wound, not her, but his jaw was tight.

"Why would you do something so foolish?" Deckard growled as he picked up a needle and threaded it. "Did you want him bleed out before he got here?"

She steadied herself, praying to her ancestors that he hadn't seen her flinch.

"No... I... I was worried the bolt would do more damage while I carried him here."

"You should have run here for me and then took me to where he injured. That would have been the smart thing to do."

Deckard grumbled under his breath and put the needle down, wiping away more blood.

"Play nice with Ku-dzu… I mean, Kuzu…" Richard's words trailed off.

Kuzunoha put down the candle holder and ran to his side. "Is he…?"

Deckard was holding a damp poultice against his side. "No.

Unconscious. He's lost a lot of blood though."

Kuzunoha watched the stranger's chest rise and fall. Strained but still breathing. Her knees felt weak and she let out a breath she hadn't realized she was holding.

Deckard's hands were covered in blood, but the poultice seemed to be stanching the red flood. She didn't know if that was a good thing or not. How much blood could a man lose before he didn't have any left?

"How do you know him, Kuzunoha?" Deckard asked.

"I told you, four men attacked—"

"You just happened to be with him at the time?" Deckard snorted in derision. "Why am I not surprised?"

Had he been anyone else she would have raged against the slight. But Deckard had earned the right to say whatever he wanted to her. She'd given it to him six years ago when she'd broken his heart. She looked away.

"This isn't about me. He would have died—"

Deckard cut her off. "He almost did anyway, Kuzunoha. With you pulling bolts out of his side and forcing him to walk here...you're lucky I was even here. I could have still been at your sister's majority celebration."

Deckard walked out. She heard him using the water pump. The room went blurry and she wiped her tears away angrily. It didn't stop the yellow from the walls bleeding together, making everything a soft orange. Richard's eyes fluttered open.

"Where are we…" he murmured, trying to sit up. She put a hand on his chest.

"No, don't move. You're with friends. Deckard will make you better."

Richard blinked and shivered. Kuzunoha wrapped a blanket around him, wishing for once that Deckard actually were a blessed. Then she wouldn't have to worry if this man she'd saved would survive.

She sighed. If Deckard had been blessed, he wouldn't have been in Hidan. There were only five or six in the entire country and at least three of those were in the main city of Cainin living with the noble families there. At least two worked directly in the king's employ, promising that the man and his family and friends would never fall to any but the worst of injuries or severe old age. Blessed paid for their gifts with being well-kept prisoners to their masters' will.

Richard just stared at her. "Are you real, Kudzu?"

She closed her eyes for a brief moment. *Kudzu* and *Kuzu* meant the same thing: a weed and occasionally slang for trash. She would let Deckard call her that, but not Richard.

"My name is Kuzunoha." She kissed him on the forehead. "Stay here. Deckard knows what he's doing."

Before Richard could respond, she left.

Chapter 4

A blood-curdling scream woke Kuzunoha up the next morning, but she should have expected it. The water in her wash basin was red with the blood she'd washed off herself and her dress. Even afterwards, the white silk and gauze looked brown. She still hadn't gotten all the blood off and her sheets were covered with little brown spots. She needed a bath drawn and a long soak. Normally, she didn't mind going to the communal bath in town, but she wanted something private today.

She wasn't going to get one with her sister and their guest, sitting at the main table downstairs.

Sheriff Dobson wasn't normally an intimidating figure. At only a few inches above her height, he would have been considered a short woman; as a man, his lack of height was nearly embarrassing. His skin was darker than her own and his eyes were usually bloodshot. He always smelled of the most expensive soaps. Rumor had it that he washed his clothes daily to hide the scent of rum. Fortunately, even being a drunkard hadn't stopped him from being competent. Today, he was looking at her as if she had become a problem. She supposed in his eyes, she had.

"Your dress was covered in blood this morning. You want to tell me what happened?"

Had his voice always been so gruff? Or was it only like that because he was questioning her?

"I helped a young foreigner to Deckard's home last night. Some men had attacked him and he'd taken a crossbow bolt in the side. What's this all about?"

"I'm certain he isn't done yet, Kuzunoha. Wait until he's finished before you begin questioning him," Himiko said. Her hair was still drying and she sipped on a fragrant cup of tea. She had apparently had time for a bath this morning.

Sheriff Dobson continued. "It was the young foreigner who was staying at the Koi. What was his name? How did you two get involved?"

Kuzunoha's ears reddened. She knew she'd developed a bit of reputation in town since her breakup with Deckard, but that was too forward for someone of his rank. "I believe his name was Richard. If you want to talk to someone who was 'involved' with him, talk to Calla, not me," she snapped.

The sheriff reddened himself, looking away. Himiko grit her teeth. "Don't be snippy, Kuzunoha. People died. If you don't want to be treated as an idiot, don't act like one."

Kuzunoha's heart started to race. She ignored the reaction, focussing on Himiko, rather than her words. Anger was better than panic. Himiko was trying to act like a big sister, or more accurately, how the matriarch of the family would act towards its most junior member. The act never failed to irritate Kuzunoha, and she was certain that her sister knew it.

Nobody knew which of them was eldest, only that they were born within a month of each other. When her father's mistress had come to present him his daughter, he'd refused to claim her. Her mother had left her on the doorstep and left town on the next boat out. It had been Himiko's mother, wanting to have proof of her husband's infidelity, that had saved Kuzunoha. She'd pointed out exactly what people would think of him leaving his child to die. Her father had grudgingly accepted her, deciding that the day she'd been left would be her birthday, though at least one servant had said she had clearly been a few weeks old at the time. He had wanted to make sure that she knew she was second to the child that was his preferred heir.

Kuzunoha let out a breath. "I saw the men go after the stranger and Calla. They were armed and I followed."

"Why would you do something so stupid? Going after armed men by yourself?" Himiko asked.

Kuzunoha glared. "I didn't want them to make trouble. I thought I might be able to help or… I don't know. I just did."

"What happened when they approached the stranger?" the sheriff asked.

Kuzunoha sat back in her chair. "They were threatening him and Calla. I don't know what they wanted, I couldn't hear what they were saying. Richard yelled something and they all drew weapons…"

She remembered the blades coming out, Richard's skill at dancing around the other men's blades. He'd moved like a dancer.

Sheriff Dobson took a note. "Who drew first?"

She thought back and finally shook her head. "I can't remember."

"What did you do?"

Kuzunoha ran a hand through her hair, feeling the dried sweat in it. She'd done what she could last night, but she still felt dirty. "I tried to help. I ran forward. He was holding his own and I don't know if he really needed my help. Then I noticed the guy with the crossbow taking aim," Her arm started shaking and she grabbed onto the table. She took a deep breath. "I yelled at him to stop. He released the bolt and then turned the weapon on me, reloading it…" Her breath caught. She felt her knife sliding through skin again and felt ill. She swallowed hard. "He attacked me and…and I don't know when I'd drawn my own blade…then it was in him and the crossbow fell to the ground…"

She pushed herself away from the table and ran to the window. The man's look of surprise seemed clear in her memory. She tried not to retch.

"I need a bath," she said when she could speak again. If she could just get clean then the scent of blood wouldn't be on her anymore.

There was a clink on the table. Her sister had poured some water from the jug on the table into a glass. Though she was still frowning, her sister pushed it towards her. Kuzunoha took a deep breath, sat down, and grabbed the glass. It was cool in her hands. It would have been more comforting if it were tea.

"So, four men dead and you're claiming self-defence," he said.

Kuzunoha put down the glass, having not sipped it. "I'm not claiming anything. That's what happened."

"This stranger was attacked first and then took out all four easily? You're sure you aren't confused as to who attacked whom?" Himiko said.

"Yes…no…I'm not confused. They attacked first. I got involved when one of them drew a crossbow. I took the stranger to the healer's home last night. Have you seen Deckard yet?"

Sheriff Dobson grunted. "He says the stranger is healing but isn't going to wake up for a day or two. I want this dealt with sooner than that. Four murders…it mars the occasion of your illustrious sister's birthday. It mars the town. We need trade, we need the boats. We can't have murderers walking free."

He didn't want to solve this. What he wanted was a scapegoat. Her eyes narrowed.

Himiko rolled her eyes. "Kuzunoha, don't make it worse. Answer him honestly."

"I am. It was in self-defence. For both of us."

He grunted again. "We'll see. One of the men was a bounty hunter. If this stranger had a price on his head, I'll find out."

The sheriff stood up from the chair. Himiko stood with him. "And my sister?"

Kuzunoha felt a chill run down her spine. He couldn't actually be thinking about taking her away to one of their holding cells. She hadn't done anything wrong.

"She isn't cleared of any wrongdoing yet," the sheriff said. "I should take her in. Barker will want to speak to her as well."

"I…"

Himiko cut her off. "Do you have to? It would be a disgrace to my father's name, especially since it sounds as if she, at least, didn't do anything wrong. I'm sure that I can keep her here and out of sight until you've finished your investigation. I'm sure my sister will do everything she can to help you."

Kuzunoha flushed and the sheriff blinked as he looked from her to Himiko. She was not an embarrassment to the family, but her sister was, nearly groveling to keep their name clean.

His frown deepened. "She can stay out of respect for your late father, Himiko. Keep her in the house. I don't want to see her while we're investigating."

Himiko kept her smile on until she heard the gate slam, signalling that the sheriff was well and truly gone. Her voice rang through the house. "I expect that the sheriff's visit to our home this morning will be downplayed by all of you and not discussed in public. If I hear any rumors too close to what happened here, I will find out which of you disobeyed."

Murmurs of 'yes, mams' answered her from the nearby rooms and Kuzunoha could hear a shuffle as both of their servants decided they had somewhere pressing to be that wasn't here. Kuzunoha waited until it was clear before she spoke.

"Himiko—"

Her sister cut her off. "One night. I asked for a single night of you not getting in or bringing any trouble down on our family name. And of all the ways to do so, you help a murderer kill bounty hunters."

"It wasn't as though I went out expecting to find four people stalking some stranger with Calla," Kuzunoha said.

Her right hand twitched, feeling as though she held the familiar weight of her blade. She shook her hand and wrapped it firmly around the cup.

Her sister's lips were a thin line. "We have that working for us. It was Calla taking this stranger home, not you."

"It shouldn't have been a problem regardless," Kuzunoha muttered.

"Sailors and traveling wretches. Our father would have been disappointed with your choices. You know that."

Kuzunoha had always considered his disappointment a point in the vagrants' favour. "Who I share my bed with isn't any concern of yours."

Her gaze strayed to the ancestors' shrine set on the far table. Sex itself wasn't looked down upon, but there was so much tradition and expectation that had to be followed for anything more permanent. She hated all of it. At least her father had finally given up on trying to arrange her and Himiko's marriages.

Himiko sighed. "I know…but Kuzunoha, we're talking about murder.

What do you know about this man you saved? Were you hurt? You said you took him to Deckard's afterwards?"

Kuzunoha let out a breath she hadn't realized she'd been holding. "The boy had taken a crossbow bolt to his side. Bounty hunters or not, they weren't trying to take him peacefully. I wasn't hurt." She remembered the men leering at her and sneering at her attempts to help Richard.

Himiko sighed and closed her eyes. "That is good. Still, I don't see why you didn't run to get the sheriff himself or one of the others? Or Deckard for that matter. Honestly, you should consider yourself lucky he'd even gone home at that point. How old is he?"

"He looked younger than us. I'd be surprised if he has more than twenty years." He'd looked so vulnerable lying on the bed at Deckard's. "He asked me not to leave him alone. I… I couldn't just leave him after he'd asked."

"No, I suppose you couldn't," Himiko said without opening her eyes. When she did, she fixed a glare on her sister. "You will have to stay here, Kuzunoha, at least until the sheriff finds out exactly what happened. He's had it out for you since you were involved with those thieves when you were twelve. Don't get in his way. Our family has a lot of political clout, especially if you stick to the self-defence argument, but I'd rather not have to use it if I don't have to."

"But…"

"No buts, Kuzunoha. You don't have anywhere to go. Stay inside the house, at least until he's satisfied about your involvement. That is an order, not a suggestion."

Her sister stood and walked out of the room. As soon as she was gone, Kuzunoha growled to herself. She'd never taken to being locked inside the house well. She doubted she would take it well this time.

She caught a shadow moving on the far wall. "Miya? Is that you?"

Their youngest maid flinched and came back into the room without saying anything. The girl looked as if she wanted to be anywhere but where she was.

"I want a hot bath drawn for me, immediately. And figure out whether my dress upstairs is completely unsalvageable or not. If it isn't, burn it and check to see when the tailor will be getting more of the material in."

"Ye…yes, miss."

The girl fled. Kuzunoha closed her eyes and tried not to feel the walls closing in around her.

Chapter 5

Richard closed his eyes as he heard the shuffling outside again. He thought he was in a healing room, but he wanted to make sure of it before gaining anyone's attention. Every healer was different and if he was in the wrong establishment, he might need to escape, injured or no. The shuffling outside continued and he probed his wound. He couldn't bend over to look at it and there were no mirrors nearby, even if he had wanted to get up.

He felt around the wound itself. The skin was tight, warmer than the rest of his body, and the entire area hurt. He was sure that he was bruised to hell, even if the hole itself was small. He closed his eyes and touched it.

Even expecting the pain, he gagged trying to remain silent. The pain rolled through him like a wave, reducing everything in him to that one point. Even his curse hadn't ever dropped him like this… after the first time. He took his fingers away and the pain receded, though much too slowly. He realized he was shaking and sweating. He concentrated on taking deep breaths.

He remembered being shot; the wooden shaft punching its way into him. The whole area had burned but Richard had been able to push past it. He wouldn't have allowed those men to take him. Death would have been preferable.

After the fight, things became difficult to remember. He did remember Kristinel aiding him in battle. He'd never heard of the goddess taking the form of a Sian Ku before, but he didn't see any reason why she couldn't. The Sian Ku had their own gods and demons, of course, and didn't hold to the teachings of the Courtesan or even that of her sometimes-consort, the Candlemaker, but surely some of them must.

Richard reached a shaky hand up to his neck. The wooden symbol of the Courtesan's sash was still on its cord around his neck.

He lowered his hand, exhausted. Somewhere, he heard a door open and a rough voice berating the occupant. Richard closed his eyes again and listened as intently as he could. Two men, one old and grizzled with gravel in his tone, argued. The younger one spoke without hesitation, his tone, serious and quiet. The voice of someone who knew they were in charge, despite appearances.

Richard relaxed incrementally. That meant that he had not been captured by his enemies. None of her servants would have been allowed to think they were ever in charge.

He finally heard both men come towards the doorway. Long deep breaths, calm demeanor, even breathing, regular heart rate. It only took a few seconds to relax his body.

When the door opened, he fought a flinch. Deep easy breaths. Relaxed.

After a few minutes, there was a grunt from one of the men. "You'll let me know when he wakes," the gravel-toned man said.

The other stayed quiet, as though he knew Richard was faking it. He cursed silently, wishing he had a weapon on him. Even so, he couldn't have used it. Not like this.

"I'll send a message when he can see you," the younger man said.

The door closed. Richard opened his eyes and looked around the dull room again. Yellow-orange walls, dim sunlight through a window, three beds. Nothing near enough that he could grab without leaving the bed.

A few seconds later, the younger man stepped back into the room. Richard made sure his eyes were closed again.

"Will you keep faking all afternoon?" the man said. "If you're worried about the sheriff, you have good reason. He wants to lock you away, near-death or no. Still, I won't let them take you until you're well."

Richard opened his eyes. He'd thought the man was younger, but he was at least six- or seven-years Richard's senior. He had a lean muscular build. His hair was the colour of wheat and had been tied into a neat tail at the nape of his neck. His clothes marked him as working class, but his tone marked him as a healer. Only healers could convey annoyance, frustration, and maternal instinct all at once. A scent tickled Richard's nose and he inhaled deeply. Beef broth with a hint of spice. Soup?

"Can he?" Richard asked.

The man shook his head. "Not yet. He could try to lock you away to force some answers out of you, but I'm a registered healer. As soon as I told his superior, Harrison, that the sheriff took you against my wishes, he would have you out and back in my care until there is undeniable evidence of your wrong-doing. But enough about that. How are you feeling? I thought you'd be hungry soon." He placed a tray Richard only just realized he'd been holding on the table beside him.

"I could…" Richard began and then shook his head as his stomach rebelled. "Maybe not…"

The man grinned and sat beside him. "You'll be hungry enough later. Some of the broth will help you get the good of the stuff in it. Tomorrow, you'll be able to sop some bread as well. Day after that, perhaps some solid food. We'll see how you're doing."

Richard tried to sit up and stopped, gasping in a breath of pain.

"Don't try," the man told him, slipping a second pillow under his head while Richard blinked pain spots from his vision. "You won't be able to bend at the waist by yourself for a few days yet."

Richard turned to glare and found a spoon at his lips. He accepted the mouthful, visions of this brusk man grabbing his jaw and forcing it open if he didn't respond fast enough. The broth was nearly as spicy as it was back in Jisa, though instead of burning his lips, the heat settled and tingled on his tongue.

"Where am I?" he asked, between spoonfuls.

"You're still in Hidan," the man said. "I'm Deckard, the healer. You've created quite the stir here."

Richard's stomach roiled again, but it had nothing to do with the broth.

He nodded and opened his mouth for another spoonful. Better to let this man talk than to give away his own secrets.

"You're intelligent to say nothing, I'll give you that. Speaking for myself, I don't care what you've done. So long as you're hurt and behaving yourself, you'll be my patient. Do you have any questions?"

Deckard put the soup down. Richard hadn't thought that he would be full yet, but he found his stomach didn't agree with him. A good healer indeed.

He let out a breath that turned into a yawn. "Just one… I remember a woman…"

Deckard snorted and stood up. "She's always had that effect on men."

"She was real, then?" Richard said.

"Very. You'd do better to forget you ever met her. Now sleep. You won't heal if you aren't sleeping."

Richard opened his mouth to complain, but sleep claimed him. Tricky healers, always mixing medicine with food. His mind stuttered on the woman though. Very real…and that meant he owed her his life. He'd have to find her again. When he was well. Her smiling face and the glowing scarf she'd used to keep him from bleeding out shone in his memory and into his dreams. Scarfs were good omens; they meant that Kristinel had not abandoned him.

Chapter 6

Finally free, Kuzunoha thought. The week-long house arrest had nearly driven her mad. It had been years since her sister had tried to punish her for anything, let alone enforce it. Berate her, yes. Kuzunoha would have simply left, but the sheriff and his men were still looking into everything that had happened. She didn't want to make things worse for the foreigner when things were already bad enough.

Four men dead, even strangers, in a city as small as Hidan was four too many. Kuzunoha was just glad they'd cleared her name of the charge. She had helped Richard…that was all.

If that had been it, why was she waking up at night, tasting the blood in the air as if it had just happened? She wished the rest of the town could see it her way. The church people were the worst. They had all come by the house, sure that she would need their aid in vanquishing the demons in her mind. Everyone else stopped talking when she came near only to start back up as soon as she was past.

By the time she reached Deckard's house, she was on edge. She wasn't a popular person to begin with. Whatever reputation she'd had before, this was it now. Aid to a murderer. She knocked sharply, trying to clear her mind of maudlin thoughts.

A moment later, Deckard opened the door and frowned when he saw her. "Are you hurt, Kuzunoha?"

She had incredible health, avoiding nearly every cold or chill that swept the town. He'd always said she had the vitality of a stag.

"No," she said. "I came to see how Richa…I mean, the man I saved, is doing."

He regarded her silently and then opened the door wide, inviting her inside without saying a word. She stepped in and he gestured to the kitchen table.

Deckard sat down across the table from her. "He's sleeping now, but we can talk. He was injured. Badly. The bolt…did a lot of damage. He'll heal but it was a near thing. I hope he'll have learned something from this."

"I shouldn't have moved him." Kuzunoha clenched her hand into a tight fist.

"Removing the bolt didn't help," he agreed, "though moving him was immaterial at that point. It didn't make the wound worse. It just made him bleed worse. Your ribbon was a good idea, but it wasn't tight enough to really help. It soaked up the blood, but the material wasn't sturdy enough to hold the wound shut. It was damaged too badly to recover, by the way."

She blinked at him. "Recover what?"

"The ribbon. I assume it was expensive. Apparently, blood doesn't clean out of silk. It would have to be heavily bleached and it was already damaged from the acidity of his blood…"

She knew about the care of cloth of course, but he never had. Kuzunoha wondered if he'd asked someone or if he only knew because the stain had been created with blood. In the end, her entire dress had been tossed, since even their best dye master hadn't been able to save the fabric. Which was just as well. Kuzunoha didn't think she'd be able to wear it all again even if they had been able to fix it. She'd always remember how it felt covered with gore.

"The ribbon was never a concern," she said.

Deckard coughed, seemingly uncomfortable with the conversation. "He will recover, though it will take a few more weeks at best…months, if he continues to be the sort of patient he has been."

Kuzunoha let out a breath. "Can I see him? At all?"

Deckard shook his head. "At this stage, it would be best to let him rest as much as he can. He should be able to handle visitors in a few more days. I can send you some notice when he is, though you probably shouldn't come again."

Kuzunoha's temper flared. "And why is that?"

He stared at her. "Kuzunoha, you were just cleared of your charges. Judged innocent of murder."

"Clearly," she said. She wouldn't be free and walking around on her own if she hadn't.

Deckard glared at her and then nodded behind him to the healing room. "He hasn't."

Kuzunoha had thought that once she'd been cleared, he would be too. She shook her head. "Why not? People attacked him in the middle of the road."

"There are witnesses who say that he drew first."

She wished any one of them had come forward to help her carry Richard here for healing. He was nearly a foot taller than her and weighed considerably more than she could carry comfortably.

"Even if he did, he was outnumbered four to one with a woman on his arm. I'd draw my blade if four men stepped out of the shadows to accost me on my way home."

Deckard leaned back in his chair. "What do you really know about him?"

"I know he needed help."

Deckard put his hands up. "No one is disputing that."

She slumped in her seat, looking anywhere but at him. "Are you sure?"

He winced. "It's not every day that someone in the community is accused of murder, Kuzunoha. They'll forget soon enough."

She didn't want them to forget. She wanted it to not matter. "Have they also forgotten that I was helping someone?"

"They're not sure why you would help him."

She stared at him and then flushed. "I am not sleeping with—"

"That's wasn't what I meant. Nobody knows anything about him. Not even Calla knows anything concrete. What do you know that they don't?"

Kuzunoha let out a breath. "He is a foreigner. He…" Pointing out that he was an excellent fighter was probably not going to help her case here.

Deckard finished for her. "… was being followed by men who wanted him dead, he had enough money to pay for his inn and all of the amenities he could want, he was carrying enough weapons to arm ten men…"

She hadn't known the last. Hadn't even expected it after she'd carried him. She wondered how much he would weigh without all the iron on him.

"I'm not asking for a lot, Kuzunoha, but I think that you should look into the company you keep."

Kuzunoha reminded herself that Richard had been right to carry so many blades. Four men had tried to kill him. He was a victim, not a criminal. "He needed help. None of those things changes that."

"Just take care of yourself. That's all I'm asking for."

She took care of herself. No one else ever had. "I always do."

Out in the streets, the air seemed colder than it had before. Deckard's words turned into ravenous wolves in her mind, chasing all of her arguments down like prey, gnawing at her resistance. Richard was attractive, yes, but being good looking didn't mean he wouldn't hurt her. She almost snorted. Quite the opposite in her experience. The good-looking ones were the ones most likely to end up hurting her.

He was very good with his weapons. There were very few men that could take out three armed attackers without getting severely hurt and Richard's only wound had been from the bolt. A soldier or a hunter, perhaps?

Who was after him? That one was harder to answer. The men hadn't been trying to kill him, or at least, it hadn't been their plan that he die that night. One had been a bounty hunter, but not the other three. Yet, they had clearly worked as a team. Hired thugs then, maybe with conflicting orders? The question then was, why?

If he had stolen something, it would have been reported, unless it hadn't been the owner, but someone else who simply wanted the object. But if he'd stolen something, it certainly hadn't been from Hidan. And while he had wealth, it looked like the wealth of a traveler. Perhaps he's taken something less tangible. He was attractive and charming after all… perhaps some wealthy woman's virtue? She smirked. She may not have known much about him, but if Calla was any indication, the woman would have been entirely willing.

She shook her head. Did she really want to look into this man's past? What could she even find out constrained to staying in Hidan? It would only be useful if she decided to see him again when he was well, if he decided to stay in town.

Somebody crashed into her and Kuzunoha grunted as she fell to the ground. She shook her head and really looked around her for the first time since she left Deckard's house.

She was about five blocks away from the docks, near the daily fish market. There was a giggle. By her foot, a boy that she didn't recognize was picking up paper-wrapped packages. When he caught her gaze, he shrank back and rushed to grab the rest of his items, bowing an apology.

Blinking, she looked around at the faces of the people around her. Everybody did their best to avert their gaze. No one helped her up. Kuzunoha's cheeks warmed and she leapt to her feet, running to a nearby alleyway.

The walls were so close together that Kuzunoha had to slip in sideways. As a child, she'd been able to run down them. Even with the walls pushing in on her, she could breathe better out of everyone's gaze. She leaned against the wall. Things had changed a lot since her father had acknowledged her, even if it was as his by-blow.

There was a difference between being just a bastard and being an acknowledged one. Acknowledged meant that she could have been made heir if he had so decided. The heir didn't have to be the eldest, and they didn't have to be true-born… they just had to be accepted as part of the family and presented to the world as such. Her father hadn't done so until Himiko had thrown a fit and said she wouldn't take over the company. Kuzunoha had been twelve and had been soundly ignored until then. Her father had brought the mayor and acknowledged her soon after.

After… everyone had known before that she was his, but she hadn't had any of the rights of family till then. It had changed everything for her.

Kuzunoha took one calming breath after another. Yes, she would look into Richard's past. If only because he had never looked at her like every one of those miserable wretches on the street had.

Chapter 7

"Stretch to the left."

Richard did, afraid that his wound would tear open again. The skin stretched but held. The wound didn't tear or bleed. It was a small win.

"Good. Now to the right."

Again, it felt tighter than he would have liked. Pain wasn't spiking through him, and that was a good sign. So long as it all held, he could leave the healer's today. He was looking forward to being away from here. Deckard was a good man, but a little too good for Richard's liking. He reminded Richard of a few of the older men he'd known back at home. Upright, with a stick named 'honor' shoved up their ass.

"A little tighter than I'd like, but still good. Stretch up," Deckard told him.

Richard took a deep breath and let it out as instructed. This had been the movement that had stopped him cold the last two times he'd tried to prove he was good enough to leave. A streak of pain ran through him as he lifted his arms above his head, but he didn't feel the skin tearing. He let out more of his breath and finished the stretch, holding for Deckard to evaluate.

The healer leaned close, feeling around the injury. It hurt, but it was an achy pain, rather than the sharp tearing he'd been feeling for nearly two weeks now. He took a breath and lowered his arms as Deckard moved back to where he'd been sitting.

He looked doubtful. "You realize that you're still not up for travelling and you should be resting as much as you can. If I let you return to the inn, you'll be under strict rules. No lifting or carrying anything for another week. There will be daily check-ups, here if you want to travel, or there if you can't."

Richard held his tongue. He didn't think that he'd ever been so watched in his life. Hopefully, he'd find out what he needed within the next day or so and he'd know then whether he had to run or not. He hoped he had enough time to stay and heal. Even with this healer's overbearing attitude, Richard knew he'd heal faster in a bed than on the road.

He nodded. "My plan was to stay in town for at least another week."

Deckard sighed. "Then be here before the noonday bell. If you aren't, I'll come to you. Come now, I'll help you carry your bags over to the inn, then. You can take small walks around the town if you need to, but be careful. You'll tire yourself out easier than you think."

Richard bit down on his tongue again. There was nothing to be gained from irritating the one man in this town who seemed to have no other goal than to see him get well enough to leave. "Thank you. I'll take care of myself and rest as much as I can for the next few days."

"Not a few days," Deckard said. "A full week. I'd prefer to keep you here, but I'm hoping you'll be a better patient for yourself than you have been for me."

Richard grinned. "My parents died when I was young and I had to learn to take care of myself. If I hadn't I wouldn't have gotten this far on my own." He hesitated before continuing. "I'm not from here, so I have to ask… is there any charge?"

In Jisa, residents carried a card with them, given out by the government; anybody who had a card could see a healer for no charge. If you were a foreigner or a jobless though, you had to pay or go to the church. The church would help to take care of you for free, but in return, they would force you into indentured servitude until you'd covered the expense. Fortunately, fake cards were always available for a price.

"All my costs are covered. However, it is customary to give a gift once you are well."

Richard nodded. He would need to remember that for later. "Do any of your townsfolk travel outside the walls?"

Deckard looked at him. "Some. Why?"

"Part of the reason I chose to come to Hidan was to make a little money but I'll need a guide. Would that girl that saved me be one of them?"

Deckard stilled. "That one has no survival instincts. If you ask around at the Koi, I'm sure you'll find someone skilled that could aid you instead. Anything else?"

Richard smiled. "Not right now."

"Good. Let's get going then."

Deckard picked up Richard's backpack and Richard put his shoes on eagerly. He couldn't wait to be out of here. The air was cold this early, but it didn't chill his lungs the way it had when he'd first arrived two and a half weeks ago. He wondered again if he would ever get used to this dratted cold.

At the Lucky Koi, Deckard had arranged a room for Richard the night before, proving to him that despite Deckard's holier-than-thou attitude, he was a good guy. The bed Richard had occupied the first night had been in the common sleeping area, a room nearly thirty feet long and the width was filled with beds with a small chest at the foot of each. The new room was less than half that size, but had a bed to itself, a small dresser beside it, and a table. It even had a lock on the door. A perfect room to rest in. He'd asked about these rooms his first day here, but they'd been having that party and higher-ranking guests had already taken all of them. Besides, he hadn't really wanted to pay the cost. Now, the ridiculous price of having a private room while he healed was a luxury that he was willing to pay.

As he lay down on the bed, he was glad that Deckard hadn't stayed. His side throbbed and he was breathing heavily. He was tired and needed to rest. Irritating enough when he wanted to find out how screwed he was.

He picked up his journal and a bit of graphite. The men in the alley had attempted to kidnap him and there were only two people who had any reason to want him that badly. Neither were nearby, but one had a much farther reach. He shook his head. He wasn't sure that anywhere would be far enough to escape her.

His breathing hitched at the thought. In his first days of freedom, he'd ran and ran, stopping only when he couldn't run anymore. Running like a rabbit wouldn't help him escape. Using his brain would.

First, he would have to find out if anyone had found out who the men were. One had been a known bounty hunter, but according to the sheriff when he'd stopped by, he hadn't been carrying papers for Richard. To Richard, that was just more reason to be worried. The Lady would use any tool that came her way, legal or no and she could be persuasive in ways that he didn't want to think about. He could ask about the men's equipment, to see if they had anything on them to mark them as hers. Barring that, he would need to find out if they had spoken to anyone here and what they'd talked about if they had.

Fortunately, Deckard had let slip that the bounty hunter had been seen working with a criminal in a less than reputable side of town. He'd check with the underground when he got a chance.

The door opened. Most town sheriffs, especially in pathetically tiny places like this, were obnoxious; idiots drunk on their own power. This one was no exception.

"Knock, knock, bastard," the man said as he closed the door behind him.

"Sheriff Dobson. I'd say it's a pleasure to see you again, but I'm a bit too tired to extend the courtesy, at the moment."

"I know you killed those men in cold blood. Don't think you're off the hook yet."

“I acted in self-defence,” Richard narrowed his eyes at the familiar threat.

“You say that. I have a few that said you knew these fellas from a long way back. What did you steal? What were they trying to kill you for?”

As if he would just tell the idiot. “I didn’t know them,” Richard said. He had faint memories of men who looked like them, but those weren’t always true memories. “And I didn’t steal anything.”

The Lady had let him go; had blessed him with a gift. He may have made the request without thinking about the consequences, but once offered, the gift could not be taken back. Now that he was free, there was no way he was ever going back.

Sheriff Dobson snorted, and Richard bared his teeth, pointing at his bag. “Look for yourself…again! Everything I own is in that bag and none of it has a bounty out on it.”

“The doesn’t mean it isn’t stolen.”

When he had been young, men like the sheriff, with their icy glares, would have scared Richard. However, he hadn’t been a child since before his mother had died, leaving him alone on the streets of Jisa.

“Even if it was, it wouldn’t matter,” Richard told the man. “You need proof to throw a man in jail, not baseless accusations.”

If this town were one iota smaller, perhaps the man could do whatever he wanted. But it wasn’t, and even Dobson had to answer to someone, so long as Deckard hadn’t led him wrong telling him about Harrison.

"I will find something on you," Dobson spat, confirming the information. The door slammed shut behind him.

Richard winced at the sound and he put his book on the counter, leaning back against the pillows. He hadn't even left his bed and he was already exhausted. No matter how tired he was, he couldn't sleep like this.

Pushing himself up from the bed, Richard shivered. His stomach roiled as he stood up and his side ached. Pain stabbed through him. Grabbing the wall, Richard used it to get to the door.

Just before he reached it there was a knock. Richard stilled.

"I've got some water for you. Healer Deckard's orders."

Richard moved the last few steps and opened the door. The man had short hair, shaved nearly down to his skull. He had a tray with a jug of water and a small candle-fed cup heater.

"The healer said you'd probably be wanting to take some of those herbs he left you for pain. Said you'd need hot water for it." The man put the water down and lit the candle inside. Then he filled the mug and set it on top. "It will take five minutes to boil. If you want to drink it at a lower temperature, but still warm, that'll be three minutes. The candles are a silver each but don't waste them if you don't have to. Hey, you don't look well. Let me help you back down."

Richard shook his head. "I'll be going to sleep as soon as I finish this and I'll want to lock my door."

The guy looked sympathetic. "No problem. Let us know when you want some dinner, okay? We'll set some of the stew and bread aside for you."

Richard nodded and locked the door behind the man. Then he methodically made his way back to the bed. The water was just beginning to steam gently when he reached it. He sat and threw in one of the bags Deckard had given him.

"Each bag needs to steep at least five minutes and then needs to be drunk within twenty minutes. Each bag can be used twice before it should be thrown out. No honey or sweeteners can be used with them for at least the next four days," he said, repeating the healer's instructions.

He pulled the drink off the heater and blew out the little candle. Then he crawled into bed, hating how cold he felt, how tired. He pulled up the covers and sniffed the drink. Vile, it smelled acrid and sharp. Pinching his nose, he downed the entire cup in a single shot. He didn't taste it going down, but the stuff had an aftertaste that seemed almost sulphurous. He gagged and drank a few mouthfuls of cold water straight from the jug to clear the taste.

The moment he set the jug back down, his eyes started drooping. Richard sighed in pleasure as the hot water seeped into him, reaching his aching side, warming the wound. The sharp claws forcing their way through him slowly disappeared. Richard pulled the covers up to his nose. His mother had always said that sleep was better than medicine. For now, if Deckard's potions would help him sleep without pain, he'd drink every one of them without complaint.

His last thought as he nodded off was of the girl again. Her dark eyes were all he remembered. They had been soft and exotic, comforting him, like a symbol of his goddess.

Chapter 8

Kuzunoha took a sip of the wine Janice handed her and let out a happy sigh.

Janice attempted a smile. “It isn’t like you don’t get this at home.”

Kuzunoha looked at her and the woman flinched.

“Don’t do that,” Kuzunoha said.

Most people didn’t like her and acted as though anything but a prim smile meant that she was secretly planning to steal their firstborn. She wasn’t as graceful or eloquent as Himiko, but that didn’t mean that she was a monster. She snorted. Not that Himiko was eloquent when she dealt with her.

Janice stammered out an apology and fled. Kuzunoha ground her teeth and took another sip of the wine. Cool and refreshing, the white wine left the barest hint of an aftertaste. She didn’t get this at home, not now that Himiko could lord it over her as another difference between them. It hadn’t been so bad before Himiko was technically her matriarch; their servants followed her orders to the letter.

Turning her mind from the wine, she looked around, hoping to see Richard. Most of the tables had occupants, but most were ignoring her, aside from a few men giving her appreciative smiles. She ignored the looks.

According to rumor, Deckard was planning on bringing Richard back to the Koi after dinner to finish healing. She'd found out little else and she was quickly running out of places to look. He'd arrived off the sea, washed his clothes and body at the bathhouse, flirted with the girls, and taken a bed here. Nobody had been willing to tell her where he'd come from or why. The only thing the sheriff had been willing to tell her was that there hadn't been any warrants out for his arrest, and that had been said in a way that had suggested the man wasn't done looking. Calla had remembered him too, but vaguely. She remembered the weapons and terror more than anything else.

Himiko entered the bar and Kuzunoha let out an annoyed breath.

"What are you doing here?" Himiko approached her table and looked disapprovingly at the wine in her hand. As one, the bar patrons seemed to suck in a breath and go quiet.

Kuzunoha made a point of swishing the light fluid in her glass and sipped it again. Kuzunoha hadn't thought that Himiko's frown could deepen. That it did felt like a personal victory. "I finished my meeting with Sheriff Dobson and decided I didn't want to go home yet."

Himiko waved at Isashi as she came in and then turned back to Kuzunoha. "Don't get into any more trouble, Kuzunoha. I mean it. The last thing our name needs is yet another disgrace."

"Disgrace? I saved a man's life," Kuzunoha said. A few people's heads lifted to look at them and she lowered her voice. "What did you expect me to do when I saw him being attacked?"

"Stay out of it, like any other sensible person would have. Or run away to get help."

"I must say, I'm glad she didn't hesitate," a voice said, just behind Kuzunoha.

Kuzunoha turned and saw Richard. Kuzunoha liked him even more now. Her sister's eyes promised dire consequences for him, if she could ever make them stick.

"You're looking better," Himiko said.

Though Kuzunoha disagreed with her sister on nearly everything, it pleased her to agree this time. She had thought Richard decent looking when she'd first seen him. After the fight, regardless of his compliments, she'd hadn't even considered his half-conscious attempts to flirt. He'd needed her help and that was all that mattered. Now, she looked.

His skin wasn't quite as dark as she'd originally thought; it was a soft shade of almond, not cinnamon. His eyes were warm as well, a bare smidge or two lighter than black. His hair was dark brown, cut strangely short, spiking out from his head. His clothes were strange in their color if not their design. Pants, shirt, vest, cloak... it was all black. All his metal was dark, like silver after it had developed a patina. She thought it might have been some type of iron. It seemed almost incongruous. Black wasn't a cheap color. With an outfit this expensive, she would have expected him to have silver, brass, or gold, not some common metal.

He was smiling at her. "Kuzunoha. That is how you pronounce it, yes?"

Her heart fluttered when he said her name and she almost shivered at it rolled off his lips. His pronunciation was horrible, of course, but she found that in his accent, she didn't mind as much. It flowed like a song. The softness behind it felt genuine.

"Yes, it is. Please, sit down."

"Good. I had worried that I'd somehow gotten your name wrong. I wasn't in the best frame of mind when you tried to teach me." Richard set his drink down and took the seat across the table from her.

"I'm impressed you retained it at all. It isn't an easy one to learn," she said.

"My sister is a bold-faced liar if she lets you use that pronunciation." Himiko wagged a finger at Kuzunoha. "We'll finish this conversation later."

Himiko stalked off to the table Isashi had chosen. The hunter positively shone as her sister drew near.

Richard seemed not to notice her sister leaving. "I'm pronouncing it wrong?"

"Ignore my sister. You are not pronouncing it the traditional way, but I like the way you say it."

He smiled again. "It is a beautiful name. I've never heard its like. Still, I would hate to get your name wrong. Perhaps I should call you by what your healer called you…what was it again? Kuzu?"

Kuzunoha didn't have a meaning in the Sian language. It had been the name of a peasant woman centuries ago who had given her noble husband a son but had abandoned her duty to him when he'd become violent. Her father had given her it as a reminder that she would never be as good as Himiko, who'd been named after an empress.

Kuzu, on the other hand, did have a direct translation: trash. The only person she allowed to use it was Deckard. He hadn't known the insult for what it was. The only language he spoke was Cantouk, though she knew he understood his people's native language as well. It had helped that it had irritated her father for her to grant him the privilege.

"No please. Call me Kuzunoha. I have never liked that nickname."

Richard shrugged. "Of course. Forgive my pronunciation until I have had a chance to study it. The Sian language isn't much like my own and doesn't roll off my tongue easily."

"Unlike my sister, I don't mind waiting while you learn. Where are you from?"

"Originally? Kaleka State."

It took her a moment to place it. Kaleka was a small island nation on the other side of the map. It would take over half a year to sail there from Hidan. Her father had always said that if you could get a foothold in Jisa, their capital, you would hardly even need to work. With the trade going in and out, there would always be somewhere to send your wares, always someone with the money to pay for them.

"Why did you come all the way here?"

"Meeting you wasn't enough of a reason?" he asked. With a sigh, he continued. "I had wanderlust. I wanted to see the world, make my mark in it."

Just like her. She reached a hand across the table and patted his. He took hers in his own. "I hadn't gotten a chance to thank you. You kept your head in a very difficult situation."

She thought of Deckard yelling at her, at how stupid she'd been. She pulled her hand back. "You mean that you were lucky our healer was awake? That he was home at all?" She looked away. "You could have died when I pulled the bolt out without making sure..."

Richard switched chairs, moving to the one beside her. "I meant what I said. I'm lucky that your friend was close and knew what to do, but without your help, I don't know that I would have survived at all."

Kuzunoha didn't meet his eye. "Speaking of which, should you be up and about already?"

"The bolt hadn't gone in as deep as we'd thought. Your friend said that my collapse was caused by having too much alcohol in my system and losing too much blood. He told me to take care of myself for a few days, but that I'll be fine to do the rest of convalescence here."

She bobbed her head in relief. "Deckard would know if anybody would."

Richard nodded. "This wasn't what I wanted to talk to you about, though. I was wondering what you do around here? For work, I mean?"

Kuzunoha looked away. “I don’t really have a job. Being an illegitimate noble doesn’t leave you a lot of options.”

At her age, she shouldn’t be jobless, sitting at home all day. Everyone her age was either married or working. She had no prospects in either of those, and while she liked her freedom, she liked to have someone around that understood her.

“Good,” he said. “I need the aid of a brave local.”

“A brave local? Why?”

He leaned in close. “I found an old book about the last voyage of a sailing boat that went missing nearly a century ago in these parts. It’s why I came here originally.”

Kuzunoha blinked. “You found a treasure map?”

“Less a map and more of a last account of her travels. She was running light, carrying the servant of a prominent merchant from Kalvettika.”

Kalvettika was only a month or so away on a fast boat. Still, ships weren’t lost near the coast often. Staying inside the reef was usually fine, but ships that went outside were never seen again.

“Why would you think she was lost around here?”

“According to the book, her crew died trying to bring her to shore near Baris Cove.”

Baris Cove wasn’t far from Hidan, but she shook her head. “If everyone died bringing it in, then who got the book out? And if they knew where it was, why would they just leave it?"

Richard smiled. "One man escaped the shipwreck and he was insane by the time anyone found him after the storm that took down his boat. Bonkers for months. They took him back to his family when the winter was over. It took years before he was able to say where the ship was and by then, he was too old for the travel. One of his kids wrote down everything he said about the incident, hoping to come out here and find it. Fortunately, he never made it."

"What about his trail? Surely a hunter could have followed it." Hunters were the best at that sort of stuff.

"According to the book, nobody could have. Not even a hunter. He was out there for weeks before they found him."

"And you expect us to be able to find it?"

"With the book, telling us where to go and you helping to tell me what the landmarks he mentions are? Yes. And just imagine. Coming home, baskets of coin, treasures found, secrets unearthed and laid bare."

Kuzunoha bit her lip. The problem was that she could see it all too well. A crashed ship, long hidden, monsters braved, and a chest full of coins and gems at the end. What kid hadn't played treasure-hunter growing up? They were fantasies that her father hadn't appreciated. Under his tutelage, they'd become fog burning away under a ruthless sun. Money was better made through trade, deals, business partners, and less dangerous endeavors. Risky ones, yes…dangerous, no.

And still, it called her.

"What proof do you even have that it's still there?" she asked, covering up her indecision.

He raised his eyebrows in a challenging manner. "Are you saying you're in?"

She could understand his reluctance. If he gave away too much, she could try to find it before he could. There were legends, myths of treasure, ships lost and found, monsters killing everyone, but leaving the holds untouched. She sighed, wishing that Grandma Zola hadn't passed away last year. The old woman hadn't been related, but she had watched over every kid in Hidan at some point. She had been a font of knowledge about the old stories. Unfortunately, Kuzunoha's father had considered it unseemly that a peasant should teach of any of his children, so she'd only gotten to listen to a fraction of her stories, usually when Himiko's mother was too sick to take care of them herself. Zola would have remembered if this ship existed.

"I'm not agreeing yet, but even I need more information than just a child's tale. What would my part be in this…scheme of yours?"

"A guide," he said, leaning back. "I don't know the area, the landmarks, or the dangers. Without a guide, I'm worried that it will take months or longer to locate. With your help, we might be able to cut it down to weeks."

She bit her lip again and he grinned.

"Come on, you aren't one of those who hides away in town all day, every day, right?"

Some, like Himiko, preferred staying inside. The city walls were enough to protect them from most troubles. So many small towns fell to the monsters during their first few years even now. Unlike them, Hidan had survived, grown, and even flourished. Staying inside was how you stayed safe.

Safe wasn't enough for Kuzunoha. The green grasses outside the wall called to her, enough that she'd found ways to get over the wall to play in those fields without anyone knowing. True, she hadn't generally gone any further than the sandy flats, the dark beach that ventured inland further than any of the others. On the far side of it, there was some farmland and just beyond that, the tannery. It was past that where the real danger began.

"I think most do, but yes…I think I've gone further than most. If we don't count the hunters, of course."

Richard grinned at her. "I knew I'd pegged you right."

"Hardly," Deckard said as he walked up. He towered over the table, the queue he'd pulled his blonde hair into making him look more severe than usual. Fortunately, his plain white-gray clothes served to make him less intimidating. "I told you that she had no survival instincts when you asked."

"She has survival instincts. What she doesn't have is an instinctive terror of being without walls," Richard said.

"Same thing," Deckard said.

"What are you doing here, Deckard?" Kuzunoha asked.

Deckard pointed at Richard's cup, instead of answering her question. "I thought I told you no alcohol for a week."

"The woman dropped it off before I even asked. It would be rude not to finish it." Richard smirked and took a sip.

Deckard stared at him. Richard put the cup further away and gestured for one of the barmaids.

"Fine, I'll get water for the rest of the night. But all this isn't getting me an answer. Kuzunoha, will you be my guide?"

It sounded simple enough, but she had a bad feeling about it. "I don't know, Richard. It still sounds... sketchy."

Deckard raised an eyebrow, "I thought you said you just needed a guide?"

Without waiting for a response, he turned and raised his voice, calling for Himiko. Kuzunoha could see Himiko apologize to Isashi before she came to their table.

"Deckard? What do you need?"

Richard looked concerned but Kuzunoha just shook her head. "Richard is just offering me a job. Nothing that you need to concern yourself with, Himiko."

Himiko laughed. "Make sure you don't pay her until it's done. She's never been able to hold down any task she's been given."

Kuzunoha didn't even wait for Richard's response. "How would you know? I've never had the option before."

Himiko ignored her. "So, what is this job opportunity?"

"He needs a guide," Deckard said. His gaze hadn't left Richard yet.

"That hardly seems necessary," Himiko frowned. "Kindler's Cove isn't that big."

Kindler's Cove was just down the hill from the local lighthouse and the one place that everyone in the city could get to without worrying about their safety. There was a pilgrimage to a nearby cave for those that followed Kittin, a goddess of divination from Deckard's pantheon. She was the most popular goddess in the area and her church, a three-story monster of stone with high arcing walls, was the biggest building in town. Kuzunoha thought a tiny prayer for her. She didn't follow the goddess, being brought up in the religion of her ancestors, but it couldn't hurt.

"I need a guide to take me a bit further than Kindler's Cove," Richard said smoothly.

Himiko frowned and tossed her hair. "How far?"

"It doesn't matter how far," Kuzunoha said.

"Of course, it—"

Deckard raised a hand, stopping Himiko. "And why wouldn't you ask a hunter? Isashi is here tonight."

"Because I don't know any of the hunters, and I would like to get to know the woman who saved my life better."

Kuzunoha blinked. She'd never had someone so clearly put their interest into words before.

Himiko glared at Kuzunoha. “Absolutely not, Kuzunoha.”

Something in Kuzunoha snapped. “Why do you think you can give me orders?”

“I’m head of the household.”

“What does that have to do with it?”

“You haven’t reached your majority.”

“It’s less than a month away!”

Himiko growled. “I don’t know how our father put up with you. This has nothing to do with me being head of the household and everything to do with you being an idiot. You aren’t going. That’s final.”

“If it had nothing to do with you wanting to control me, you wouldn’t have brought up your status.” Kuzunoha spun on Richard. “I accept. Come to my house tomorrow morning. We’ll make arrangements then.”

“I forbid it,” Himiko interjected.

Richard put up his hands. “Ah, I won’t be able to make it tomorrow.” He winced. “I’m still not well yet. I will let you know when I am better.”

Deckard muttered under his breath, “At least someone at this table has some sense.”

“When you’re well then,” Kuzunoha said imperiously.

Richard smiled. “I’m sure I can find my way there.”

Kuzunoha nodded and stomped out of the bar.

Chapter 9

Richard looked at the house again. It was big. A lot bigger than he'd thought a noble's house would be in a two-horse town. It was also pretty. Expensive materials, kept up, new coats of paint when the old got ratty. It was too good. If the inside looked anywhere near as nice as the outside, he just may have gotten in over his head.

Calla had been available and eager, but comparing her to Kuzu would be like comparing a candle flame to a campfire. He'd thought she was his goddess come to ground when he first saw her, though he'd never heard of Kristinel taking the form of a Sian Ku woman before. After realizing that Kuzunoha was only a conduit, one that the goddess had worked through but just mortal, he still wanted to know her better. All of her. Richard was attractive, but he wasn't the sort who would normally interest a woman like her. He'd hoped to woo her into bed with his money, his charm, his mysteriousness.

He looked at the house again. Money was not going to work. He mentally revised how much he had hoped to offer her and sighed. If she had a mind for business at all, hiring her was going to be expensive in and of itself.

He let out a breath. Just how far was he willing to go just to sleep with her? She was gorgeous, like a doll dressed in silk, even if she was shorter than any grown woman he'd ever known. Her height hadn't stopped her from killing someone to save his life. A goddess coming out of the dark, doing everything she could to help him.

From the information he'd dug up since his return, no one had found the boat yet. If it did lead to some sort of treasure, he might be able to afford a ship for the next part of his route. He might even have enough extra to cloud his passage, further confusing any pursuers.

He shivered. He hadn't been able to figure out what his attackers had done in town after they'd gotten here. He needed to get out, but he needed money and information first. Mice would flee without thought or plan when spooked. Lions planned, hunted and, most importantly, survived.

The entire situation was too perfect for him to ignore. Fated. He knocked.

A pretty woman, Sian Ku like Kuzunoha, answered the door. Her clothing was sky-blue, a robe design that fell to her ankles, leaving her shoulders bare. The robe did have sleeves, long enough to just cover the girl's slender fingers. Two green ribbons dangled from the top of the sleeve, presumably to tie them out of the way while cleaning. She was cute, in that same foreign way that Kuzu was, though not attractive enough herself to be a conduit. He smiled at her, raising his eyebrows suggestively. She blushed and glanced away.

"What do you need, sir? The mistress of the house has already gone this morning."

"Actually, I was looking for the younger mistress."

The girl gave a little bow, before ushering him into a house that appeared even nicer on the inside than it did on the outside. The walls were wooden for the most part, separated by the same paper room dividers he'd seen in the bathing house. The floor and furniture had been stained a deep nutmeg brown. Here and there, red accents gleamed, reminding him of tiny petals floating on the wind. Soft looking pillows, dyed in vibrant colours too bright to have been washed much, had been placed on a few of the couches.

When he'd been working as a thief in Jisa, this place would have been above his pay grade because they would have been paying for protection. In that city, it was just easier.

The girl stopped at a small table at the entry to the living room and gestured for him to sit in the small chair beside it. "I'll wake my mistress for you."

"She isn't awake yet?" It was nearly mid-morning. He wondered how late she usually slept.

"No..." The girl couldn't meet his eyes. There was something about shy women like her. Adorable.

"What's your name?" he asked.

"Miya…sir." She swallowed and her chest heaved.

"I'm Richard, a follower of Kristinel. I don't suppose you worship her here, do you?"

Her eyes widened and she shook her head. The words worked for most women who hadn't been brought up on the island of Keleka. There was a vast difference between sex and worship, but these people didn't know that. They heard the goddess was a courtesan and that her adherents were known for their sexual virility. It was a stereotype that worked in his favour at times like these. He stepped closer to the maid and brought her hand up to his lips, kissing it.

"I'd love to introduce you to her worship, sometime."

"Sir!" An older woman's voice interrupted him and he looked up. The glaring woman was no taller than Kuzunoha, about thirty years older, and wider than some of the doorways he'd seen here. As a rule, Richard liked women. This one, he could do without. "If you're looking for women like that, you should go to the bathing house, Arise from Ashes. Miya, you should know better."

Miya's cheeks were pink and it wasn't entirely out of embarrassment. "Sorry, sir." She pulled away, still gasping like a fish on a hook.

"I'm not," he whispered.

The flush consumed her face and she nearly fled up the stairs. "I'm going to...to go and find my mistress for you..."

"Follow me to the dining room, scoundrel," the crone said.

"I am sorry. It won't happen again."

Where she could find them, he amended silently. She pointed to a seat at a simple black table set with flowers arranged in a low vase. He sat but she didn't move, staring at him from behind one of the other chairs.

"Thank you. I'll sit here and wait for your mistress."

When she still didn't move, he returned the stare until she grumbled and walked out of the room.

The ship, *Sight to Sea*, wouldn't be too difficult to find. Or at least, not any more difficult than any other ship that had been missing for half a century or more. She'd been carrying a coin box of a rather impressive size, and the notes, though disjointed, would be enough to help him narrow down an area.

A glass clinked in front of him. Miya smiled at him and he picked it up and took a sip of the dark maroon fluid in it. Not wine, or any sort of alcohol. It had a light fruity taste, like raspberry and blackberry, but something else too that he couldn't identify—a tang that he didn't associate with either fruit. Fruit juice, rather than a morning wine, but he'd never tasted juice so smooth before. There wasn't a smidge of pulp in the glass. He'd never seen anything this clear, other than a good white wine or the water in Divers Cove.

He sighed. If Kuzu's servants wrung out her juices in cheesecloth before they even made it to the table, then he'd have to rethink how much he'd hoped to offer her of the treasure. He'd originally intended to offer her money up front and a small percentage of the treasure. Now he might have to offer her a full share. He supposed that in that case, there was some benefit; if they found nothing, he wouldn't be down to coppers.

"Thank you, Miya. How long will your mistress be?"

Her breath caught and she glanced around nervously. "Sir, I... can't."

"Of course not," he said, hiding a smile. He hadn't meant to put across that sort of request. “Please, call me Richard. I wanted to apologize for my forwardness. You are lovely and I wasn’t thinking, mentioning it before we’d gotten to know each other. If you would like to see me, I’ll be staying at the Lucky Koi for the next few weeks.”

She glanced away but her eyes came back to his, as if drawn. She nodded and he watched her hips sway as she left.

Kuzunoha arrived soon after the meal was set on the table. She looked half asleep, her long hair drooping around her. Even tired, she stopped in front of a tiny shrine tucked into the corner. She clapped loudly, bowing slightly, and then moved her hands to form a symbol, some sort of triangle with her fingers. Then she came to sit down at the table.

“Good morning,” he said.

She grumped as she collapsed into her chair. “Is it? I haven’t been awake long enough to know.”

Not a morning person, apparently. Even just up from bed, she was beautiful. It was her lips he noticed the most. She’d been wearing lipstick the colour of cinnamon at the Lucky Koi that night, a week ago. Her natural colour was a lovely maroon pink.

Miya slipped a plate of food in front of Kuzunoha, with an addition Richard hadn’t had. Pancakes. A small glass jar of honey accompanied it. She slathered the thin cakes with butter and then opened the jar. He could smell it and his breath caught. Not honey, but maple syrup.

A memory he hadn’t thought of in years returned: maple syrup overpowered the rosemary and garlic his mother hung in the kitchen, and his mother's face, unlined, cooing at him. A good memory.

Without a thought, she drizzled the syrup all over the pancakes and closed the jar again.

"May I try some?" Richard asked.

Maple trees only grew in a few places and it was stupidly expensive everywhere else. Hidan wasn't one of those places. A jar that size was an investment of gold, not copper or even silver.

She blinked at him, looked down at his plate, and shot Miya a look. "Make him a set. Now."

"Mistress, your sister said—"

"I invited him and you will treat him with every courtesy."

"Yes, mistress." She stole one last glance and then fled into the kitchen.

"Your sister disapproves of me that much?" Richard asked.

She rolled her eyes and took a bite of the pancakes, maple syrup dripping wasted onto the plate below. "Yes, but that isn't what Miya meant. Maple syrup is expensive so we don't generally have it when others are here. However, my sister had some this morning. I am not missing out and neither are you. After all, technically you are a business acquaintance and father used to make sure it was offered when we hosted them. Besides, it's Himiko's favorite so she makes sure to always have some available. She's less diligent in getting the things I enjoy." Kuzunoha cut off another slice and put it in her mouth.

He didn't mind reaping the benefits of sister rivalry when they included things like maple syrup.

"So, we are going to be associates? I'm glad," he said. "It appeared as though you may have only agreed when your sister forbade it."

Kuzunoha picked at her food. "I won't back out. Himiko…. she thinks that this is below me. My father believed that no child of his should be working for someone of a lower status than our family. That leaves me precious few places to go. My father was… quite well-loved."

She sounded sour when said the last and he didn't respond. A moment later, Miya walked in and slid a plate of three pancakes in front of him. He caught her eye before she could turn away.

"Thank you. I appreciate it," he told her.

Her smile made her entire face light up. She turned and strode into the kitchen. Once she was gone, he slathered the pancakes with butter before drizzling syrup over them.

"What businesses do your family run?" he said, putting the folk into his mouth.

The syrup was as sweet as candy with a hint of smokiness. He could have melted into a puddle right then. Not that the rest of the food wasn't good, but this was a luxury few ever had. He took another bite, as if he needed to make sure he wasn't dreaming.

Kuzunoha was cocking an amused smile at him as if he were overreacting for her benefit. This girl, in this slip of a village, ate them every week or so. To her, they were no big deal. She sipped her juice, as peerless and devoid of pulp as his own. "Dyed silk and glass."

Richard sighed. It didn't matter how small the town was. With those two industries supporting it, they would have more access to the essentials than some larger cities. Or at least, her family always would. Asking why she wouldn't want to do the work she was trained for was probably too forward. He hesitated and then asked anyway.

"What were you trained to do?"

She put down her fork and turned her eyes away and grumbled. "My sister's replacement."

Richard nearly choked. That would leave her with nothing unless her sister was willing to give one of the companies to her. He didn't know much about her sister, but he didn't think that she would give up any of her control easily.

"Your father didn't provide you with any additional training?"

"No, he learned early that by pitting us against each other, he got better production out of us. It was good for Himiko, but for me..." She shook her head. "That's why I want this to work."

"Let's discuss our arrangement then. How much will you want for being a guide?"

"We won't be splitting the prize? Fifty-fifty?"

"It is my book, my treasure. I had thought to offer you gold rather than a cut. It's a safer investment than a percentage." He couldn't help but try, even knowing the tactic was likely doomed to fail.

"I don't want safe. I want to be your partner, not your employee."

He smiled but covered it with a sip of the juice. Maybe she didn't want the detriments of being noble, but she wasn't willing to give up the perks completely either.

Before, he'd wanted to have her in his bed. Now, he wanted to know her as well. "Thirty-five percent."

She raised her eyebrow. "You're bringing the book and the survival skills, but I'm not completely unknowledgeable myself or you wouldn't be hiring me. Forty percent."

He had expected her to go higher, which was why he'd started low. That she wasn't being greedy meant he'd read her right. She was professional, but even inexperienced, she wouldn't end up being a liability on the road.

"With the addendum that if I choose payment in something other than coins, it will take priority," she added.

"As in... jewelry or such? You would accept in trade rather than just money?"

"Yes. Speaking of which, what do we know about this ship?"

Richard smiled. "Here's what I know. The ship was called 'Sight to Sea'. Her Captain was known for taking illegal cargo on occasion. Despite that, she did some passenger travel as well. On her last voyage, one of her stops was supposed to be Hidan, but she never made it. I don’t know much about all her cargo, but I know that she was carrying some rich man from Kalvettika delivering gifts and money somewhere.”

“And its thought that the ship crashed somewhere near Hidan?”

“I found a book that had information on it. Apparently, they were hit by a storm and there was only one survivor. The man was raving mad and sent to live with a nephew in a nearby town. That man’s grandson wrote about the stories he heard from his great uncle.”

“And you think we have a chance at finding this ship?”

“Better than just a chance. A good one. When people went looking for it, they were searching the sea. I think she came to land.”

“Where?”

Richard sighed. “Somewhere near here… I’m still trying to translate out the book and the stories. It was enough of a lead for me to come here, after I’d collaborated some information from a few buddies I’d made on the boat ride to Mortin’s Port.”

“You’ll need time to finish translating it?”

“I wouldn’t want to leave before I’m healed anyway.” He admitted. “We can probably leave two weeks from now.”

That should give him enough time to be well enough for light travel and searching, especially with Kuzunoha with him. He’d have to slow down to her speed for the first few days anyway, before she realized what real travel could be like.

"That will give me time to find supplies for our trip and whatever else we require. Do we have an accord?"

He smiled, pushing his empty plate away from him. "We do. If you'll excuse me though, I have to return to my rooms. Being out still tires me more than I'd like."

"No problem. Would you like me to write up an agreement and bring it by your rooms on the morrow?"

"Please. We will both need to be able to read it. I read Sentar, Dorrani, and Cantouk." He could also read a smattering of other languages, Trill and Govin among them, but he would never be able to check the wording in those accurately. It was thoughtful of her to offer to write it up. He really was starting to ache. He'd have to drink more of that dratted healing tea when he got back to the inn.

Her eyebrows rose at that. Most could only speak one language, two the most. Speaking and reading in just the ones he'd named would be impressive, even if she knew more than one herself. "Cantouk, then. Unless you need help returning to your rooms, I'll see you out and then begin writing it up and find out when Justice Kilmar will be available to witness the signing for us."

"I can make it on my own. I'll see you tomorrow then, partner." He held out his hand and she clasped it in her own, shaking firmly, a grin lighting her radiant features.

Chapter 10

Kuzunoha walked into the store, hardly able to contain her glee. A few things to buy, a few things to check about this shipwreck and they could be out. The longest part would probably be Richard's translating of the book. The man who had written it down had miserable handwriting. Kuzunoha had considered herself a good hand at deciphering text, but this book was in Dorrani and beyond her ability.

First on her list of things to do was picking up supplies. Sleeping sack, utensils, and cutlery, backpack, hardier clothing—suited for days spent in the wild rather than hours—tools, toiletries... she still felt embarrassed thinking about that last one. There were a few items that Richard had asked her to check on prices for as well: pots, pans, foodstuffs, and even a collapsible canoe. Items that they would both end up using and sharing the costs for.

She paused outside her destination, watching as a few of the people loitering outside the front doors of Talvert's shop saw her and shuffled away, the tallest one whispering while they moved out of earshot, "Kuzunoha was the one that helped that foreigner."

Soon she wouldn't just be the one who helped the foreigner—she would be the one working with him. Would that make their comments easier or harder to bear? Not knowing the answer, she stepped into the shop.

The scent of spices hit her like a bat to the face. She had the urge to claw the scent out of her nose. A sneeze would have given her relief. Instead, the intensity of the smell overwhelmed her nose. Her head throbbed in time to a bard-in-training—just enough out of tempo to grate on already abused nerves.

“Kuzunoha, we don’t often see you in here. What can I help you with?”

Kuzunoha shook her head. Talvert was a tall man, second in his line to carry his father’s name, Eric. No one ever called him by it, though since there had been three boys born within two years of each other with the same name. One inevitably became Tall Eric, while the other became Dancing Eric, after he’d fallen on his nose and broken it trying to impress a girl at the fair. Talvert, having no identifying embarrassments or notorieties, simply became Talvert.

“Just a few things to pick up. I thought you might have what I was looking for,” she told him, looking around the store, waiting for the pounding in her head to subside.

Kuzunoha didn’t often bother coming to the general store herself since the servants handled weekly shopping and the rest. Still, even she could tell that the store hadn’t changed much since Talvert had taken over from his father. The shelves were over-stocked, boxes and extra merchandise filled up every corner and the shelves, laid across every wall and more running perpendicular in the centre of the room, were filled with a smorgasbord of brightly coloured food and bric-a-brac.

“If we don’t have it in stock, I’m sure we can order it in.” His smile was genuine and Kuzunoha felt herself relax. "What's your first item?"

She moved a finger up to her lip. "I think the first thing I'll need is a good bag."

He nodded. "Purse, backpack, or sack?"

"Backpacks and sacks. Waterproof preferably."

Talvert pursed his lips and looked over to the northern wall. "Nothing we have out right now would meet your standard."

He knew her well enough to know that she was picky about quality; in exchange for her pickiness, she almost never haggled. She bit her lip at the anticipated delay, but Talvert held up his hand.

"I do have something in the back that might do. I was going to ship it back, since the foreigner that ordered it left town before picking it up from me. It might work for you though. Would you like to see it?"

Kuzunoha tilted her head in a half bow. "You have me intrigued. Yes, I'd like to see it."

"Check out what we have on the northern wall and let me know what you think of those. I'll grab the bag and meet you over there."

He was right about the backpack selection. Most were made using a thin leather that stretched under her fingers or a softly woven cotton. They were bags made for use in town, not out on the road. There was one bag made with a silk covering of a flower design. Pretty, but badly made. The stitches were already pulling at the fabric.

She turned away in disgust as the bell over the main door rang. She turned and caught her breath as Deckard walked in.

Like the bag, he was unimaginably pretty. Unlike the bag, he was well made and still the most attractive man she'd ever known. His hair hung low on his shoulders, making him look like a deity come to ground. His physique was muscled, surprisingly so for a healer, and he stood at least a foot taller than her. She turned away, but not before she caught his frown at seeing her.

"Good afternoon." His words were for Talvert, not her.

"Ah, Deckard. Here to pick up your package? I had two items left to wrap. Why don't you look and see if there's anything else you need? We got a new type of bandage in with the last shipment I can add in. They're in the back by the bags."

Deckard stepped near to the back, picking up the bleached cloth in one hand. He squeezed it and she wondered if he could tell their quality like she could silk, just by its feel.

"Kuzunoha? Picking up a new bag?" he said without looking at her.

"I've agreed to be Richard's guide, so I'll require one."

At that, he did turn to look at her. "You're going? Your sister didn't convince you it was foolish?"

"Of course not, Deckard," she said. Realizing how that sounded, she tried again. "He needs a guide an—"

"Why can't you just listen to your sister for once?"

"Listen to her? And you?"

"You've never listened to me."

She winced and pushed her hair behind her ear. "Deckard, this is hardly something to worry about. We won't even be going as far as Croptal."

Most likely. Richard seemed certain that the boat had crashed somewhere nearby, no more than a week or two's journey walking.

Deckard rubbed his forehead. "This stranger arrived in town and within a week killed four men. Does that seem 'safe' to you?"

"Deckard, it was three men and it wasn't his fault."

The sheriff may not have liked having to count him innocent, but you couldn't arrest a man for being attacked in the city streets.

Deckard closed his eyes. "I'd forgotten. How are you doing? You haven't been by to see me. Have you at least spoken to one of the priests in town?"

Kuzunoha didn't like remembering the man she'd killed, didn't like talking about it at all. She'd seen his face in her dreams again last night. What she'd done had been necessary to save Richard's life. Still, it felt like even more of a wedge between them. Deckard healed for a living. She, apparently, destroyed men's lives, killing them when less direct ways like simply ruining their lives by cheating on them, weren't available.

"I haven't. It was just one man, Deckard, and a stranger at that. I'll be fine."

"One or ten, I'd feel better if you'd talk to someone about it," he sighed. "How did you manage to convince your sister to allow this anyway?"

"Himiko doesn't get a choice." Kuzunoha's mouth curled up towards her nose. "It's my choice, my decision, Deckard. She doesn't get a say."

"Kuzunoha..." Deckard took a step towards her and she recoiled.

"Deckard, I have your package ready. Would you like any of those bandages as well?" Talvert asked from the front of the store.

Neither of them moved.

"You have to talk to Himiko before you do this."

Kuzunoha looked away. What was she supposed to say? That Himiko had forbidden it or that she didn't care? He would know all of that already. There had been a time when he had known her best.

Or she thought he had.

She gestured towards Talvert.

"Your package is ready, Deckard," she said.

He regarded her a moment longer and then turned to the shopkeeper. "Thank you, Talvert. I've decided to take your supply of the new bandage type here, if that's all right. Let me bring them to you."

Kuzunoha sighed. It took nearly five minutes for Deckard to finish his business and leave. He didn't look at her again.

Talvert approached her, carrying a black and red bundle. "He seemed tense."

"Isn't he always?" she asked. Everyone in town knew they'd been together. Nowadays, she was simply an old inconvenience to him.

He gave a light smile. "You said you were going somewhere."

Kuzunoha shook her head. "I've got a job as a guide. A couple weeks on the road, right around Hidan."

"That's usually hunter work," he said, cautiously.

She shrugged. "Richard wanted to get to know me after I saved his life. The area right around Hidan is safe enough that we shouldn't be in any real danger."

Talvert put out a hand. "Richard? You mean the stranger? Is he well enough for that sort of exertion already?"

She blew out a breath. "Hardly. It'll be at least another week. We're studying the places he wants to go while he's here in the meantime."

"Ah. Say no more." Talvert put the bag on the counter, moving a clump of buckles out of the way. "This is the best that we have in stock. I assume you'll want something that will stand up to the elements?"

It wasn't actually black and red but had a colour like fall leaves: oranges, reds, and deep browns. It was softer than some of her outfits, but it looked strong, made of some type of leather she didn't recognize.

"Good bison leather, silk thread, reinforced with more bison leather ties," he told her when she asked. "We give you a thin spool of both to make repairs if needed, though you'd have to put it through more than the regular paces. Bison hide is strong. Its inner covering is silk from your family's own warehouses. It comes with a water-resistant pouch for your clothes, and ties together at the top to keep most water from getting in. It has a multitude of pockets and comes with this matching belt pouch to keep small items closer to hand. Finally, the straps go over your shoulders and have these two additional ties. They cross your chest and stomach to distribute all the weight. It will make carrying up to sixty pounds of equipment feel like feathers."

"Nice. How much?"

"It sells for ten silvers."

She winced inwardly. She had it, but that was hardly the point. Every other bag on the wall would have gone for maybe ten coppers…except perhaps the silk bag. That one, he might try to get two or three silvers for.

"Sell me on it."

He smiled and coughed into his hand. She smiled, remembering her father telling her that it was one of his tells. *Be wary but read through the tell and you'll be able to tell just how much he's exaggerating.*

"You're paying for the high quality. Bison hide is much stronger than cow and you know how much stronger good silk is compared to cotton." His breathing was even enough, just a little bit of excitement. He had stuck out his chest; showing pride in his work.

"Waterproof?" she asked.

"It's been waxed and I'll include an extra stick for you to repair on the go. It won't help if you're submerged, but it should be fine for most rain."

Kuzunoha shuddered. Every couple of years they would get a storm in off the ocean that would soak you so fast you might as well have been submerged if you stepped outside. He winced, probably remembering those storms as well.

"I'll be honest, miss, I don't have anything that will help if you're getting that wet."

"Shouldn't be a problem during this season. Do you have some of the sealable bison bags I could pick up for it?"

"Double protection, huh? I don't have any right now, but I can see about ordering some in. It may take up to three weeks. They cost one silver sol each. Will that be okay?"

Expensive as well, but they were going after a ship. If she wanted the best protection, she would need to pay for it somewhere along the way. "Please. I have a few other items to pick up as well. You may need to order them as well, so I'd rather get it all at once if I can."

Eric nodded, smiling and took her bag up to the front to start wrapping it up. "Not a problem at all. What's next on your list?"

Chapter 11

"Kuzunoha, we need to talk." The words were in Siangu, the language that their father had insisted they speak at home. Since he'd died, they had used it less and less.

Kuzunoha stopped going through her clothes and looked towards her door. Himiko was there, wearing a traditional Sian Ku outfit: black wide pleated pants, with a long red shirt with black accents that called dragons to mind, all in silk. It was a mirror to the green version her father had worn. Her sister was probably hoping to invoke the ghost of their father, praying it would make Kuzunoha more pliable. Himiko had never paid attention to their heritage lessons the way Kuzunoha had, or she would have known that Kuzunoha could never be moved that way.

Kuzunoha put the shirt she'd been holding back into her closet. She wouldn't let Himiko scare her, but there was no point in antagonizing her before they even began. She gave her sister a small bow. "Yes, Himiko?"

"I spoke with Deckard today. He told me you were thinking about leaving town. I hadn't put much stock in it since you and he are hardly on good terms. Yet, here you are…packing."

Damn Deckard. He had stayed out of her life since they'd broken up. Now, he wanted to get involved? Had he stayed out of it, Kuzunoha could have waited until everything was ready to go and she was heading out to leave the city with Richard, when her sister couldn't do anything to stop her.

"Richard requires a guide for the area. He has hired me," she answered, coolly.

"I forbade it. Did you forget?" Himiko growled.

"No."

"Then why are you still going forward with this?"

Himiko had entered the room and towered over Kuzunoha, trying to use her half a foot height intimidatingly. It wouldn't work. Kuzunoha had always been the shortest one of the family. Her lack of height didn't make her afraid—it made her want to fight harder.

"I've accepted the job. I'm not giving it up."

"He isn't noble. You can't work for him."

"That was father's rule, not an actual law, Himiko." Even if everyone in town did seem to think it was. She'd tried once to go against his wishes and had found the stablemaster tentatively willing. Her father had threatened to destroy the stables when he'd found out that she'd taken a job mucking out stalls in exchange for riding lessons. Since then nobody had been willing to break that rule, even after her father had died. "I can work for who I want, so long as they'll hire me. He did."

Her sister's eyes went wide and her face turned a blotchy red. "Kuzunoha, I am trying to do what's best for you. He's dangerous, a murderer.

It's bad enough you had him in our house. I'm not going to let you go haring off into the forest with him."

"You're only annoyed that he had breakfast here. It's not like I brought him up to my room."

If Kuzunoha had time to think about that, she wouldn't have said it. She liked sex, but her father had always been more traditional about it. Peasants could sleep with whomever they wished. Nobles, or those brought up in a noble house, shouldn't. Kuzunoha had thought that Himiko shared her outlook, but she'd come down hard on her for it lately, ever since her sister had decided that she needed to act like a proper family matriarch would. Yet another thing she did that failed to live up to her sister's ever-rising standards.

Himiko covered her eyes with her hands and ground her teeth. "Perhaps, I would have preferred that. My maple syrup stock wouldn't be almost gone then."

Kuzunoha blinked at the argument. She hadn't expected Himiko to notice that Richard had some, let alone bring it up. Apparently, Kuzunoha wasn't the only one feeling petty tonight. "It's not like he's eating us out of house or home, Himiko. Not with one meal."

She bit her tongue to prevent making a comment about serving steak and eggs instead the next time he came over. If she pushed too hard, Himiko would find some way to retaliate.

Himiko massaged her forehead. "Forget about the maple syrup. It isn't important. Kuzunoha, that man is dangerous."

“This isn’t a permanent job. It’s a short-term thing. We’ll be buying supplies and then we’ll be gone for a few weeks. That’s it.”

“You could be working for the family. All you would have to do is ask.”

Kuzunoha almost snorted. She’d tried that once before too. Tim had offered her a job working as a lowly clerk. She wasn’t going to bring that up today. Choose your battles, someone wise had said. “Himiko, Father trained me for one position only. So, unless you’re leaving the family business to me, I don’t have a position here.”

“You know, I never wanted this. I wanted to own a bar, maybe with a few rooms for guests and a decent-sized kitchen,” Himiko muttered under her breath.

If being an innkeeper was Himiko’s dream, she should sell the company to Kuzunoha and buy one. She was certain she hadn’t hidden the sentiment when enough when her sister growled at her.

“Dad left it to me, Kuzunoha. There are other things you can do.”

“Name one,” Kuzunoha challenged. Himiko narrowed her eyes and didn’t answer. As the silence started dragging, Himiko flushed.

“Just let me talk with Tim and we’ll find a spo—”

“Never,” Kuzunoha spat.

Her father had raised her hopes over and over, promising her that she would be more than her sister, better in every way, if she just worked for it. His death had shattered her hopes. She was nothing but a spare and it was Himiko who'd been named heir in his will. The only thing Kuzunoha had received was a weekly dividend from the house, whether she worked or not.

Well, Kuzunoha would prove him and Himiko wrong. She would make something great of herself and she would do it without Himiko's help.

"Then choose something else. Something that isn't him," Himiko growled. "Father said that you should consider marrying for the family. Maybe I can find you a husband. Then you can be his problem."

Kuzunoha had wanted to marry once. Part of her still wanted a husband and a child one day. But if anything could break her, a loveless marriage of convenience would be it.

She didn't even try to warm her tone. "I don't care what future he wanted. That won't be mine."

"You can't be a child forever, Kuzunoha. One day, you'll have to accept that you have a familial duty to uphold," Himiko said.

To accept any of it would mean accepting all of it. She refused. Pushing past her sister, Kuzunoha ran to the one person who might understand what she needed right now.

Chapter 12

Richard moved the woman's hair out of her face as she lay in his arms. She was pretty, and of Sian Ku ancestry—she had dark hair and a golden tone to her skin. He'd always had a thing for exotic women.

Even more than her beauty, she was warm, which meant that the skin that she was cleaving to was warm as well. It was too cold in this blasted country. Where he'd grown up, there was no snow, only a muggy scorching heat that settled into your bones and warmed you for hours after the sun set. Here, the sun seemed pale and dying.

Miya snuggled closer, hiding her face by leaning into him and kissing his neck. He felt the tip of her tongue flick out and touch his neck, just before her lips followed. It wasn't the first time she'd used that trick and he had to admit, he liked it. He settled back again and pulled the covers up again. Her movement had knocked them loose enough to let in the chilly air that seemed to be the room's highest temperature.

"Oh, Richard, it's already too hot. Let me up and I'll open the window for us," she said.

He shivered. Under the covers, he was finally warm again. Not like back home, but warm instead of just above freezing. Regardless of how much he'd like to see her standing naked, it wasn't worth the loss of heat. She moved slightly against him and he grabbed her.

He smiled and cupped her breast, tilting it up to him while his other hand moved lower, exploring. She gasped, shivering and closed her eyes.

"I can think of much better ways to use up that energy, rather than wasting it on opening windows."

"Richard...sir..." She bucked and gasped again.

"That's what I like to hear." He purred, shifting the covers over his shoulders and climbing his way back on top of her. Miya let out a gasp, her eyes as wide as her beautiful lips were and opened her legs wider for him.

The door to his suite opened. "Richard, Dorif said you wer—"

He paused, an unvoiced growl in his throat. Who would enter a rented, unlocked room without knocking? Cold air snuck under the covers and his good mood vanished. Kuzunoha's head poked around the opening door. His shoulders dropped and he raised an eyebrow at her. Only an entitled lord's daughter would think that she was too important to knock.

"Kuzunoha, I'm a bit busy right—"

Both girls shrieked loud enough to be heard all the way through the floor to the bar below. Kuzunoha recovered first, partially covering her eyes with a splayed hand. "I'm sorry, Richard. I didn't realize. I'll lea—wait." Her hand dropped and she frowned. "Miya?"

The woman under him shrieked again and nearly kicked him out of bed in her dive for any anonymity the covers could give her. Richard shivered and picked up some clothing from the floor, yanking his pants on. Stupid people in a stupid frigid country, living in temperatures that no sane person would want to be naked in. He wished again for the warmth of his homeland. One day.

"Kuzunoha, get out."

He pushed her into the hallway, less gently than perhaps he could have. The chilly wooden floor numbed his toes. He looked back at Miya, her wide-eyed expression peeking out from covers pulled up above her nose.

"Don't move, Miya. I will return in just a moment."

He shut the door behind him. Kuzunoha's stared hard at the door, as if she believed it would allow her to see through the polished wooden walls to his bed again. Her cheeks were pink, but he didn't believe it was all out of embarrassment.

"Since you are determined to hold this conversation now, what is it you need?"

"Richard, what were you doing with my maid?"

He raised an eyebrow. "I should think that was obvious. Though what I do with anybody, on their off-time, in the privacy of my room," Richard stressed, "is no concern of yours. What do you want?"

Kuzunoha flushed at the reprimand but held his gaze. In a different situation, he would have been pleased. She'd been thinking about him in a way that made his attention to her maid irritate her. That was good since he wanted to have her in his bed as well. On the other hand, women were notoriously unwilling to leap into bed with a man that they'd just walked in on.

The banked fire in her eyes made him wish that she hadn't seen him though. Fire like that in a woman made her active, unpredictable, and fierce in a way that promised nibbles of teeth where other women would only flick their tongue.

"You're right... I thought..." She paused. "It doesn't matter what I thought. I'll return later."

Richard rolled his eyes. "I am already out... if it's something quick, I may be able to do something before I... return to my business."

She smiled at him, relieved. Part of him preened at her smile. The other part berated him for being too nice. Much too nice when he couldn't decide whether he wanted her to leave or stay.

"I…" She wouldn't meet his eyes, now for an entirely different reason. "My sister…I just needed someone to talk to about it. It's fine. I'll come back another time."

He closed his eyes. Sister rivalry. On the one hand, maple syrup. On the other, things like this. "Any difficulties that will stop our arrangements?"

She took a deep breath. "No. Nothing that she could arrange fast enough. It was just…troublesome."

He felt like a heel. She'd come by, hoping to talk to a friend. Instead, she'd found him busily engaged. He shook his head. Right now, he couldn't be her ear. "Then ignore her. Another week or two and we'll be gone. As soon as we find the ship, you'll have a lot more influence to wave back at her, all right?"

She nodded. "True. Another two weeks and she can't do anything." Her hands were squeezed into tight fists, but he didn't think she was the sort who would go looking for a fight.

"Did you need anything else?" he asked.

"No. Thank you and I'm sorry for...interrupting."

He smiled. "Normally, I'd invite you in for a drink and discuss what had happened. Right now… is clearly a bad time. Why don't you come over for lunch tomorrow instead?"

"Tomorrow won't work," she said, not quite meeting his eyes. "Talvert asked me to come and pick up the boxes from him."

"The day after then?" he pushed her, wishing he were well enough to help. He could take his injuries into account when having sex, ensuring it stayed slow and sensual. He couldn't do that with moving boxes. Fortunately, Kuzunoha didn't seem to notice his lack of an offer to help.

"You won't still be..." Her cheeks flushed. "Busy?"

Ah. That made sense. He smiled ruefully. He would be lucky if Miya agreed to come back. "I promise you, Kuzunoha, I don't double-time. If I say I will make time for you, I will be there."

"I'm glad to hear it." She smiled. "Please... will you tell Miya I'm sorry?"

He smiled. "Thank you, my lady. Happy hunting."

She glanced at his door. "I feel like I should be saying that to you."

She gave him a salute that proved she'd never been in an army and headed down the stairs. He smiled and composed himself again. It was time to solve the other mess: the woman who was probably desperately searching for her undergarments among the discarded clothes everywhere in the room.

He put his hand in his pocket, feeling the soft cotton under his fingers. Fortunately, she'd be searching a very long time. Time that he could use to convince her to stay and finish what they'd begun.

Chapter 13

As Kuzunoha walked towards Talvert's shop, she saw Himiko step out of it with the smuggest look she'd seen in months. A weight pulled on Kuzunoha's stomach. She resisted running in the other direction. Himiko didn't do her own shopping, any more than Kuzunoha did, but she may have had other business with Talvert that had nothing to do with herself.

She let out a breath. Himiko couldn't do anything to stop her, but still, Kuzunoha wondered if she was taking her seriously enough. Shaking her head, she walked over to the store.

The shop was as full as it always was. Every item was three to five items deep and shoved onto the shelves in no discernable order. She smiled at Talvert when she entered and saw a set of boxes set to the far side of his counter. Three of them were large enough that she would probably have to take them out separately. They had to be hers. She made a quick calculation. She could hire a horse and wagon to help transport the boxes for five silver with an extra silver if she got the gentleman to help her with the loading and unloading. She didn't have money to waste it, but with Richard still injured, she couldn't ask him to help out.

"Talvert, thank you for wrapping all of this up for me," Kuzunoha said, reaching for her money purse.

Talvert winced. "Actually, those are stock for the store. I have a box and a half for you, but…well, I wanted to talk to you about it."

Her sister had definitely been here, interfering with her sister's business. Kuzunoha smiled at him, trying to keep the expression genuine. "Of course. What would you like to talk about?"

He wouldn't quite meet her eyes, playing with the strings of his white apron. "Miss Kuzunoha. How is the bag I sold you?"

"Perfect," she said, knowing that would work his way around to what he wanted to talk about. "I love the design and its been holding up quite well so far."

"Good…good. Have you spoken to Almeric yet?"

Kuzunoha let out a measured breath. The roads outside of town could be dangerous and she'd gone to Almeric for a set of leather armor. Even the simplest set still needed to be fitted to the person it was meant for. "Of course. Why?"

"There's been a bit of a delay on stock right now. It's going to take a lot longer to get in."

"Here, as well as with Almeric?" she asked, holding out hope that the feeling in the pit of her stomach was wrong.

He looked nervous but nodded. Kuzunoha gritted her teeth.

"How long will it be? And on what?"

"Everything... especially medical supplies. As for time"—he paused—

"I really don't know. It could be months."

Months. Richard had said that they would discuss how far they were tomorrow and decide when they would leave then. This wasn't an ordinary stock issue though. If she let it go, it would be a failure on her part. She could see her future now. Dreary, dull, working as her sister's underling for the rest of her life. She would eventually be married off for the good of the family while her sister married whom she wanted and ran the family business.

She set her jaw. "I'm sure we can work around that. I can see you still have some of the items I'll need here," she said, looking at him and not at his inventory. "Perhaps I can take those away with me immediately."

A last chance for him to rethink his decision. He swallowed and averted his gaze. "Maybe we should wait. With delays being as they are...well, maybe you'll want to wait on them."

"Oh? Why would that be?" Her cheeks hurt from holding the smile.

"Just think about it," he said, instead of answering her.

Just think about it… long enough for her to hopefully rethink her situation. She felt a rumble at the back of her throat and stopped the growl before it formed. "Maybe you're right, Talvert. Perhaps we can talk about other things." He smiled and she closed her trap. "Like what my sister offered you."

"She didn't offer me anything." His feet weren't in accordance with his mouth and he stepped back.

"Gods be damned, Talvert." He flinched. "You've never gotten involved before, not even when that black fabric came in and everybody wanted it."

It sounded civil enough, but it had been a bloody war between her and Himiko. Her hair still hadn't grown back to its prior length before the paint incident.

"What changed?" she asked.

He shrunk back. Maybe he was remembering the paint too. "Your sister and the healer are worried because you're leaving town with a man no one knows. The only thing we do know about him is that he has money and he's dangerous. I can understand you wanting to break away from your family, but this isn't the way."

His tone was gentle, supportive. He almost made the argument sound reasonable. But there was one thing that Kuzunoha couldn't believe. Deckard would never try to control her life. He'd made it quite plain that he wanted nothing to do with her.

"Deckard and your sister just want to help. Why don't you talk to Jack instead? I hear he's been making some good in-roads with his business running that new warehouse of his on the docks. He would be more than willing to take some capital and offer you a position, I'm sure. Up to your rank, too."

The man was smiling as if he thought he'd found the perfect solution to the situation. As if she would be happy working as a secretary to the Kerlow family. No matter how much she liked Jack, she wouldn't enjoy working for him. Besides, this deal with Richard would be her chance to prove to the world that she was capable and more than what society said she could be.

Really though, it was Deckard's involvement that frustrated her the most. He'd told her to stay out of his life. She had, even after she'd realized how stupid she'd been. She'd thought that there had been an unspoken promise that he would do the same.

"Let me see if I understand this. You won't sell me the items I need because the boy I used to date said he doesn't like me going away for a week?" she asked.

She'd expected Himiko getting involved. She'd planned the arguments she'd need to use against her sister. Deckard's betrayal hurt worse for her not having expected it. Talvert looked confused. "It has nothing to do with him being connected to you, or about Himiko being your sister for that matter. Look at that business with the dead men. That's suspicious in and of itself. The sheriff still hasn't even been able to find out where they came from."

"Deckard doesn't have any control over my life. No more than Himiko will soon." Kuzunoha spat.

"Lady, neither of them want to control you. They just want to keep you safe."

Kuzunoha clenched her fists. She was going to kill them both.

Chapter 14

"It's not even illegal," Richard said. Kuzunoha narrowed her eyes and he shrugged. "It's a low blow, I grant you, but he is allowed to decide who he wants to do business with. Legally, he doesn't even need a reason to not sell to you."

Kuzunoha felt the hard wood of the wall behind her and stared at the greens and soup on the table. It was a good lunch. She could smell the savory spices from where she stood. Unfortunately, she had no appetite for it right now.

"You'll have to convince one or both to back off and have them explain their change of heart to your store owner. If it doesn't then we can see about more drastic issues," he finished.

Kuzunoha punched the wall of Richard's room and then grabbed her knuckles, wincing. The wood hurt a lot more than she'd thought it would. "How am I supposed to do that?" The wall wasn't damaged, which irritated her. The room was very natural looking, untreated wood for the walls, undyed linens…even the tables had a natural feel to them. "They won't listen to me."

He had seen how her sister acted towards her. "What about your ex, Deckard?"

She closed her eyes and leaned into the wall again. The wood felt smooth and cool on her forehead and the faint scent of cedar surrounded her. As it always did, the sharp scent was calming, grounding her for what she had to do next. She pressed her knuckles against it. “How did you even find out about that?”

Richard shrugged. He was sitting on the bed and his shirt was a shade of purple she’d never seen before. She wondered how they made the dye. “It isn’t exactly a secret. The entire town remembers when you were together.”

“That’s simplifying it, I’m sure. How many of them remember it and hate me?”

“Seems to depend on whether the individual is young and female or not.” He joked as though the thoughts of everyone else weren’t a concern.

She wanted to laugh. Instead, she pushed away from the wall and felt a rivulet of blood run down the back of her hand. The skin on her knuckle was torn.

“So, what happened between you two?”

She deliberately misunderstood. “Himiko and I? I thought it was obvious.”

Richard gave a significant cough. “Normally, I’d just leave it at that. However, if you won’t go talk to him, I’ll have to. At this rate, they won’t sell me anything either, which also means I won’t be able to leave if I need to.”

“What? Why?”

"I need supplies to travel as well. Not everything, of course, but I'd like more food, bandages and ointments before I go. There's less issue if I take a ship but it will be a pain, and will leave me unprepared if anything happens, even if I can pick up anything I need in the next town over."

Kuzunoha looked out the window, grumbling. She wanted both of them out of her life. Everything would be so very easy with them gone. Or if she just left…she put that specific thought back in its box. She had to stay. At least until this was over. If she didn't, they won.

Richard touched her arm. She hadn't even heard him get up. He pulled her to the table and started wrapping up her hand with gauze. "There are a lot of rumors about why you broke up."

"Yeah?" She tried to sound surprised. When she didn't say anything else he tapped her hand as if reminding her to go on. She sighed. "I slept with someone else. He was a little bit older, a little bit more mysterious..."

Richard smiled. "A little less safe."

She leaned away. "At any rate, I got caught. Deckard left me in the dirt." She didn't add 'where I belonged.' It wasn't necessary.

"And he's still trying to do what's best for you…you two have a weird relationship."

"We don't have a relationship," she told him. "He's just being a pain in my ass."

"Family will always be a pain in the ass."

Kuzunoha didn't think your ex was supposed to count as family. Instead of raising that point, she grumbled. "They don't think I'm capable."

"You'll be out of your element, I'll give you that, but we shouldn't be doing anything out there that you wouldn't have to deal with here. What else?"

She didn't answer. She didn't have to.

Richard sighed.

Kuzunoha ripped her hand out of his and slammed it on the table. Her hand protested, throbbing. It started bleeding again and she grit her teeth against the pain.

Richard looked at her, his eyes wide. She blushed. He pointed to her hand. Red was already seeping up through the white of the gauze. Great.

Richard got quiet. "Do you think I stole the book?"

His fingers tapped on it, an irrepressible little dance that clicked away in the background.

She shrugged. "That or you slept with the wrong man's wife. Either way, why you're running doesn't concern me. It doesn't change what we're doing here."

Richard stared at her and she guessed that he hadn't expected that answer.

"It wasn't either of those," he said quietly.

"Armed men don't come after people they don't want something from. That doesn't concern me though. What does is you. From what I've seen, you hold a few weird beliefs, and you clearly have someone looking for you. Still, keeping things to yourself doesn't make you untrustworthy."

"I didn't take anything from the one that sent the bounty hunters. She… wants me back for other reasons. I don't like talking about it." He paused. "You don't seem to mind my secrets."

"You have a history you want to escape…" Kuzunoha said, not meeting his eyes. She only hoped that when she escaped hers, it didn't come with bounty hunters attached. "And you protected me that first night, when that thug decided that murdering his target and the townie girl helping him was a better way to get what he wanted. That protection makes me inclined to trust you. Anyway, what have you found out about the ship."

"The ship's captain was a woman named Jezebel Cartine, but the patron who had commissioned the trip was Morioka Norio."

"Do you mean Norio Morioka?" When Richard looked at her oddly, she shrugged. "In Sian Ku, the family name comes first. Morioka is a family name. I was wondering if we were dealing with a foreigner or someone who lived here."

Richard shook his head. "It isn't important. They hired the captain in Kalvettika and by the time they neared Hidan, they were only carrying him and his treasure. A huge storm hit the day before they arrived. That's where the tale gets a bit muddled."

"Muddled?"

Richard grimaced. "According to the book, the ship hadn't sunk…he says they'd made landfall before everything went wrong."

"If they'd landed, someone in Hidan would have noticed." The hunters, if no one else. Hidan's surrounding coastline simply wasn't that big. "Why would they land in a storm?"

"That's part of what I can't understand either. Trying to land a ship in a storm like that is just asking to be driven onto shore, or into those cliffs that you call the shore. At least on the water, they could try to navigate the waves to avoid the worst of it."

The shore around Hidan was never wide to begin with and many times the water would come right up to the cliffs. The cliffs were nearly fifty feet tall and treacherously steep in most places. Every time the storms came they chipped a little more away from the cliffs, which would make the cliffs even worse to land near since they could have rocks hiding just under the water.

"It makes no sense, regardless of how high the water comes. A ship that doesn't sit too low in the water could get near the beach. The shore itself drops off after ten feet or so. It still doesn't make sense though, not in a storm. Even smugglers wouldn't attempt that."

"Are there any pirate coves around here?" Richard asked.

Kuzunoha nearly snorted. There had never been pirates around Hidan. The holy well had been a gift for keeping the people of Hidan safe. Even the pirates were more likely to barter than attack a town that guarded a holy shrine.

"Not in my lifetime," she muttered to herself. That was the key, wasn't it? This ship had disappeared before her lifetime, probably before her father's lifetime. "There was an old woman who used to tell stories. Her tales didn't often involve pirates, but there was one. A pirate named Sun Silver hid from the Belish Navy for three days straight. After the third day, the Belish Navy gave up their search. As they did, Sun's ship slipped out of a sunbeam and harried the navy until they reached Havenhare."

"They hid in a sunbeam?"

"Technically, they slipped out of…" Kuzunoha closed her eyes, trying to remember her exact wording. It had been something poetic. "A sun-touched mirror."

It hadn't made sense then and it still didn't now. "That effectively cuts out any natural caves. Still, are there any around here, other than the holy site?"

The beach was visible from the holy site, but pirate cave it was not.

"I'll dig up a few of the old maps of the area and see if I can find anything. At the very least, we'll probably want to get a canoe, if Talvert won't sell us one. That is one item we may be able to get from Jack. One of his ships may have one that we could borrow. Regardless, if they didn't beach themselves, then the ship must be somewhere in the water. I'll look for likely places."

"The ship couldn't have been too far though. Where did they find him?"

"Tonoro's Hill."

He paused but she nodded, gesturing with her uninjured hand. "I've been to it. It's a three-day walk, but it isn't shoreside at all. Even with our few marshes up here, it's all landlocked."

Himiko's mother had taken Kuzunoha and her sister before she'd died. Kuzunoha had loved exploring the cave there. Afterwards, she'd climbed over the city wall as often as she'd needed. Getting out, even if she stayed in the flower-filled plain outside the walls, had been its own reward.

"We can start there, at least, and move our way to the shore," Richard said.

She breathed a sigh of relief. "I'll get on my part so we can actually start leaving then."

"And you'll do that by…"

"Talking to Deckard. There must be some way to change his mind. And if I can change his mind, I may be able to push him to help me convince Talvert to ignore my sister again."

"I still have something I need to look into as well. Why don't you join me for dinner tonight?"

"Of course. Here?"

"In my room again, yes."

She'd meant at the Koi in general and her face heated. She couldn't stop her glance towards his bed. The last time she'd stepped in this room, nearly a week ago, Richard had been there with her maid, of all people. She looked away, trying to deny her flush. Richard coughed to get her attention.

"I'm sorry, but I wasn't issuing an invitation."

She'd never been so embarrassed in her life.

"We're business partners." His tone was cold. "I wouldn't want to change our agreement, muddying the waters, so to speak."

Her cheeks were blazing now. She couldn't decide if she was angry at him for reading her so clearly or embarrassed that she'd just been turned down.

"So, if we weren't business partners..." She broke off and headed for the door. That was too forward, even for her.

"You are very attractive." His gaze was hot, but he reined it under control. "Perhaps later. I hope we can still do business together."

It wasn't a no. It was a 'not right now.' Her mouth felt dry and she swallowed, her hand just above the door handle. She could tell him that she would rather share his bed than his treasure. Another wave of heat rolled through her.

She took a deep breath, hearing Richard step up behind her. She bit down on her tongue and the pain cleared her mind. If she took him up on that offer, her sister and Deckard would win. She would never get out, never get away. She would have confirmed everything they believed about her.

Turning, she caught Richard's hand in hers. He'd been reaching out to touch her. Slivers of cold blossomed along her back where she imagined his fingers.

"You're right, Richard. I was incredibly rude to even suggest it." She swallowed. “Perhaps we can discuss the matter again when we aren’t partners.”

Richard looked surprised and something flashed in his eyes, there and then gone again so quickly that she couldn’t identify it. “Yes. In the meantime, we can consider our dinner tonight to be our victory celebration.”

It took her a moment to realize what he meant. Deckard. She groaned. They hadn’t solved anything, and despite her earlier bravado in simply thinking that talking with Deckard would convince him to stop meddling in her affairs, she didn’t actually think it would be that easy.

“Or at least a shoulder to cry on?” she suggested, annoyed at the slight whine in her tone.

“Kuzunoha, I have great faith in you.” A smile tugged at the corner of his lips.

“I’m glad,” she said, seeing Deckard’s lips caught in their usual frown, rather than Richard’s smile. “Because what I have faith in is Deckard’s stubbornness.”

Chapter 15

Her hand lay on the inside gate latch, stinging from the light touch on her cuts, but she couldn't bring herself to open it. The house was well built, stone with a well-kept roof. It was the fourth largest home in the village. His mother had been given it when she had become one of Hidan's healers. Deckard had taken it over from her when she'd died.

It hadn't changed since she was five. It wasn't painted, the mortar old and crumbling. Once a week the woodcutters refilled the wood along the west wall, so it was always well stocked, even in winter, so Deckard could bring in bundles to dry before burning. A small cellar was carved out of the dirt and Deckard among other things, it had a furnace in it that could be used to heat the entire house, though he preferred to use the stove in the kitchen to do it if no one was ill. She took a deep breath. There was something about the property that just smelled right; a clean scent that she didn't associate with anything else in the city.

She moved near the door and heard pots banging together. She hesitated and then growled. She wasn't going to get anything done like this and she was embarrassing herself. She opened the gate and strode up the walkway to knock on the door.

She regretted it as she heard a feminine voice. She'd forgotten about the woman he'd been with a few weeks ago at her sister's majority celebration. "I'll get it, Deckard."

The woman that opened the door was dark-skinned, with curly brown hair and warm eyes. Immediately, the pleasant smile on the woman's face dimmed. She looked older when she wasn't smiling, maybe Deckard's age. Kuzunoha reached for the girl's name so as to not embarrass herself further. It was a traveler's name.Timi…no. Tieni, that was it.

"The silly girl from the Koi. The one Deckard hit with the door?" the woman asked, clearly not expecting an answer.

Kuzunoha ground her teeth. "My name is Kuzunoha. You're Tieni from the kompania."

They were traveling folk, unable to settle down in any city; Thieves more often than not, as well as entertainers. Her father had always said that most kompanies were also bandits when the towns didn't give them enough money for their performances.

The woman smiled widely. "I'm not surprised that you've heard of me. I came into town with a kompania and I still perform in the Koi on occasion. What is your favorite song, girl? Perhaps I'll give you a show if you have coin."

Kuzunoha smiled as toothily as possible, imagining that she was a cat showing its fangs. "I'm not a fan of windbags, gasping for breath as they try to keep an audience entertained."

Tieni sucked in a breath. Her dark eyes looked closer to a fiery orange as she folded her arms over her chest. "Well then, you have no business here at all."

"Ah, but I do." Kuzunoha caught the door as Tieni tried to close it. "If I wanted to see you, I'd frequent the Koi. Since I'm at the healer's..."

Tieni raised an eyebrow and then smoothed down her shirt, a flimsy bright thing that flowed over her loosely, slipped off one shoulder. That shoulder was thickly muscled. More thickly muscled than most non-hunters.

"He's currently engaged, unless you're injured, Kit-kit."

"My name is Kuzunoha, not..."

Just behind Tieni, Kuzunoha saw Deckard, wearing nothing but a pair of pants, walking out of the bedroom. He pulled on a bleached shirt over a leanly muscled chest. He'd tied his hair back today and it shone like wheat, hanging just long enough to touch his shoulders. The blue of his eyes caught the light and she stepped back.

"Tieni? Am I needed?"

Kuzunoha saw Tieni smile at her. Kuzunoha realized that she'd moved back, lost ground. She fought an instinct to run. She wouldn't run from Deckard—she owed him that much. Technically, she owed him happiness as well, but she couldn't give her blessing with Tieni. The woman seemed like a grasping worm. Deckard deserved better.

He saw her and stopped, his expression hardening. "Kuzunoha, what are you doing here?"

She raised her hands. “Nothing that I—”

She didn’t even finish before he’d moved forward to grab her hand—the one Richard had wrapped. “How did you get hurt? Get in here. What were you doing?”

Tieni’s eyes flashed, but she moved aside before Deckard pushed her. Kuzunoha had to stop herself from grinning. True, Deckard was only doing it because she’d been hurt, but the alacrity with which he drew her into the house made her happy. As he sat her down, Kuzunoha saw that Tieni was grimacing, her arms folded over her chest again.

“Deckard, I’m going out. Don’t forget about our dinner tonight.” She leaned in for a kiss. Then she whispered, loud enough that Kuzunoha could hear her, “We can finish this later.”

Deckard kissed her back. “Thank you, Tieni.”

Deckard started unwrapping her hand, but Kuzunoha watched Tieni saunter out if she owned the place. “I don’t understand what you see in that girl.”

“She isn’t a girl. She’s a woman.”

The comparison, even if he would argue that it wasn’t one, rankled. Kuzunoha stood. “This was a bad idea. I’ll be fine.”

Deckard grabbed her hand and she hissed as his finger clamped down on her knuckles. “Sit down. Kuzunoha. You’re hurt, I’m not going to let you go like this.”

She sat back down, looking away. "It doesn't hurt that much."

He reached the bottom layer of the wrapping. She hissed as he tugged her skin up with the bandage. Deckard stood and then returned to the table a moment later with a bowl of warm water. He wet the bandage before gently massaging it off.

It looked worse now. The skin was brown and flakey with dried blood and the scrapes looked red around the edges. Deckard put some alcohol on a cloth and cleaned her knuckles. It hurt but the pain felt like a benediction. "Kuzunoha. What did you do?"

She tried to meet his eyes but couldn't do it. "I punched a wall."

He laid a hand on hers. "Why would you do that?"

"I was…" Would she ever get a better opening than that? "Angry. Talvert is withholding my items."

"Why would he do that?" Deckard didn't seem to be paying attention to her.

"He thinks you're very wise," Kuzunoha said, instead of answering him.

"I don't see how those two things are related."

He sounded confused. She risked a glance. "You told him you don't approve of my plans."

Deckard shifted. Now he was paying attention. "I don't. I made that clear. I may have healed Richard, but even I can't deny he's shady. He plays his cards close to his chest and managed to kill four men while drunk in the dark. I don't like the idea of anyone getting involved with a man like that. Regardless, I don't see why we're even talking about this."

"Because you and my sister have convinced Talvert that I'll be murdered if I leave town with him."

Deckard said darkly. "You're leaving town with a man you don't know. Himiko worries."

"You know how she is. I could be doing anything and she'd be against it because she didn't suggest it."

He pushed away from the table. "So go. Talvert will sell you what you..."

"No, he won't. That's what I came here for. That isn't what worries me though. What happens when Almeric says that there is a problem with the weapons or armor I've purchased?"

"Kuzunoha, have you thought for a moment that Himiko and I may be right?"

"I can't stay here, doing nothing for the rest of my life."

"So, get a job with someone here in town."

"With whom?" She threw up her hands. "I'm still a daughter of the Tanaka family. They won't let me work, knowing who my father was. You remember what happened when I tried last time."

They were both standing. When had that happened?

"What am I supposed to do about it? You can't make your own decisions. You're still a child."

"I'm an adult, Deckard. I make my own decisions."

"You make bad ones!"

It was a slap in the face. She slumped into her chair and a moment later, he followed suit. Neither would meet the other's eyes.

"How am I supposed to prove that I'm capable of making good decisions if you and my sister won't even let me try?" Her tone was low and angry.

"Is that what you think I'm doing?" he said just as quietly.

She didn't answer him. She didn't think she needed to.

"Richard is still a bad influence," he said.

It was enough. "Thank you," she said. Then she smiled, trying to lighten the mood. "We'll leave the interfering to Himiko from now on."

He didn't smile. "I rather like Himiko, you know. She has a good head on her shoulders."

Her heart dropped into her stomach and she stood to leave. "She's easy to like."

Chapter 16

"Miya?"

Her father had hired the maid when Kuzunoha had been budding into womanhood. Miya had been the pretty one then, two years older with the body of a woman. Kuzunoha had been sure she would outpace the girl, but Kuzunoha had stayed slim and tiny and Miya had stayed pretty and curvy, more like Himiko than herself. Kuzunoha could see why Richard had seduced her. "What do you need, Miss?"

"Please run a bath for me and then I'll need you on hand to dress tonight."

It was her majority day tomorrow. She would be an adult, officially and her sister would give her her autonomy. It meant less for her than it did for Himiko, of course. She wasn't inheriting anything, she didn't have anything waiting for her but without it, she had no power to make her own decisions. She would still be a child before the law. If Kuzunoha had left before, her sister could have sent others after her, forced her return, could have attempted to punish Richard for going with her. If she didn't want to burn her bridges to everyone and everything in Hidan, she needed Himiko to give her her freedom.

"Of course. What would you like me to set out?"

"The cherry tree dress."

Miya gaped at her. "Miss? The white and pink one?"

The dress was an heirloom, brought from Sian Ku when their family came over, generations ago. Her father had wanted the dress to go to Himiko, but in a perfect instance of happenstance, her sister had grown too tall for it. Their father had begrudgingly given it to Kuzunoha.

More than adequate for a simple dinner with Richard, but she wanted to wear it; wanted everyone who saw her to remember that she wasn't a child anymore. A larger part of her just wanted to look better than her sister had at her majority.

"Yes, I think I'll also want the orange and red sashes for it tonight."

"Yes, miss," Miya said, nearly tripping over herself in her haste to get away.

After the bath, with the expensive robe settled around her, Kuzunoha grinned. Its colors reflected a blooming cherry tree beside a river. She knew that the large ribbons that she had chosen to go with it would suit perfectly. Even Himiko wouldn't compare to her tonight.

She heard the door to the house open and slam shut. Miya jumped, rushing out of the room the moment Kuzunoha gestured that she could leave. She hoped she could get out of the house before Himiko got here, but Kuzunoha could deal with it if she didn't. It wasn't as if she didn't need to see Himiko tomorrow anyway. It was tradition that the head of the household give some sort of gift to any member that reached their majority. Knowing that they would need to talk soon usually resulted in both of them ignoring the other even more than they normally did. Her sister had always been contrary. She had just finished applying the lightest amount of kohl to her eyes when Himiko burst into her room.

"What did you do, Kuzunoha?"

Kuzunoha turned to her and knitted her eyebrows together. "Please be more specific, Himiko."

Himiko gnashed her teeth together loud enough that Kuzunoha could hear it. "You got to Deckard. He showed up at my office and said that you were my problem to deal with. That it might be better if I let you leave."

Kuzunoha hadn't expected Deckard to do anything like that. For a moment she just blinked, confused.

"Have you considered that he might be right?"

Himiko's expression suggested that she wasn't going to. "You're being stubborn and dragging the family's name down with you. Treasure-hunting." Himiko snorted. "I thought you were gullible, but not that gullible. And why are you wearing that? Kuzunoha, that heirloom has been in the family for over one hundred years. I certainly hope you aren't primping this much to go meet with him."

Kuzunoha's eyes narrowed. "Who I meet with and what I wear during those meetings isn't your concern."

Himiko entered the room and slammed the door behind her. "That's where you're wrong. You're a member of this family, which means that everything you do reflects back on me. That's why you get away with so much. Nobody wants to discipline a member of the Tanaka family."

Kuzunoha wanted to grind her own teeth together. "Excuse me? I don't think..."

"You can't keep on this way. It's time to grow up. How can I trust you with part of our family's heritage when you clearly don't respect any of it?"

"How can you say that? I am a grown woman. You're the one trying to keep me a child."

"You are a child. One that can't even keep a job."

"I don't call what Tim offered me a job," Kuzunoha said. Himiko pounced on the words.

"You still quit." Her sister said.

"A clerk, Himiko. He gave me a job filing and rewriting out reports. Don't act like you don't know that."

"To each their skill level," her sister quoted at her.

Kuzunoha clenched her fist. Her father had made sure that she could do her job well enough to run the company. She had more skill than that of a simple clerk.

"I learned from father, just as you did. If I didn't learn correctly, then maybe its because hadn't taught me correctly.

Himiko's mouth thinned to a line. "Kuzunoha, if you leave with him, I will tell Harrison that you've been kidnapped."

"Himiko, everyone knows that I want to do this." It didn't mean that her sister couldn't do it.

"That doesn't mean you can do it. You're a child, Kuzunoha."

"As of tomorrow, I am not."

"You will be given your majority when I feel you are capable of making adult decisions."

"You would deny me my majority?" Kuzunoha was speechless. "You can't do that."

"I can, Kuzunoha. You forget, I am your guardian, not just your sister. You do not have my permission for this venture." Himiko stormed off.

Kuzunoha looked in the mirror. A perfect little doll in a perfect little dress. She wanted to break the perfect little image with her fist.

Could she burn everything? Leave Hidan for good after finding this treasure? She would have to if her sister decreed her an invalid before the law. If she left, she might be able to hide her shame from employers, but she would never be able to hide from her ancestors. Every child she had would carry that shame. She remembered Richard's words. *As soon as we find the ship, you'll have a lot more influence to wave back at her.*

She finished packing her backpack with a few things that she didn't want to lose, her few important keepsakes. Then she looked at herself in the mirror again. She looked ridiculous. A backpack, too heavy for her sharp frame strung over her shoulders, while wearing an outfit that wasn't suited for heavy wear. She'd be better suited wearing her regular clothes.

She left the room anyway.

Miya was waiting near the front door. "Mistress?"

"Clean my room and extinguish the lights. If Himiko asks, tell her I've gone out."

"But..." The girl glanced up towards Himiko's study.

"If she doesn't ask, you don't have to tell her."

"But…" she said again.

Kuzunoha took a step forward and Miya flinched. The girl nodded too fast.

Kuzunoha opened the door. A cool breeze hit her face, bringing scents of fire and cooking food on the air, as well as all the less pleasant scents within the town: horse manure, piss, and the sickeningly sweet scent of rot. She steeled herself.

Miya had been with them so long. She was one of the few remaining pure-blooded Sian Ku in the village; when Kuzunoha's father had been alive he had refused to hire otherwise to work as house servants. She kept her hair only long enough to sweep her shoulders, and her eyes were much darker than Kuzunoha's. In the dim light coming from outside, Kuzunoha couldn't tell where the brown ended and the black began in them.

"Miya, how is Richard in bed?"

Her maid turned red, from the black collar around her neck all the way up to her hairline and said nothing. Kuzunoha winced a little herself. She hadn't meant that to sound as cruel as it had. "I'm sorry."

Kuzunoha stepped outside. She had a dinner to get to and then later, she would need to figure out a place to sleep.

Chapter 17

Richard finished putting the final touches on his room. He'd aired it out all day and cleaned up; he'd even asked the maid to polish the wood floor. It hadn't cost him much to get the tiny personal table removed from the room and one of the tables from the Lucky Koi brought up. He'd ordered dinner for two, noodles and a sauce, with a salad on the side.

The food still seemed out of place, full of salt and other preserves. Growing up in Jisa, they'd always had fresh fish, fruits, and vegetables year-round. Here, the growing seasons were short, like their blasted cold summers. It surprised him that anything could grow at all.

Regardless, everything was ready. Now all he had to do was not sleep with Kuzunoha. It was the sort of plan that was just crazy enough to work. Act professional and ready to take on anything, but don't let it get too personal. All he had to was pretend he wasn't crazy about her.

There was a quiet knock on the door and he straightened his outfit again. He didn't own courtier's outfits anymore, but he'd had his own clothes washed and he'd polished every bit of metal on them. Cold iron didn't shine up well, but he'd done his best. As always, he was armed—his weapons hidden, but accessible. Three daggers, plus another four throwing knives. A smaller amount than he'd normally carry, but he had to be prepared.

He opened the door, smiling. His jaw dropped.

It was Kuzunoha, but not the Kuzunoha he'd expected.

She usually wore robes tied with thick heavy ribbons. Miya had said that they were a type of plain daily dress from Sian Ku. This dress was similar but hung differently. The cloth was thinner and the belts tighter. They were a resplendent white that you couldn't get if you weren't noble and the pink and blue threads running through the design were lustrous on the stark background. They hung to her feet, stopping just above her ankles. She wasn't wearing boots of any sort, but a strange platformed sandal with toed socks. He found the socks strangely comforting, as if they were proof that he wasn't the only one who found the weather here abominable.

She had just the slightest amount of kohl around her eyes and some lipstick on her lips. Her hair was tied up with silk strands and silver sticks, decorated with tiny gems. Elegant, easily put up, and so satisfying to remove.

Her expression was determined, which he found strangely disconcerting.

Richard took a deep breath, trying to slow his pounding heart. He didn't know where all the air had gone. A small part begged him to give in, a roaring in his ears that he could ignore only with effort. It was too easy to fall to thoughts of pushing her on the bed and opening that dress.

"Kuzunoha, I'm glad you're here. Sit. I'll tell them to bring up dinner."

He opened the door and moved into the hallway. It was cool after her heat. He put his forehead against the wall and the chill wood welcomed him instead of making him shiver.

A large body moved up the stairs towards him. Lifting his head, Richard saw one of the innkeeper's sons, a thick-set man with dark hair and skin lighter than Richard's, walking towards him carrying two steaming plates of pasta.

"She has that effect on everyone. I would have died happy if she had turned the smile she wore downstairs on me."

Richard knew that feeling and remembered the first time he'd felt it. He still remembered her, blonde hair and nails shining blood red. He clenched his fist. He would die before he went to another on his knees. But something the man had said caught his attention. "She was smiling downstairs?"

When the guy nodded, Richard took the plates and stepped back into his room. Maybe there was still a chance for both of them to enjoy the evening.

Kuzunoha was on his bed, playing with one of his other daggers. The cold metal touched her fingers and he felt himself relax.

"What is this metal?" she asked, toying with it. "It's all you use, but I've never seen it before."

"It's cold iron," he said, putting the plates on the table.

She tilted her head. "Like in the old myths about fairies?"

"Yes. I traveled through a few of the old forests on my way up here. My guide suggested that the more you carried, the less likely one was to take you."

Not that the suggestion had helped his guide in the end. Fey were good at convincing people to stab themselves in the foot. A truly good servant would then apologize for bleeding on the floor and offer to clean it up.

Kuzunoha was naïve. She laughed with the carefree abandon of someone who thought fey were silly. "Does it work? We don't have those types of monsters around here. Only goblins and their ilk."

"Oh, they are very real, Lady."

"Truly? The only story I've heard told of a fey gentleman and his fight to keep his true love, a mortal girl, with him."

If the fey had cared for the girl in the story, it was clearly only as a toy. Richard shivered and touched one of the body-warmed hilts at his waist. It was comforting in the way only a tool of violence could be.

Kuzunoha sat up straighter. "Wait. You mean you've seen one? Not just superstitions you've heard?"

He pulled his hand away from the knife with difficulty. "Enough to make me believe that any love they felt was nothing but a facsimile of emotion."

He hazily remembered terrified eyes in a dark forest, a kiss, and then the man gasping, claws in his belly. Kuzunoha was at his side, but he hadn't heard her move. Not a good sign. He breathed deeply. He was in Hidan, not in the Karnesian forests.

"A bad experience?"

"I lost a... friend." It wasn't the whole story or even the right story, but it would do for the nonce. He pushed her away and moved to the table. He picked up his fork and viciously stabbed the dinner. Nothing this evening was going like he had planned.

He sat and took a deep breath. The pasta smelled rich and heavy from the creamy white sauce. The scent of the freshly baked bread with it was heaven. It was as far away from dark, cool forests as one could get. The salad was odd, full of cauliflower, carrots, celery, and radishes. He shoveled the forkful of pasta into his mouth and chewed.

Kuzunoha sat down across from him and picked up her fork.

"I spoke with Deckard," she said. "He was amenable."

"And your sister?" he asked.

Kuzunoha put down her fork and looked out the window. Her lower lip trembled. "She said that if I left with you, she'd call it kidnapping to the sheriff."

"How legal is that?" he asked, putting down his fork. He thought that anything legal could be done against her, but perhaps he had simply been blessed growing up in Jisa. That idea scared him more than a little. Kuzunoha had been about to take a bite of the pasta, but she put her fork down, sighing.

"Honestly? I'm not sure. She's the family matriarch now and my legal guardian. If I leave without her giving me my autonomy, it could mean trouble."

"How old are you?" He said, thinking quickly.

He'd known that she hadn't attained her majority yet but hadn't considered how that would affect her. He'd been on his own since his mother had died when he'd been nine. Nobody cared how old you were on the street. They cared how big you were and whether or not you could defend your turf.

"I'll be twenty-one tomorrow," she said.

"Twenty-one? Not nineteen?" Nearly four years older than him. How in the hell did anything get done if you had to wait until you were twenty-one? "But if you'll have passed your majority?"

"It's non-negotiable, but I think I've found a way around it. At least of any trouble for you. If I leave town without seeing my sister I can argue that I knew it was an empty threat, that I knew she'd never really do it. Then if she does, all the trouble will fall on me, not you."

That was a very fine edge to skirt. "Will your sheriff listen to that argument?"

"He might. The mayor though… likes my sister. If she's willing to go to him, he might change the law or just make her continued guardianship of me legal. I… have to be willing to ostracize myself completely if I want to leave after that. But that would my choice and not your trouble."

Dangerous…was it too dangerous to still go with her? Now was the time to back out if he was going to.

"We just need to pick up our items up from Talvert. Unfortunately, even with Deckard backing off, he isn't willing to discuss it. So, how would you feel about me involving a friend and having us leave tomorrow, or the day after at the latest?" Kuzunoha finally ate the bit of pasta on her fork.

He wasn't averse to the idea of leaving town sooner rather than later. It might even be prudent depending on what he found out tonight at his meeting. "A friend? Won't Talvert know that he's buying the items for you?"

"Jack owns a boat. He could claim it was supplies for the boat. I'd buy them from him, but unless he happens to be arranging a trip, he probably won't have any on hand."

"Who is this guy?"

"He's a member of Hidan's other ruling family. The Kerlow's control the docks and Jack personally works with the church to provide tours of the holy site. He offered me a job once… but I was still hoping to take over the family business at the time. I… even if he offered again, I don't know that I could accept working under him."

Richard sat back and she finally ate the pasta on her fork. She stabbed at a bit of the salad next.

"We could use his aid. Would he be willing to help for free?"

"He's a give-and-take kind of guy..." Kuzunoha said, before wincing. "Let me try that again. He's a good guy, but he'll insist on some form of payment."

"If he requires payment for more than the items, it will come out of your cut and not mine," Richard said. "There's a large chance that we won't find the treasure. I won't indebt myself to your noble friend over this."

Honestly, if they found the treasure and the man was being reasonable, Richard would be more than willing to pay half. He wouldn't do it without knowing the specifics first though.

Kuzunoha swallowed a bite of bread and followed it up with a generous sip of wine.

"Of course," she said. "At this point, I don't care what money I make. I am going to prove to Himiko that I'm not her little sister anymore. That I can do whatever I damn well please." She paused, looking at him. "You're not eating?"

He'd been watching her eat. Delicate, but strong, her movements called attention to the dress and the skin just underneath it. Whenever she leaned over her plate, her other hand moved her dress away from her wrist. It was erotic and yet there wasn't any reason that tiny bit of skin showing should be.

He swallowed without really tasting his food. "I am. I was just trying to figure out what this would change. Will you need me to go with you to talk to your friend?"

She shook her head. "No, he knows me. It will be easier to convince him alone."

"And how did things go with Deckard?"

"Surprisingly…" She said, a small smile crossing her lips.

That didn't explain anything and she knew it. Her instincts had taught her to off-balance people and then take an inch whenever she could. No one would argue her the inch, after all. By the time you realized that inches became feet or miles eventually, it was too late. He set his chin. He'd dealt with Asani, the bitch that got him on the run in the first place. He hadn't even noticed that one's machinations until she was at his doorstep, metaphorically speaking.

If nothing else, at least he knew how to handle her type now, even if Kuzunoha wasn't as destructive as Asani had been. Each woman was crafted just a bit differently. It was that unending newness that he enjoyed the most.

"I mean, how are things between you now?"

He hadn't been sure how Deckard would react to her demands. He'd thought that her ex may have still been carrying a torch for her, regardless of the traveler girl he was currently keeping in his bed.

"Well enough. He was annoyed, and he'll be more annoyed if I have to ask him for help again. Still, he listened earlier…perhaps miracles do happen."

"Then, is there anything else you need from me?"

"Actually, I do. I don't suppose you know of any places to stay, do you?"

He nearly laughed. She wasn't trying to seduce him. She was trying to drive him mad.

"If you're sleeping here, then you'll be in my bed."

His voice was thicker than he'd intended. She flushed, glancing to the bed. She turned back to him so quickly, she may have injured her neck. She gave a small bow. "No. I'll... figure out something else."

His gut roiled but he just shrugged. "Did Himiko kick you out?"

"No, I left. My bag was mostly packed anyway. But I couldn't stay there anymore, Richard. I want...something more. Some...place that isn't hers."

Richard understood. It was stupid, but sometimes you needed to be stupid. Pride was a fickle beast. He couldn't support her in this, though. If she stayed here, the sheriff would be here by morning. He might end up seeing the man anyway. He also had his meeting later tonight to go to. Too many good reasons not to keep her here.

"I'll see if I can find someplace else to stay."

He nodded and felt a tug in his belly. He couldn't guarantee her safety in the common room downstairs with the ship that had just arrived, dropping sailors hoping for warm berths into the inn and he'd seen the other two rooms like his had been taken as well. He didn't know this Jack fellow at all, but he did know one person in town who would do everything he could to keep her safe while asking for nothing more from her.

"You should go see Deckard. He has that extra healing room, after all."

Richard swore one day that he would see exactly how far down that blush went.

Chapter 18

Jack's house was small and practical compared to Kuzunoha's family's house, though it was larger than even the healing house. His father had commissioned it for him when he came of age. Jack's brother, Raphel, would live with his father and in the family manor when their father passed on.

Her family's manor was supposed to hold all family members, including grandparents, parents, and children. It was the Sian Ku way. It would probably never be that full again. Their father had never said what had happened to their grandparents, but she knew that both had died before he'd had even come of age.

She wondered if her father would have built her a home like this if he'd lived. Kuzunoha snorted. Most likely he would have kept her at home, expecting her to do the same as Jack's sister, to marry one day and live with her husband's family. She sighed. She couldn't deny that part of her wanted that future: a manor house with a tall man that loved her and a small child with unreasonably blonde hair atop their dirt-smudged face.

She walked up and knocked on the door. A moment later, it opened. Jack was wearing a set pair of soft pants and nothing else. He was thin and soft-featured, though his eyes, as always, had a hardened smile to them. Not that Jack was cruel, but he was shrewd and fond of saying he'd seen entirely too much during his childhood.

Kuzunoha understood how that could be. Bastards, even girl bastards, weren't usually brought up with the love and unlimited support of their parents like true-born children were. To be thought of as half as good, you had to do something twice as well.

For Jack, that had never been a difficulty.

"Kuzunoha? What are you doing here? Especially this late?" He smiled as he noticed the dress.

"Not quite the reason you're hoping it is," she said, smiling.

"To my eternal disappointment," he joked. "Speaking very seriously though, that dress is incredible on you. Would you like to join me for a drink, at least?"

"I'd love that. No company tonight?" She had heard that he was seeing one of the girls in town, though she didn't know which one.

"Actually, I do have company. However, she'll understand that you're not here to take her place."

She followed him in and he poured them both a glass of whiskey over some cool stones. He handed her the glass and they clinked them before drinking them down. Jack smiled and poured her more.

"Still a good drinker, I see."

"Of course. I haven't stopped just because I don't tend to...visit as often as I used to."

After Deckard, she'd rebounded with Jack. The sex had been a balm to her heart before they both realized that it wasn't going to work. Still, she had a lot of good memories of that time, most of it in this room, talking late and drinking.

"Anyway, sit. Is this business or pleasure you need?" he asked.

She sat down on the couch, different from when she'd visited last time. This one was a cream and green colour. "I'm looking for someone to help with a business endeavor of mine."

"An investor?" he asked.

He had to be joking since she'd never known him to be that out of touch with what was going on in town.

"No…I'm certain you've heard of the guide job I've taken with the foreigner."

He moved from the couch, where he'd been about to join her and moved to the blue chair on the other side of the table instead. He sat down, sipped his drink once more, and set it down.

"The one that murdered those people? Don't roll your eyes at me like that," he said in his own defense. "It's the only thing people know about him."

"My sister has decided that I shouldn't be going. Normally, that wouldn't bother me. This time, she's been talking and has convinced Talvert to not sell to us. Not a gods-damned single item worth more than a copper sentine."

"So, what can I do about—?" He paused, working out what she was there for. "You want me to get you what you need from him?"

She nodded.

Jack coughed into his hand. "This would be easier if you only needed black market items. I could take those directly out of the stock I keep. For what you're probably asking for… If he figures out that I'm buying for you, he won't sell to me."

"Tell him you're stocking up early or for another trip. He won't know, since you buy so much already." Jack made a noise that said he conceded the point.

"Tell me more about this expedition," he said, raising an eyebrow at her. "I've heard the jist of it around town. Hidden treasure that you'll be fighting monsters and pirates hand-over-fist for. Personally, I'd like to know why your friend didn't come directly to see me about it. I have a boat for charter and I doubt you're looking for a sunken ship."

"Richard doesn't think we're looking for a ship lost at sea." She said. Then she shrugged. "I honestly think he chose me simply for convenience. I'd saved his life and he wanted a local to help him search."

"I can't say I like you taking up the task. It's a bit too close to cutting in on my territory, you understand." The fact that he wanted a cut of the deal was left unstated, due to their friendship.

She rolled her eyes, trying to play it off. "I can promise you that searching for lost treasure around Hidan isn't going to become a common thing. This is a one-time thing, not a new job for me."

He frowned, but accepted her excuse, as though it had been simply her escorting someone around that he'd been interested in. Probably because there was more than one way to skin a rabbit. "What was it carrying?"

"An important passenger, carrying traditional gifts for a newborn."

"Tea towel toys and blocks won't be worth much." Jack pointed out.

Kuzunoha shook her head. "Sorry, traditional Sian Ku gifts for a newborn."

Jack still looked blank.

"Money for the parents to spend on the child, money for the child themselves, and family heirlooms. The most expensive items will be the dolls."

"Dolls?"

"Sian Ku works of art," Kuzunoha said, almost wishing she'd

brought hers. "They aren't made for playing with. The heads, hands and feet are made of fine plaster, and painted. Wood is used for the body. The clothes that are made for these dolls are often worth more than any actual clothes that may be sent."

"Are they worth more depending on who created them? You said the person was important."

She scrunched her forehead. "Not really. Not to say that there aren't expert doll makers, but they aren't usually signifiers of family. They may have a crest on some of the clothing. At any rate, I don't think that even one of our families would still pay for their return. Not unless the families were exceptionally close."

"Why would they send gifts if they weren't?"

"It's a birth." Kuzunoha laughed. "Everyone that you've met is supposed to come by and offer a gift. It's our way."

"What happens if you don't find it?"

She hadn't been expecting the question, but her mouth set in a hard line almost immediately. "We will."

"And if you don't?"

"Then we find nothing."

"That isn't a good investment, Kuzunoha. I can see why your sister is worried."

His lips thinned into a line and Kuzunoha nearly growled. "Jack, please, I expect this sort of uselessness from Himiko but not you. I am not going to make money. I'm going to prove that I can."

"And can you?" he asked.

She stuck out her chin. "My majority day is tomorrow."

"Which your sister is clearly blocking, else you wouldn't be here, right?"

She didn't dignify that with an answer.

He smiled. "Fine. It's your sister and your trouble when she catches up with you. However, it will make my fees higher. I know your sister… if she suspects that I helped, she'll try to take me out along with anyone else who helped you defy her."

She nodded.

"Do you know how much you'll need, what supplies can be picked up where, how long purchasing them should take me?"

"Yes."

They discussed the details of what she wanted and what he wanted in return. "I should only need one day to collect all this. I will want one other thing. First rights to any items you're selling and fifteen percent off what you could sell them for."

She sucked in a breath. The request wasn't completely out of line, but it was still too high. Also, Richard had said that it would come out of her percentage. She could afford it, even if it was expensive.

"Fifteen percent? Much too high. Five percent if you want exclusive first rights."

"Ten percent." He haggled. "They're first rights to a treasure you keep insisting is minimal, which means that you have a guaranteed buyer interested in at least seeing what bring back."

"Seven percent. They're still first rights."

"Eight and a half. You have to get your partners agreement first. My time is worth something."

She narrowed her eyes, but finally, nodded. "So long as Richard agrees, it's acceptable."

"Good. In that case, I have but one other question. What if you die?"

"What?" The question took her by surprise.

He amended his question. "I know you. You would never back out of a deal once you've made it. You simply don't agree to those that irk you too much. On the other hand, if you die out there, I will lose you..."

She flushed. It was… more intimate than Jack ever really got. She tried to reassure him.

"The dangers are minimal, Jack. Even the birdos aren't very active right now and the water is still too cold for any fishmen, even if they did happen to notice Richard and me travelling."

There were creatures in the water that occasionally took out unwary fisherman boats, although most of them only came up this far during the warmer months. A particularly cold winter would easily freeze the top layer of water. It wasn't a problem for boats that could crash through it, but it seemed to impede the monsters' movements.

Jack shook his head. "It was only four years ago that your father died to their predations, Kuzunoha."

Kuzunoha stiffened. Her father had died to the creatures in the street and she had never left her dagger at home since then. He knew that. "I am better with my blades than you are. I can take care of myself."

"That is true." He put his hands up in a gesture of defeat and then looked her up and down. "Will you be leaving that here with me?"

She blinked. He was pointing at her body. "Leaving what with you?"

"That robe is an artifact of your family, correct? Leave it with me. I have a lockbox you can use to keep it safe while you're gone."

Kuzunoha thought her heart had missed a beat. She grabbed the silk tightly, as if Jack would tear it off her.

"But...this is an heirloom."

"And I assume you don't want it lost if you don't come home. I assume you want to avoid going home if you can at all help it."

He did have a point. Her sister would never forgive her if something happened to it because she took it out of the city with her.

She sighed. "I agree. I'll bring it to you tomorrow."

"Why wait? Leave it tonight. I have some sturdier clothes here you can wear. You can return them whenever you get a chance, perhaps tomorrow, so that you and your business partner can sign to the contract."

She realized that she was clutching the silk too tightly. She sighed and forced her hand to open. Even if she took it with her, where would she leave it? The box was at home and she didn't even have a place to stay. Deckard wouldn't have a box to put it in. If she went to him. Did she have a choice? Unless she wanted to stay with Jack. No, Deckard was a more suitable choice if only because Himiko wouldn't come looking for her there. She just might if she found out that she was staying with Jack.

"You're really looking forward to meeting Richard. Why?" she asked.

"Kuzunoha, I still care about you. I want to look in the eyes of the man you've fallen for and confirm for myself that he's up to the task."

Kuzunoha grumbled. "We are business partners. Nothing more."

"Truly? Then why the blush?" Jack asked, a chill in his tone.

Kuzunoha put a hand to her cheeks and looked away from him, as if she could hide it by looking away. "Think what you want, but we aren't sleeping together."

He paused and then hugged her. "I'm sorry. I worry about you."

She was too tired to deal with yet another person who felt she needed to be protected. She wasn't made of glass. "I know. Sorry. We'll be by tomorrow morning. Let's get me out of this. Your girl had better not be in the bedroom naked and waiting for you." She stood, annoyed.

He grinned at her. "Cersei's in the kitchen. You remember my assistant, right? I can guarantee that she won't be in my bed, waiting for me. Let me grab you some clothes."

Chapter 19

Deckard kissed Tieni again and she pushed against him, her hands searching his body. It was nice having her by his side, in his room. They hadn't been dating long, but they had become comfortable.

There was a knock at his front door and he grimaced. This was the part she hated.

"Sorry," he whispered, pulling away from her lips. He'd need clothes, pants at the very least. Fortunately, he always kept a set right by his bed. Tieni's shoulders dropped.

"Do you have to?"

"I'm a healer, Tieni. I need to be available, regardless of the hour."

"But...Deckard. I turned down playing at the Koi for tonight. A ship landed earlier for today. You know how much I could have made playing. They asked for me specifically. You can ignore it for a few minutes, surely?"

He lived in one of the three homes in Hidan set aside for healers. He had an individual well, a tub for heated water, thick stone walls, and even a solid wooden roof. Repairs were made by grateful people, food and new clothes left at his door... he even had a stipend from the mayor that he could use to buy herbs, new supplies like bandages, ointment bases, and oils. In return for all that, he was essentially always on call. He didn't get time off. Even when his girlfriend had taken time off specifically to spend with him.

He couldn't leave someone outside, hurting, no matter how much he wanted to stay with her. She just didn't like it. She reached out to him. He caught her fingers and kissed them. "Tieni, I'm sorry."

It was his path, the same one his mother had been on. Sometimes he wished he could give it up. Become something else. He stood. Whatever he wished for when being a healer was inconvenient for him, he wouldn't be getting it.

The air was cold on his skin and he grabbed the pants and threw them on. The stone floor was chilly and he made a mental note to throw an extra log on for the night. It may have been spring, but the cold weather hadn't released its hold yet.

He opened the door. Kuzunoha smiled hopefully at him. His mood dropped along with the temperature as a cool breeze chilled the stone even more. She'd asked him to leave her alone. Despite his better judgment, he had agreed. He'd even done more than he'd agreed to, talking to Himiko about it. It wasn't fair for her to show up at his house later that same day after he was already in bed. "What do you want?"

"I'm sorry to wake you up. Can I come in?" She shivered. The shirt she was wearing was too thin for the weather, and the pants were hardly better, drawn up to her thighs in an attempt to make them wearable. Why was she wearing them? Kuzunoha hated pants, and Himiko's adoption of the style was all it took to set her against it. The entire outfit was cheap, undyed dock clothes with someone else's stains. He'd known her for half his life and she'd never worn undyed cotton or owned something passed down by anyone but perhaps her sister. Even her sleeping clothes had been dyed and embroidered. When she'd bothered with them at all.

"Get in here. Why are you wearing pants?"

She shivered and moved to his kitchen table. Deckard threw a new log into the oven and started a fire to warm her. Afterward, he hung up a pot of water. Tea would warm her better than just the oven and wouldn't waste the log that way. Besides, she would do better if he wasn't looking at her.

Kuzunoha shivered again and he felt an irrational spurt of anger.

"Thank you, Deckard, I…"

Tieni walked out of his bedroom and her words died away. He flushed. Tieni was wearing one of his shirts and nothing else. Her legs seemed to have no end and the shirt only barely covered her. She looked like a prowling cat. He liked it, but then, like most men, Deckard liked women in whatever they wore and if it was the right woman and the right situation, then naked was always a plus.

She strode up to him and wrapped a hand around his waist. Without looking at Kuzunoha, she lightly kissed his lips. "Who is it, Deckard? We may not have been asleep, but it isn't as though we weren't busy."

It took effort not to roll his eyes. There was a battle going on in his kitchen and it was being fought silently with clothing instead of swords and shields. He understood why Tieni wouldn't like an old girlfriend coming around, but did she really have to be such a child about it?

Kuzunoha flushed and stood, pushing the table back a few inches in her haste. She crossed her arms in front of her and looked anywhere but at them.

He wasn't sure if she'd lost or if she was going to concede the battle without fighting.

"I should have realized that you would be here. I didn't think…" Kuzunoha glanced back at him. "I should have. I'll leave...just...yes, I'll go. Sorry."

He sighed as she leapt away from his table towards the door. Time to change the rules. It was his kitchen, his house. He wasn't going to let anyone, even Tieni, get away with scaring one of his guests or clients.

"Kuzunoha, sit down. My front door is always open, even if...other doors may be closed." He looked at Tieni. "How about you hop back into bed. I'll join you as soon as I can."

Tieni's eyes flashed and Kuzunoha paused, her hand already on the doorknob. He raised his eyebrows at his girlfriend. He wasn't going to turn away someone in need, even if he and Kuzunoha did have a difficult past. If she said anything else, Kuzunoha would flee like a colt the first time it was saddled. He'd have to chase her down. The faster he helped her, the faster he'd be back in bed with Tieni.

She rolled her eyes and kissed him again. There was an urgency to it, but when she pulled away from him, she was smiling.

"I'll be waiting for you then," she said. He liked her saunter as she moved and he turned back to Kuzunoha as Tieni closed the door to his room.

"It isn't important. Not important enough that I disturb..." Kuzunoha gestured to the bedroom and stared daggers at the front door. "I'll find somewhere else, it's fine..."

"Somewhere else?"

She sighed and wouldn't meet his eyes. "I... I can't go back home tonight, Deckard. Himiko was in a rage when she got home. We fought and she… threatened to not give me my majority. I just...I can't stay there anymore."

"And you came here?" He didn't think that Himiko would actually deny Kuzunoha her majority. It was odd for Himiko to overreact, but then again, it was with Kuzunoha. Anything was possible when it concerned those two.

"I didn't know where else to go," she said.

Kuzunoha had always been like a porcupine. If you could get past the quills, you'd see how cute she could be. If you irritated her...well, she wasn't shy about showing her displeasure. She wouldn't have anywhere else to go and with the ship that came in earlier, the Koi would be full.

"How long?" He heard himself ask as she finally returned to the table.

"Ever, maybe?" She glanced up at him but looked away before she even met his eyes.

"What?"

"No, I mean, not here for ever…but…Deckard, I don't know if I can go back home again. Not to live permanently."

Her hair fell around her face, framing it in darkness. He fought back an urge to push it behind her ear like he would have when they'd been dating. Instead, he stood and checked the water. It was just starting to boil so he grabbed two cups and brought them to the table with some tea leaves. He put one of the mugs in front of Kuzunoha.

"It isn't the green tea you like so much, but it's all I have tonight. Can you start at the beginning for me, please?"

Kuzunoha sighed but obediently took a sip. His measure of Richard went up as she reiterated what her night had been so far. Still, it didn't answer the most pertinent question.

"So, why can't you go back home?"

"I'm an adult, Deckard. I need my own home, a place... well, a place that's mine. She'll never respect me so long as I'm still living off the family's wages on the family estate."

He wanted to point out that they probably wouldn't get along any better with her out of the house either. Himiko and Kuzunoha got on like oil and water. What comforted one would be a deadly insult to the other. "Kuzunoha, do you even know how to get a house?"

She shook her head. "No."

By the Seven, she was frustrating. She probably hadn't thought any further than her adventure. "Most times, a person's parents will help to build their children homes when they marry, if their home is too small for the entire family to live in."

He didn't mention the abandoned houses. Monster attacks and the occasional bandit raid claimed victims. It was sickening to leave the houses standing so long, a grim reminder of loss and a danger, but sometimes the spirits of the deceased had to be placated before they would go peacefully to their eternal rest. A difficult procedure, depending on what the spirits felt they'd left undone in their lives. Everyone remembered the interloper who'd tried hiding in one of the homes to avoid paying for a room at the inn. He'd gone mad and killed six people before they had been able to capture him and soothe the spirits that had possessed him.

"I can worry about that later, then. Right now, I just need a room for tonight. I'll be leaving the city tomorrow evening most likely. Since you have company already, I'll go. I don't want to inconvenience you. Thank you for the tea," she said, turning to the door again.

"What about Richard?" Deckard said, biting on his tongue hard enough that it hurt. He didn't trust the man, didn't want him anywhere near Kuzunoha.

"He said if I was staying with him, I'd be sleeping in his bed." Then she flushed. "I wasn't..."

Deckard cut her off, his voice level. "I can't give you the healing room. I do have a cot, a pillow, and a blanket you can use for tonight After that, we'll have to talk."

Her relief made him want to tear his hair out. How did she end up in these situations?

About ten minutes later, Kuzunoha was set for the night and Deckard retired to his room. He looked at Tieni. She was in his bed, glaring daggers. She would have heard him moving the cot, even if she hadn't heard the conversation. He slid out of his pants and under the covers.

"Kuzunoha will be staying here for a few days. She has nowhere else to go," he told her.

He would have to talk to Himiko tomorrow if he couldn't convince Kuzunoha to do so. It wasn't quite in his job description, he was a healer, not a priest, but she would want to know where her sister was staying. Deckard wasn't going to try to solve the family's problems, but he could do that much.

"You'd tell me if I should be worried?"

He gave her a small kiss. "Tieni, it won't happen. Ever. She cheated on me. I don't ask for much, but monogamy is at the top of that list."

Saying it brought its own bitterness. Kuzunoha...the last time Kuzunoha had stayed here she'd been in this room. His. It felt wrong, having her outside. Not that he wanted Kuzunoha in his bed again. Ever. He meant that. It didn't mean that it didn't still hurt. Tieni's expression softened as he slid over to her.

Deckard kissed her again and her hands started caressing him. Frustratingly, his thoughts went to Kuzunoha again, just outside the door. His chest tightened. He may not have had feelings for Kuzunoha, but he couldn't stop thinking of her immediate presence. With a disappointed sigh, he stopped her. "I've never liked...an audience."

Tieni grumped and moved to the other side of the bed. "So, you're kicking me out while she's here? I should have just stayed to work at the Koi tonight."

"No," he said, fiercely, grabbing her. "You are always welcome. I just...don't enjoy it. Please stay. I want you by my side tonight."

The tension drained from her and he pulled her close. He blew out the candle and she slid into the crook of his arm. With Tieni lying warm and solid beside him, he stayed awake, listening to the sound of her breathing.

Chapter 20

Richard counted the minutes to five after Kuzunoha left before he got up, armed himself, and locked the door behind him. He didn't know if Kuzunoha's idea would work. If it didn't, a prison stay would keep him in town and from moving further afield, especially if those idiots he'd killed had gotten off a message first.

He grumbled under his breath as he walked down the stairs into the Koi proper. It was busy tonight, or at least as busy as a bar in a tiny town like this ever got. There were nearly thirty people in the place. From their clothes and the scent of salt and fish, Richard assumed that most of these men were fishermen, rather than sailors. They were all talking at once it was a cacophony of sound in such an enclosed space.

He hurried to the front door and felt a small stitch in his side. He slowed down. He was getting better, but in this case, not overdoing it was the right move.

The man who'd brought up his meal saw him and held the door open for him. His grin was almost conciliatory. "I saw Kuzunoha leave. Couldn't keep her for the evening?"

Richard grinned back at him. "She would have stayed if I asked, but her sister is demanding her home earlier."

The man shrugged. "Himiko's always been the more responsible one. She got on her sister's case a year ago over a guy she was with. He wanted her family's business more than he wanted her. Kuzunoha hadn't seen through him yet but Himiko was there to keep her on the straight edge."

The man was talkative. Richard may as well make use of it. "I have a question for you. Do you know how old she is?"

"Old enough to know what she's about." He grinned, then the smile dropped off his face. "Oh, you mean, seriously? She and her sister are pretty close in age, so she should be hitting her majority soon. Himiko had hers just a few weeks ago. Not that it does much for her, just gives her the ability to drink and make her own decisions."

"Have you ever heard of someone blocking someone's majority?"

The guy laughed. "Is that even possible? Even with their arguments, I can't see Himiko going that far. She's the nice sister. Too nice for her sister, honestly. That woman puts up with crap that no one else would."

So at least Kuzunoha's argument of not believing the threat would be believable. Richard nodded. "Thanks. She mentioned it was tomorrow, but I didn't know what rights it entailed. We get ours at nineteen where I grew up." Though as a general rule, anything you wanted could be found for a few more clips of coin once you were sixteen.

"It doesn't do much—lets you drink hard liquor and own property—but it's always a big deal here in Hidan."

That gave Richard something to think about. If it was true that the elder had gotten herself all the businesses and family property, it would leave nothing for Kuzunoha. When she'd said that her father hadn't left anything for her, he'd taken it with a grain of salt. Now he wondered if all her old man had left her was a stipend so long as she was behaving. He would have to find out about that… he could ask Kuzunoha later. The man's other words rang through Richard's mind too. *Too nice for her sister, honestly.* Had any of the men here, other than Deckard, ever tried to learn more about the woman they hoped to bed? One of the reasons Richard never worried for company was his ability to get them talking. Nothing got women more riled about a man than thinking he saw more in them, dug deeper in their secret sides, than anyone else had.

His meeting was taking place in a pathetic, run-down shanty in the bad part of town. The wood was rotting and the floorboards bent and creaked under his weight. He could understand the creaking being a good defense, but if the floorboards were as bad as they looked, they wouldn't hold two or three men standing on them at once. If a fight broke out he'd have to get off of it as soon as he could.

Still, he had a reputation here in town after defeating his assassins. He shrugged. More like a reputation for being ready and able to kill, but he preferred the first description. Anyway, as long as they weren't waiting for him to make a wrong move, it meant they'd likely be more careful before making any rash decisions. Though that reputation also meant that if they decided he needed to be taken care of, they'd bring more than enough men to do so.

A loose board on the wall by the front door moved slightly to the side. The guy inside didn't make any stupid mistakes, like putting his face right in front of the peephole. He felt a little better about the meeting now. Dealing with professionals meant that he wouldn't have to assume that a double cross was already in the works. He'd prepared for one, regardless and didn't see the need to change his plan on an if though.

"It looks awful cold outside tonight," the guy inside said.

Which meant they had gotten the message he was coming. Good. "The cold isn't too bad, it's the heat I can't handle."

The guy closed the window and Richard heard him unlock the door. When it opened, he saw the inside was lit by a few candles, all well covered to hide their light. The door closed behind him, locking him in. Richard put his hands into position so that he could grab throwing daggers if he needed to.

A big man with thick-muscled arms as wide as his neck sat on a divan couch. His beard and mustache were neatly trimmed, but his hair was an oily black nest. To his right sat a blonde woman so plain looking that Richard knew she was probably a bodyguard rather than a consort. Her hair was long, and set in a complicated hairstyle held by two stiletto blades.

Four other men were sitting against the wall on hastily set chairs. None of them looked armed, but Richard didn't make the mistake of thinking that they had no weapons. Instead, he brought his hands up and ran one through his hair. The plain-looking woman smiled approvingly and everyone relaxed incrementally.

The man who'd opened the door went around the room, unhooding the candles and the room brightened considerably. There was a low table in front of the divan, a card game partially in progress. He smiled, nodding to the man on the divan. He'd played with his sort before; though he was a gentleman, despite all evidence pointing to him being a small fish in an even smaller pond.

"You would be Carlos?" Richard asked.

The man gave a single nod. "I hope you're doing better. I heard that you'd gotten yourself quite injured by those thugs."

"Not badly enough to take me out of the picture." Richard held his hands wide. "Shall I twirl to prove it?"

The man snorted a laugh. "That won't be necessary. You want a seat?"

Richard nodded and a simple chair was brought for him. When he sat, the chair tottered but would hold so long as he didn't fidget. It would make it even more difficult to get up quickly if he needed to fight, but now that he'd taken it, he couldn't refuse the seat. Instead, he took a few coins from his pocket and put them under the offending chair leg, making it sit relatively flat. Then he sat back with a smile.

"Thank you for that. It's still easier on me while I'm healing."

"Wouldn't want to inconvenience you."

Richard nodded and threw a few of his other coins onto the table. These men survived by knowing everything that happened in Hidan's underground. No matter how small the town, someone would have their fingers on the pulse and make sure that the wrong people were never robbed or inconvenienced. If anyone would know about his assassins, it wouldn't be the sheriffs. It would be this man.

"Thanks. Now, I came by for a simple card game and some good company. Will you deal me in?"

"Of course." The man picked up his deck of cards and tossed all the money on the table off to the side. "Tell me who started the trouble?"

Richard snorted as Carlos shuffled the deck and tossed the first one his way. "Those idiots who attacked me. Wish I knew more about them."

"I'd be wanting some revenge, if it were me," Carlos agreed.

"Well it was my best coat their damned bolt ruined," Richard said, negligently, picking up his hand. Carlos laughed.

"There were four, said they came from Michael's Den, but they didn't come by ship or by raven's wing. Our man who watches the walls was waiting for a shipment and he saw them come over the Northern side. The tall one had arranged the room under the name 'John' but one of my men heard the stout one call him 'Andreas'."

Richard looked at his own hand. Not bad. A pair of fours with a high queen, a red seven, and black two. He loved playing a good card game.

Perhaps if the information didn't cost too much, Carlos and his friends wouldn't mind playing an actual game.

"What did they come in for?" Richard asked. He slid the seven and two across the table. Carlos dealt him another two cards. A six and another two. He threw a few more coins onto the pot. "Raise."

Carlos dropped one and dealt a new one to himself. He threw a few coins in. "Raise."

Richard looked at the pile of coins. Apparently, he hadn't greased the table enough for this info. He glanced at his cards and threw in a few coins to meet the bet. "Call."

Carlos smiled. "They said they were looking for a thief. Needed him alive, though clearly they had a disagreement about that part. They wouldn't say what their thief stole, what his name was or where he'd stolen it from. They found you right quick though, even for a town this size."

As if finding a stranger in Hidan could be difficult. None of them had ever been in a city the size of Jisa where you were lucky to know your own neighbors by name, let alone during the trading season when their population nearly doubled every year. "When was that?"

"Day before the pretty's majority party," Carlos said.

Richard put down the six and two. "Did they do anything else?"

Carlos dealt him another two cards. Richard had to stop himself from smiling. A red queen and ace smiled back at him. He threw in another handful of coins.

Carlos considered his hand carefully. Then he laid down a single card and claimed a new one. "They hired one of our men to deliver a message." He paused again and threw down double the coins that were on the table.

So, this was personal for him. Richard knew better than to ask if the boy he'd chosen had been family. "Damn shame. What was in the message and where did they send it?"

Carlos' fist smacked the table, making the coins jingle and jump. "A simple task, taking a message to a certain grove outside Hidan. We thought there was another agent and this a simple job. Anthony hasn't returned home. He would not have turned tail."

Richard threw in a few extra coins. Their boy was probably dead then. They'd know it already. "The message?"

"Found nothing of our man or the message. Call." Carlos' eyes looked dull at the words.

"Lay 'em out," Richard said.

Carlos composed himself and laid out a pair of sevens and a pair of fives. "I hope that somebody kills 'em for what they did to my boy."

A wave of pity ran through Richard and he gave one decisive nod. If he did find the one that killed the man's boy, he'd do what he could. "Fold."

"Who were they?" Carlos asked.

Richard felt a shiver go through him. It was unprofessional, but he could understand the man's need to know. Richard decided not to say. They wouldn't survive, even if they believed him. She was coming. He had to leave town soon.

"Wish I knew. I know who hired them though. You won't find the boy again."

Carlos shook his head, looking dejected. "Bad luck, that. I think we're done cards for the day. Have a safe walk back to the Koi."

Richard headed out, glad of the cold air. He'd go find Kuzunoha tomorrow morning. He had until then to decide what he needed to do.

Chapter 21

Having Deckard making her breakfast on her majority day had been a very pleasant fantasy when she'd been dating him. He'd been shirtless after they'd enjoyed their night of passion, and she'd be hovering over his shoulder, grinning from ear to ear, while he cooked.

It was her majority day and Deckard was making her breakfast. Nothing else was right. For one, in her fantasy, he'd still been dating her and hadn't had his irritating girlfriend joining them.

"So, you managed to get yourself kicked out of your own house? Impressive," Tieni said.

Kuzunoha glared. "I wasn't kicked out. I left."

Deckard turned around. He wasn't frowning, but he had one eyebrow raised and she immediately felt chastised. She was a guest and here only at his mercy. Well, if she was lucky, when she came back, wildly successful, she wouldn't have to stay here. She would have enough money to take her own room at the Koi while she figured out what she was going to do if Himiko did go through with her threat. Deckard brought a plate with eggs, toast, oatmeal and dried berries to the table. Kuzunoha slid two of the eggs onto her plate. Tieni glared at her.

"The one who cooks get fed first. Then his girlfriend. Visitors get what's left."

Kuzunoha seethed. She hadn't done anything to mend the rift between her and Deckard—how could she? He'd never asked anything of her since he'd found her in the arms of that sailor, Koan. Despite the sudden roil in her stomach that made her lose her appetite, she kept the eggs on her plate. It would have been rude to put them back.

"Be nice, Tieni. She's still my guest," Deckard said as he leaned down and kissed the other woman. Her arms curled around him, invitingly.

"You shouldn't have to cook more before you even sit down to eat," Tieni countered into his lips.

Kuzunoha's appetite evaporated. Screw the propriety. She pushed the eggs onto his plate with her fork. "Actually, I don't think I'm hungry."

Deckard sat down with a sigh. Most likely of relief. "Do you have any extra clothes with you?"

She hadn't brought her bag from Richard's. Stupid that. She should have taken it with her, but she had known it would be safe there and she'd thought she could simply wear the dress until she could get it from the inn. Now, with Jack's clothes scratching at her skin, she regretted her choice. Also, she didn't understand why he would wear clothes made with such rough cloth.

"I left my bag at the inn. I have to see Richard today anyway, so I'll grab it then."

She would have to check what she hadn't packed. She'd been mostly ready to go, but she had expected to have time to go over everything in her bag once more. She knew that she'd left her boots at home, assuming that she'd wear them the day she left and that they would be her footwear for the entire trip. She'd have to buy another pair, even if they would be uncomfortable as sin while she worked them in.

"Good. When will you be heading out?" Tieni said.

Deckard closed his eyes, sighing heavily. Kuzunoha bit her lip. Surely, Richard must have woken up by now. She stood. "I'll go now."

She was not running away. This was a tactical retreat. She vastly preferred to frame it that way. Perhaps she could find a room elsewhere if they couldn't leave tonight. Deckard was her failsafe, but she shouldn't rely on him anymore. It was clear he thought she was nothing but a bother.

"Make time to talk to your sister," Deckard told her.

"Tell her to let you back into your house," Tieni muttered.

Kuzunoha closed her eyes for a moment. "I doubt that my sister has even registered that I'm gone, Deckard."

Since she hadn't stayed with Richard, her sister would have no issues, even if she was angry at Kuzunoha for staying away for the night. On the other hand, it wouldn't be the first time Kuzunoha had stayed out for the night, not even the first time at this house. She glanced Deckard's way. His expression suggested that her sister's inattention notwithstanding, she'd better make time.

Her hand had just touched the knob when Deckard spoke. "Whether you find a place for tonight or not, you'll be welcome here, Kuzunoha."

Kuzunoha wasn't sure if that feeling in the pit of her stomach was relief or frustration. She wondered if Tieni would still be there. She opened the door in a rush and almost ran into Richard. He was raising his hand as if to knock.

"Richard?" she asked stupidly.

He held up her backpack. "I was hoping you'd listened and decided to stay at our illustrious healer's home."

"You suggested that?" Deckard said as he pushed his plate back and stood.

Richard pushed his way in and put Kuzunoha's bag into her hands. His grin was nearly ear-to-ear. "Of course. Who made breakfast?"

"I did. You've been resting?" Deckard asked.

Richard sat down at the table, in front of her plate. "I've been in bed every moment that I'm not helping Kuzunoha plan this trip."

Kuzunoha couldn't believe his audacity. Having your company join you in bed hardly counted as resting. Certainly Deckard wouldn't have considered it so.

Kuzunoha couldn't deal with this anymore. "Deckard, may I use the healer's room to change?"

Deckard gestured her away. "I'll check on you before you leave, then. You didn't seem to be having any trouble carrying that bag."

She closed the door behind her and checked her bag, raising an eyebrow in disgust. She only had two robes—blue and grey— one pair of thick socks, three sets of underwear, and a breast binder packed. It was a start but not enough. She thanked the gods that she had packed her sturdiest clothes, at least. The material was cotton instead of silk, thick, and had no excess frills or stitching. They were some of the most boring things she owned, but they would survive the trek that her nicer ones wouldn't. Silk may be hardier, but not with the frills and embroidery or the emphasis of fashion over functionality. She would still want her wool overcoats, if she could get them, along with her boots and at least two more robes, if she could.

By the time she finished changing, Richard was finishing his plate. He smiled at her wickedly as she walked into the middle of their conversation.

"Is the priestess that strict?" he asked Deckard.

Deckard shrugged but didn't say anything. Kuzunoha winced. Apparently, they'd decided to talk about embarrassing stories from her childhood. And of all of them, to bring up the Pressia one… She and Pressia had never seen eye to eye, even before the incident with the frog. To this day she still wouldn't accept any of Kuzunoha's apologies.

Tieni gave Kuzunoha a scathing look. "She sounds like a woman of impressive taste. I'll have to introduce myself."

So much for hoping they hadn't been talking about her. "We should get going, Richard."

He nodded. "Of course. Deckard?"

Tieni answered before Deckard could. “Just get her out of here. You can come back later for him to look you over.”

It took another moment, but they left.

Chapter 22

Richard saw Kuzunoha perk up as soon as Deckard's door had closed behind them. Her shoulders relaxed and she walked more self-assuredly.

"You look beautiful, as always," Richard commented.

Being outside of Deckard's presence made the difference. Or perhaps it wasn't Deckard presence that diminished her, but Tieni's. The woman had been sniping at Kuzunoha as often as she could. He hadn't expected Deckard to have the gumption to have his current woman in his bed while an old girlfriend slept under the same roof.

"Always first and everything else second," she muttered under her breath. Then she sighed and smiled at him. "Thank you. I didn't sleep as well as I could have, but it will do. You?"

He'd called on Miya after meeting with Carlos. It had been nice to rid himself of pent-up frustrations and while she'd lain in his arms afterwards, he'd figured out a plan. His captor wouldn't expect him to stay in the same place. Most likely her servants would ask around to see if he was still there and where he'd gone. Richard had set aside quite a bit of his dwindling supplies to lay a false trail. A boat paid to take him and the girl he was with to Kalvettika. With any luck, they'd follow the trail, only realizing they'd been sent on a goose hunt. He still had to pay the Captain, but he would have time before they left.

"I had a bit of trouble, but once I did, I slept well," he responded. "I've done my research and I think I've figured out where the ship is. Now I just want to talk to one of the dockmasters and we'll be set to go."

They were looking for a cove with a waterfall, five days away from here. It would have to be deep to hide a thirty-foot tall mast, plus the ship itself. Unless the mast had been one of those that could be lowered to get it inside. They would have to check them all, but he would start with the taller caves since the book hadn't mentioned any damage to the mast, just the beams and sails.

She let out a breath. "Good. I spoke to Jack last night and we came to an arrangement. He… wants first rights to buy..." She stopped walking, turning her head to follow something.

"You say that like it's a bad thing?" She didn't answer; he'd lost her attention.

"Miya?" Kuzunoha made a gesturing movement with her hand.

He had been turning to see who she was looking at, but he made a point of not wrenching his head around at mention of her name. Miya had joined him again last night after he'd found her in the Koi when he returned from his meeting. In fact, he'd walked most of the way to Deckard's with Miya this morning, but he'd thought she'd have gone home already. Where in the Consort's light had she been hiding that Kuzunoha had seen her and he hadn't?

"Yes, Mistress?" Miya asked, pink-faced as she crossed the street towards them. She refused to meet their gazes. It was adorable.

"I'm glad you're out this early," Kuzunoha said. "I need you to go home and pick me up two more of my robes. The green and brown ones, cotton, not silk. I'll also need three pairs of socks, my warmest ones, and both pairs of boots. You know, the thicker winter ones. Also, one of my wool overcoats, whichever one comes to hand first. And my gloves, if you haven't put them in storage yet."

Miya blinked at her. "Of course. Where will I bring them?"

"To Deckard's, if you can't find me."

"Of course, Mistress. May I tell your sister what time you'll be back?"

Kuzunoha's grin was a wolf baring its teeth reminding a pack member to know their place. "I'll be staying out for a few days. That's why I need the clothes."

Miya's eyes narrowed as she looked at him. Then she bowed to Kuzunoha and left. His goddess had always said love and pleasure were separate and he believed that. He only wished he knew how to convince women who didn't follow Kristinel's religion of that truth.

Kuzunoha continued walking. She slowed down near the church and took out two copper coins.

A jovial man, dressed in the amber frock of a priest of the dead god of the Corvidae, called to her. “Ah, Lady Kuzunoha. Will you be coming to the sermon today?”

She smiled at him. “Unfortunately not. I do have a donation though, if you don’t mind performing a blessing.”

His sigh was almost theatrical. “Ah, one day you’ll join us, child.”

The priest took her coins though, running his hands over her body, about an inch above her skin, calling upon one of the less known prophets of Hieros to offer her wisdom. A moment later, they were on their way again.

“Don’t you follow your own people’s deities?” he asked, remembering her gesture towards the little shrine at her home.

“I do,” she said. “But I see no reason to not hedge my bets. All of them can’t be right, so I give service to all of them when I can.”

Richard couldn’t even imagine the mental gymnastics that would take. “Have you heard of the goddess, Kristinel?

She blinked at him. “The goddess of the west, is she not? Something about love and fertility?”

The market around the church to Hieros was busy and everyone stepped out of their path. He could see that Kuzunoha noticed, though he didn’t think that any of these villagers would notice how uncomfortable it made her in return.

“Not quite. She is the deity of lust, yes, but also of paper, creation, and new beginnings. In my home country, she is the chief deity."

Kuzunoha tilted her head and he was reminded again of how he'd thought she was Kristinel herself come to earth. She wasn't that beautiful or unreal now. She hadn't lost that touch of divinity, but she wasn't carrying the goddess within her now. Perhaps he saw more than just her beauty when he looked at her—a heady thought.

"Why lust?" she asked. "I can understand paper and the ability to create objects seemingly out of nothing. But lust doesn't seem to match the other items in her care."

Richard smiled. "Kristinel teaches that lust creates bonds between people. That said, she also believes that the world is unfair and will always be so. You make the world bow to you, or you will bow to it. Therefore, lust is a tool like any other and one that is so often overlooked. It is Kristinel's favoured weapon. There can be no greater gift to her than to whisper a secret learned only through plying that gift."

Kuzunoha raised an eyebrow. "Why worship her, then? She sounds…less ethical than most."

If her words hadn't been said by her detractors for eons, he may have taken offense. Instead, he kept his smile. "Not so. There is no greater dishonour to her than pure dishonesty. Lying is forbidden to her most devout worshippers." Which was why most of his own people had learned how to obscure the truth almost as easily as they breathed.

"Interesting," Kuzunoha said. She looked thoughtful. "You are one?"

"Of her most devout worshippers? No. I am only a follower, not one of her chosen. I do follow her tenets when I can, though. She has some very interesting festivals and—"

"The sailor was her consort, wasn't he?" Kuzunoha asked. "I seem to recall that somebody told me that. She had a sailor for a consort and he became the deity of the sea?"

Cardinte had been human before he'd become the deity of civilization, which was why his symbol was often bits of gold fitted into an obsidian backing. "He created a boat out of the paper she gave us, folding it hundreds of times to make its shape. They say Kristinel was so pleased that when he was found outside of his village by creatures bent on destroying him, she made his boat ten times its size, and he sailed out of their reach. From then on, he sailed the seas, bringing the gift of maps and seafaring techniques to all of the tribes of the Kenedra, the people that lived on the island that became Kaleka State."

"Very interesting. I would love to find out more later…perhaps on our trip?"

"Of course. Now, what was this you'd mentioned about first-sell rights?"

"Jack has contacts on the docks. In addition to his other jobs, he's the one you go to if you need something less than legal. He's a bit put out that you asked me rather than him and he thinks that he'll be able to sell the dolls and the rest of it back to a specific family. He won't charge anything to buy the items for us, but he does want the right to look over anything we're planning to sell and buy it without ending up in a bidding war. He's also going to want a discount on it. Like you said though, I'll cover that."

He didn't like the idea, but the other option was not buying supplies and trying to live off the land entirely while they were out there. A bidding war would have gotten them more money, of course, but essentially Jack was offering himself as a middleman, assuming that he could run the bidding war and profit off it. Since Richard preferred to keep himself to the shadows as far as that sort of work went, he'd accept it.

"How much?"

"Eight and a half percent."

Lower than it could have been and while it was steep for one to cover entirely, he could also offer to take some of the cost himself at the end.

"And is he what happened to your robe?"

He'd considered not bringing her bag just so he could see her in it again. He had been more relieved than he'd thought to see her put on her robes again. Something about her looked wrong when she was clothed like a poor dock worker.

Kuzunoha's voice was even as she answered. "Jack offered to keep it for me."

"What?" Richard almost stopped walking but Kuzunoha didn't even slow down. "Why wouldn't you just take it home?"

"I didn't want to go home and I didn't want to hire someone to take it over, since that would alert my sister that I'm leaving. With Miya coming to Deckard's with my other items though, I can give it to her, and she'll make sure it's cleaned and returned. Miya can even tell her I sent it back already."

Richard didn't think it was as easy as she seemed to think it would be, but he smiled. He'd see what the situation was before he left the man's house today. "But he's agreed to help?"

She nodded. "Yes. I assume he'll have words for you along the vein of 'you'd better take care of her,' too. Ignore it. Nobody here knows just how capable I really am."

She stopped in front of a large house, plain and less well kept than Kuzunoha's mansion. The colors and paints were mismatched and it was clear that while it was kept up, the upkeep happened less frequently. Kuzunoha stepped up to it, knocking. "Jack, we're here."

A thin man with paler skin than Kuzunoha opened the door. He had unremarkable brown hair and eyes, though the care he took was obvious. His eyes snapped hungrily on Kuzunoha but were frosty when they turned to him. The man smiled at Kuzunoha. "I hadn't expected to see you this early."

Which told Richard a lot about this bastard, mostly that he was one. Almost-nobles like him were the same everywhere. They wouldn't talk to someone below their imaginary station when they could talk to someone that they did consider their equal. A real noble knew he could afford politeness to strangers and lose nothing in the bargain. This one still needed to feel like he was on better than other people.

"I found my appetite was...lacking this morning," she said, grimacing.

"After we finish signing, I can have Cersei make something more to your liking," Jack suggested, leading them into a parlor. He walked back out and returned a moment later with a scroll and a writing tablet with a tiny bottle of ink. "I only had time to write it once."

Kuzunoha's eyes narrowed, almost imperceptibly. "It will only take a few minutes to copy it. I can do the work while you speak to Richard if you'd like."

"I would appreciate it. You have a defter hand than I have ever had." Jack handed the tablet to Kuzunoha, then held out his hand. "I apologize for the delay. You are Richard, correct? Hidan's been buzzing about you."

Richard nodded as he took the offered hand and found the grip unnecessarily tight. He squeezed back, just as tightly. Jack's eyes narrowed.

Kuzunoha finished reading the contract. "Everything seems in order…except my dress. I've decided to take it with me."

"On the open road?"

"I met Miya on the road and have asked her to bring me a few items from home. I'll give it to her to return home."

Jack looked like he'd swallowed like sour milk. "Are you sure? I assure you it will be quite safe here."

"Yes, thank you thought. I brought your clothes back as well."

"If you insist. It's your choice. I have more paper in my drawing room desk. Why don't you rewrite it and then make a copy? We can head out to have it authenticated afterward."

Kuzunoha looked at them warily and her gaze asked Richard if he'd be okay if she left. The little minx knew her boy was playing games. It was cute, if unnecessary. He'd been playing this game since he was ten. He smiled to show her that he could handle her friend if he got out of hand and she let out a breath.

"I'll be back in a moment." Her expression suggested that they should play nice.

"It looks like we'll have to make this quick," Jack said as soon as she was gone. "You will be taking my future bride into the wild. I expect her back. Sleep with her if you want, but don't get any ideas about her being yours."

"Kuzunoha told me she wasn't promised."

Even if she had been, he didn't want to marry her. Other things, certainly, but even Kristinel would consider a marriage made at this point to be hasty or ill-omened. The best marriages were when the couple had known each other for months or even years and knew they could work together.

"She doesn't know it yet. She will though, sooner or later."

Would the arrogant lordling punch him if Richard laughed? The idea that this prick could even meet Kuzunoha as an equal was preposterous. No need for him to shatter the poor man's dreams. Richard would let the peacock prance if it made the dumb bird happy—and didn't inconvenience Richard in the meantime.

"Oh, I don't think that will be a problem," Richard told him, unable to stop the smile that crept on his face.

"Good," Jack said. "You seem an enterprising young man. I have a proposal you might want to consider."

Somehow, Richard wasn't surprised. He probably thought himself quite brilliant. Those were some of the easiest people to con. "I'm listening."

"If you do find something and decide you don't feel like sharing it, I would be willing to compensate you. For keeping her out of trouble while on the road, let us say."

The man had no idea how to read him and Richard didn't have the time or the crayons to explain where he'd gone wrong. On the other hand, it meant that even if they found nothing, this trip wouldn't be a total bust. For him, at least. "How much compensation are we talking about?"

"Enough for you to live comfortably for a few months...in some other city."

Richard nodded once, just before Kuzunoha came out.

"How are you boys getting along?" She was carrying a sheaf of papers in one hand, swishing them from side to side in her haste to dry them off.

"Splendidly," Jack said, smiling widely.

Richard restrained an urge to kick Jack in the teeth. Later, perhaps. Instead, he smiled at Kuzunoha. "At the very least, we understand each other better." He certainly understood the arrogant peacock better.

"Do you have your list of supplies somewhere in that pile as well?"

"I do," she said, handing the pile to him. "How long will it take you to purchase the materials?"

"A day, perhaps two at the most. Where are you staying?"

"Please send it to the Koi," she said.

"And we'll want receipts," Richard said.

"Of course," Jack said, willing to be conciliatory now that he believed they had an understanding. "I wouldn't want anything distracting you while you're on the road."

Chapter 23

Isashi had been enjoying the golds and blues of an early sunset when the scent of rotting meat surrounded her. She steeled herself. and grit her teeth. There were two things that would smell like that out here. One was a benign hazard and the other was an unknown threat.

She took another sniff, twisting her face at the scent. Derrina berries grew on a small bush in the wilds around Hidan. They started as tiny white pearls and grew to a purple ball the size of an adult goblin's bulbous eyeball. The berries were coveted by healers for their pain-relieving properties and by alchemists, for the paralyzing poison they could be made into when the berry was overripe.

Isashi followed the scent. She was only four hours or so outside Hidan. Helpful plant Derrina may be, but this one was too close to the city. While most wouldn't be stupid enough to eat the berries, anyone that did wouldn't live very long. The plant's scent of carrion drew predators and the berries would put anyone who consumed them to sleep. Thorny roots would then wrap around the creatures and squeeze them to death, burying them under the plant if they could. They needed blood and decay beneath their leaves to grow well. The plant was only dangerous if you had fallen asleep beside it. The vines moved slowly while they tangled their prey. It would need to be burned out.

When the scent became strong enough, Isashi slowed and judged that it had to be in the next clearing. If there were any monsters near it that hadn't been knocked out yet, she didn't want to startle them into attacking her.

She looked into the clearing and her heart fell into her stomach, making her gag.

Two dead bodies lay on the ground, human, and not monstrous. She took out a cloth and made a mask to cover her nose and mouth. Then she took out the gloves she kept deliberately to deal with dead bodies and moved quietly into the clearing.

Both bodies had been rotting for weeks now— two, maybe three judging by the damage. The first was wearing the clothes of a Hidan native. In particular, one of the vagrants was a Hidan native, though didn't know his name, she knew of his uncle. He was one of the people she refused to deal with. He had his fingers in every shady pie that cooked in Hidan. The sheriffs kept him around to talk to if something particularly bad happened. She sighed. He was also openly racist. She wouldn't deal with him. Someone else would have to have to tell him.

She moved to the other body. Though it had looked human from a distance, now she realized that the green skin tone wasn't due to rot, but was its natural colour. Its eyes had been plucked out, and its hair was a colour closer to blue than black. She counted. Five fingers, five toes per hand. The ears were pointed and the creature was covered by something like the fur of a caterpillar.

It wasn't human, but it was too close to human for comfort. A shifter. She sat back on her heels, frowning. Some of the most terrifying stories involved shifters. They looked human right up till the point when they turned on you. Most monsters lacked human intelligence and could be identified at a distance. A small few looked human, or near enough. They could put on the trappings, but they would never be human, would never be as accepted as the eledar were. Isashi shivered.

Isashi backed up and evaluated the scene again. The boy had come and not fled, thinking he saw another human. The creature had attacked him and there had been a fight, but clearly both had taken wounds. She couldn't tell who'd won. The human looked like he'd been poisoned by something and the other looked as if he'd been stabbed in the stomach. A particularly horrible way to die. After falling, they'd separated, both hoping to catch their breath, not knowing that they'd both taken deadly wounds.

She would have to bring the sheriff out to handle the boy's remains. She would need to bring the hunters as well. She was the youngest hunter in town, despite doing this job for over ten years now. Regardless, with something this odd, they would want to see the truth with their own eyes.

She stepped to the edge of the clearing and saw something white sticking out of the grass. A half-destroyed missive. The writing was difficult to make out. It had been written in a fast, heavy hand and tiny bits of ink-marked sand still stuck to the sheet. Clearly, it hadn't even been given the time to dry.

Have tracked your lost property to Hidan. He's holed up in the inn, too busy to take him. We'll move as soon as we can. Keep the messenger, if you like. A gift in return for your patience.

It wasn't signed, but it had a date on it—the first of Blonimem. Nearly a month ago, just two days before Himiko's majority day. Isashi's mind ran with the possibilities. The stranger, Richard was the only likely one they could mean. It also meant that she had misjudged the age of the bodies.

Keep the messenger. A gift…

Slavery was illegal in Hidan. There were a few indentured servants of course, but there were laws to make sure that they were given more than a fair chance to leave their servitude if they chose. Even if the stranger had been indentured, it still wouldn't have made him property. Neither would it have given his captor an excuse to keep the boy who had been hired to deliver a message.

She checked his body. Four gold coins and an impressive amount of silver. They'd paid him well to deliver a message to someone outside of town. Had the shifter been the one whom the message was meant for? Or had he come upon the boy out in the woods and attacked unprovoked?

She sighed and pocketed the money. It would go towards the boy's funeral rites. Knowing the boy's uncle, the family would only come forward after everything had been paid for.

Isashi set up signs for her fellow hunters so they would know that one of their own had already found the grisly scene and she set off at a run towards Hidan. She needed to know more. Especially if Kuzunoha were involved.

Chapter 24

The sweat dripped down Kuzunoha's back under the light leather armor. Or at least, it was supposed to be light. After a day of wearing the stuff, her opinion differed. She shook her head, took another breath, and tried to hold her arms straight. They shook and she took another deep breath but they didn't stop. She lowered the crossbow.

"How do people do this?" she complained, resetting her feet on the uneven ground.

They'd left the city that morning, full of hope for this trip. Now, having walked the entire day, all Kuzunoha wanted was to sit down and relax, and maybe have Miya run a bath.

Richard laughed. He was sitting down, ten or so feet behind her, stirring a pot. She'd never been so envious of someone doing a menial chore before in her life. With effort, she ignored Richard and stretched, seeing just how high she could go.

"You're done?" Richard said. His tone implied 'already,' which she found annoying.

She shook her head, not ready to give up. "I'm stretching, then I'll try again."

"Don't take too long. You don't want to lose any bolts if you can help it. In this light, you'd never find them again and we have a limited amount."

The forest around them was mostly green this time of year and while they'd found a good-sized clearing near the cliffs, if one of her bolts flew the forty feet to the trees, she'd have trouble finding it among the tall grasses and detritus, but not because of the light. It would be another hour, perhaps more before it got that dark.

"It isn't that dark yet." She pointed out.

"Maybe to you."

"And we have thirty bolts. That's plenty even if we lose one or two," she reminded him, wincing as she raised the crossbow to her shoulder again. Her arms were burning, but at least she could aim now. What hadn't started hurting from their travels had begun hurting with the crossbow training. She would need to stretch again before bed. If she went to sleep with her muscles like this, she wouldn't be able to move tomorrow morning.

"It depends on how many attackers there are." He mixed the pot again and didn't look at her. "I'd still feel a lot more comfortable if you'd run."

Snarling, she shot at the dummy Richard had created for her out of leaves, a spare gunny sack and some sponge carapace. The crossbow did most of the work but she still hurt too much to aim well. The bolt went through the dummy's leg instead of its chest and made an unholy crack as it snapped. She ground her teeth and huffed out a breath. "I won't leave you. I'm not craven."

"If you feel that way, we'll keep up with training. Tomorrow, though.

This is ready and I believe your hour is up."

She put the crossbow down on her log seat gratefully and walked over to the dummy. As she separated the sponges from the leaves, she noticed that she'd been better near the beginning of the hour. None of her latest shots had gotten near the muddy bull's eye he'd drawn on the chest. Peeking out from the leg, a stone was shattered. Bits of the quarrel were scattered around it. Nothing was going to be salvageable from that one.

She swore and left the remains where they were, lifting her hands to check the sun. It had fallen another finger. Sitting, she took out the bottle of wax Harold had included with the crossbow and waxed the string, the only things she'd been able to get without Jack's help. She used the last rays of the sun to ensure that it hadn't gotten dirt in it and then repacked the weapon and the remaining ammunition into her bag. Most weapons didn't work when needed because they were badly kept. She refused to put them in danger because she couldn't take care of hers.

"The weapon still good?" Richard asked. He had a bowl of the thick stew he had made and filled one for her. It hadn't smelled appetizing while it cooked and was now a lurid, greasy brown. He handed her a bowl and she shrugged. It was road food and all she would be getting.

"The weapon is fine, but I destroyed a quarrel on a rock we missed."

Richard grunted, swallowing a spoonful of the stew. "Hand me the target."

She ate a spoonful and made a face. It was good but bland. It didn't have much meat in it either. Still, it was food and her stomach grumbled for more. She passed Richard the target.

"Yeah... Do not shoot at anyone I'm engaged with in combat," he finally said.

"I'm not that bad."

"When was your first time shooting this thing?"

She stuck her spoon into the bowl and mixed it around. The wind was starting to pick up, even with the tree cover around them. She shuffled her seat closer to the fire. "I practiced with it a few times before we left."

She had preferred fighting with the bladed weapons. Perhaps because she had finally stopped seeing faces when she practiced.

Richard looked at the bag again and set it beside him. "Not as bad as I thought then. The rule about not shooting anything near me still applies though. You're as likely to hit me as you are to hit the target. That will change, but until it does, I'd rather not be shot again."

"How is it? Your wound."

Richard touched his side. "It's mostly fine now. It's a stretchy kind of hurt mostly and I do still get tired if I do too much. How about you?"

She frowned. "I wasn't hurt."

Richard gestured. She realized she was massaging her calf. She stopped and took another thick spoonful of the stew. The wind died and the thick scent filled her nose and she wolfed down the next bite. It smelled better the longer it sat, apparently.

He sighed and reached into his bag. He took out a large metal container and set it on the ground on top of the dummy. The firelight flickered against it, but the tin was old and it was covered with scratches and dings. She frowned.

"Finish eating and then we'll sit for a few more minutes with the fire," Richard said, picking up his stew again. "When it goes down enough, we'll get you into the tent and I'll massage this into your muscles."

"I'm fine," she protested.

Richard shook his head. "I'll admit that I'd expected less of you when we first set out." He pointed at her with his empty spoon before using it to scoop more of the stew into his bowl. "But I'm used to this sort of travel and, despite our taking it easy, I can see you're hurting. If I don't use some of this on you then you're going to be stiff or worse by morning. We need to be ready to go soon after breakfast. This will help."

"What about you?" she said, eating another bite. The forest was darkening around her, but she felt completely at peace. There had been no indications that there were monsters nearby, and while the hunters usually kept the area within a days travel clear, there was always the possibility that some were lurking. With their safety for the night covered, she could relax a bit. She was really looking forward to seeing the moon rise above the trees soon. The moon always seemed bigger when she viewed it from outside of the town's constricting walls. She scraped the bottom of the bowl, realizing that it was nearly empty.

Richard poured her another helping without her asking. She gave him a dirty look but there was no heat behind it. She was starved, even though she didn't remember feeling hungry when she'd sat down.

"You'll be extra hungry for the first couple of days. When you get used to eating more, I'll stop. And if you want to return the favour for me afterward, I certainly wouldn't argue."

She nodded and ate, thinking about Richard rubbing his hands over her and then her returning the favor. She bit her lip. The tent would certainly be warm. She shook her head. Partners and nothing more. Until they finished this trip. She glanced at Richard and realized that he'd been speaking.

"Sorry, what was that last part again?"

"I was wondering what your sister will say when we get back?"

"Hmmm," she mumbled shoving a full spoon into her mouth. "She'll have realized that I left already."

"Well, of course. You went to see her, didn't you?"

"Not exactly."

Richard gave her a look that suggested she continue. She grinned. "I had Miya deliver her a note. She wouldn't deign to open it until after she finished working. And I suggested that Deckard would be able to answer any questions she may have had about my whereabouts."

Richard chuckled. "In that case, it might be better if we can be up and away before dawn."

Chapter 25

Deckard was bending over Tieni, his head lowering to her chest when someone pounded on his front door, shouting his name. Tieni threw her head back and glared at him when he froze. They'd both hoped to make up for Kuzunoha's prior intrusion tonight.

The voice yelled again. "Kuzunoha? I swear if you're in there and you don't open this door, I'll..."

Tieni growled as Deckard rolled his eyes and crawled out of the covers. "Deckard, you promised—"

He touched Tieni's lips while he grabbed his pants. "It's Himiko. I'll be back in just a minute, I promise."

He kissed her, hard. She groaned but fell back onto the bed. Her eyes were still flashing though.

"Now, stay here this time. I'll be right back."

He was nearly there when Himiko started pounding on the door again, shaking his doorknob so hard he was worried the lock might fall out. He frowned. Lord's daughter or not, she'd been raised better than that.

"Himiko, give me a moment. This isn't a good time!"

She stopped pounding, but Deckard nearly felt the waves of frustration rolling off her as he opened the door. Himiko was taller than Kuzunoha by half a foot, which still made her inches shorter than Deckard. Her hair was a color Tieni called raven and he called black, and was cut in a wavy style that played around the bottom of her ears. She was more athletic where Kuzunoha was all rounded curves. Honestly, the two didn't look much alike, though, in annoying traits, you'd hardly find a difference.

"You caught me at a delicate time, Himiko." He stressed the *delicate* part.

Himiko ignored him, straining to see into his house. "Where is Kuzunoha?"

"Not here. Why...?"

"Of course she's not here. That's why I am. I swear, if I have to send Sheriff Dobson after them, to bring her back on her heels and arrest that delinquent, I will. He is going to be in jail for a long time and Kuzunoha knows it will be her fault."

"What are you talking about?" Deckard asked.

She looked annoyed. "Honestly, I thought better of you, but even you've been letting her have her own way."

"Himiko. Your sister is an adult."

A chill wind flew in through the open door. "She's a child and he took her out of town without my permission and against my wishes. That's kidnapping."

Deckard shook his head. "Himiko, that isn't how majority works."

"I'm her matriarch and I haven't given her my permission."

"You're her sister and older by barely a month, Himiko." While Himiko was telling the truth, he had thought that Kuzunoha was simply exaggerating like she always did about her sister's behavior. She couldn't expect that her sister would simply accept Himiko's promotion to family matriarch without any trouble, could she?

"That is hardly the point." She thrust a piece of paper towards him. "She's not just inconveniencing my family or our servants now. She's troubling you by staying here, me by having to go through all the trouble of bringing her back, Talvert by…"

The letter was brief and to the point.

Himiko,

I am going to look for the treasure with Richard. Deckard should know approximately where we've gone but don't bother him over this. He's been more than kind in helping me. After I return victorious, I'll contact you about getting my majority day rights given to me and getting my stuff from the house. I should only be gone for a few weeks.

Kuzunoha

P.S. - In case you're wondering what happened to the cherry tree dress, I sent it back with Miya days ago.

Deckard rubbed his forehead. That wasn't what he'd meant when he'd told her to tell Himiko she was leaving, but considering how angry she was, he understood Kuzunoha's underhanded way of carrying out his request.

"Why do you think that she needs that permission any longer? She turned twenty-one yesterday."

"I haven't seen her yet and haven't given her permission to become an adult yet," Himiko said.

"You do know that isn't actually necessary, right? She's twenty-one, regardless of whether she's spoken to you or not."

Himiko blinked at him. "But…it's tradition! I can deny her those rights… that's how this works."

Deckard rolled his eyes. "Himiko, while I agree she should have spoken to you, she didn't and now they've already left. Early this morning, actually. They're probably camping by now if they've any sense. Regardless, what can you do about it now? The gates are both locked until morning."

Himiko didn't answer the question. "The only reason I left her with you was because I assumed you'd keep hold of your senses and tell her to come home. Sooner rather than later."

Deckard put a hand to his forehead. "Himiko, she has to grow up sometime. She's left town with someone who can protect her for a few days. I may not think much of this Richard fellow's morals, but I can't say that he's not skilled. He'll see she stays safe."

"We'll be lucky if she gets back alive," she growled. "Honestly, I thought that you, at least, wouldn't fall for her foolishness twice."

Deckard took a step forward, forcing Himiko out of his doorway before he even realized how angry her accusation had made him. Himiko looked shocked. Good. She had reason to be mad, but no reason to take her ire out on him. He let out a breath, calming himself as he spoke.

"Himiko, your sister is gone." Himiko tried to say something, but he raised his voice. "She will be back in a week or two and as much as you want to keep her safe, causing an uproar over this won't help your case. What would your father think of you having to involve the entire city just to discipline your sister?" She didn't answer immediately so he started to close the door. "Now, go home."

"Deckard, you know Kuzunoha can't be trusted to make her own decisions."

What was it he'd said to Kuzunoha a few days ago? That she'd made bad ones. Kuzunoha had been right. She wasn't ever going to learn to make good ones if they didn't let her.

"If you still can't trust her to start making her own decisions, then when will you?" Her lips straightened to a line. "Allow her to figure out the consequences for her half-baked ideas on her own. Either way, this isn't my issue. It's between you and your sister, not me."

"How can you do this? How can you not help?" Himiko snarled.

Deckard snarled back. "Easily. I am a town healer; I'll deal with her when she's injured. Until then, she can take care of herself."

"You dated her," Himiko shot back, her voice rising.

"Kuzunoha is not my girlfriend, Himiko. My girlfriend is waiting for me in my bed. Do whatever you want about your sister."

He slammed the door on Himiko's surprised expression and stomped back into the bedroom, stopping only when he saw Tieni. He took a few deep breaths. He had to be calmer than this; had spent months training to remain calm. A healer couldn't let anger or panic take him. While healing, he had to be calm.

But he wasn't healing right now.

"Deckard…" Tieni said his name as if she was asking a question of him. She'd never seen him angry before. Her eyes were wide, but he couldn't read fear in her expression. He shut the bedroom door, flinching when it slammed. He turned to the door, leaning against it. The wood chilled his bare skin.

"I've had it with their whole family. I don't care anymore," he said.

Tieni walked up behind him and wrapped her arms around him. She didn't say anything, didn't try to make it better. Somehow, the simple comfort that she offered him let him heave out a sigh. Turning, he wrapped his arms around her naked body and kissed her. The kiss soothed away his anger, pushing it back into the darkness. He sighed again and set his forehead gently against hers.

"From now on, you let me answer the door. I'll make sure they know not to bother you unless they're injured." She promised.

It wasn’t an idle threat. She was almost as tall as he was and her muscles were toned. She’d been trained to use a sword as well; the calluses on her hand told him that much.

“I love you.”

He touched her chin gently, angling it upwards so their lips could meet. She responded easily, kissing him—slowly, sensually. Powerfully. With a grin, he picked her up and carried her back to the bed.

“Please?” she whispered, breathlessly.

“Yes.”

Chapter 26

"Thank you, Revered," Isashi said, handing the priest the gold. "Here is the money for his funeral rites."

It was too much for the rites, but the priest would take the extra and look after the details for the boy. If Carlos came looking, he would come to the priest, not her.

"Thank you, Hunter." The priest gave a nod. "He was not a fervent member of our flock, but we will miss him. The prayers will be said, a candle will be lit, and the body moved. I do wish that we could have found out what creature touched the body first. I do not know what animal to put on his headstone."

She looked hopeful, but Isashi shook her head. She knew that members of the Dreven sky-buried their dead and watched to see which animals visited the body, believing they were spirits, taking parts of the soul with them to their afterlife, the same way their creation deity had been killed and put together to form a different goddess.

"I am sorry, but I could not say. Perhaps the surgeon might?" she suggested.

The sheriff had brought out one of the healers that Isashi didn't know well, half-Dreven, half-Sian like Isashi herself, to look over the bodies. All she'd done was confirm what Isashi had guessed: that both had fought and died thinking their wounds less severe than they were. Neither body looked as though they'd been picked at much, so perhaps the monster's poison had been more than natural… something that magically left a scent, scaring away all but the most desperate of scavengers.

The older woman frowned but nodded. "Thank you. May Tormu quiet your soul and give you peace."

Tormu was the Dreven deity of innocence. Isashi nodded and gave a quiet thank you as she turned to leave. She'd heard that Tormu offered hope and peace to those who were world-weary. She grinned up at the sky. Her family had always prayed to Nandemo, the Sian Ku god of the twilight and between places. They were on the tail end of twilight now, and if anyone could lead her mind, either from or to trouble, it would be him.

For the moment, she decided on trouble and headed to the Koi. It was busy, as usual. Even on days when there were no extra ships in port, it was the most popular bar for people to go to after a long day. People who stayed there tended to find out the latest rumors about what was happening outside of Hidan. It was a coveted form of gossip, if you could keep up with it all.

She looked around for the stranger. He wasn't in the main room, but Himiko was, frowning into a pasta dish. Her friend smiled when their eyes met and Himiko waved her over. Despite her day, Isashi's mood perked up immediately.

“Isashi? What are you doing back? I thought that you were going to be gone for weeks.”

Isashi walked over, envious of Himiko’s outfits. Her friend was wearing a tight blue shirt with long loose sleeves, that she thought was the most gorgeous thing she’d ever seen. She was even more pleasantly pleased when the chair remained firm as she sat. The chairs were always a bit lop-sided here, but she’d gotten one of the few even ones of the bunch. It was good luck. Perhaps not on the level of a green-eyed tabby cat meeting your gaze, but lucky nonetheless.

“I had to come back early. I found something”—she paused—“less than pleasant. I had to come back to report it. It’s taken me all day and I just finished dealing with the priest.”

Himiko’s fork clattered out of her hands to her plate. She grabbed the table as if it were the only thing keeping her from falling off the side of the world. She’d never looked so panicked at the news. “The priest? Which one?”

“Revered Olivia, from the church on Taskit Street. Why?” Isashi touched Himiko’s hand.

Himiko shuddered and closed her eyes. “Olivia…the Dreven’s church. Amiterri bless us.” Amiterri was the highest goddess of the Sian Ku religions and the patron of Himiko’s family.

“Himiko, what’s wrong?” She couldn’t imagine what she’d done wrong.

“I thought you may have found Kuzunoha out there,” Himiko said, her eyes still closed.

"Himiko, if I'd found your sister out there I would have taken you aside and told you, not mentioned it like I did. Now, where did your sister go?"

The younger Tanaka had been talking about leaving, of course. Something about finding a treasure. Isashi hadn't thought she would actually do it. On the other hand, it meant that the fellow she was looking for probably wasn't here either. Damn it.

Himiko distracted her by sticking out her bottom lip in a pout. Though Himiko tended to the less dramatic, she was acting her annoyance out now. Despite the severity of the situation, she was adorable.

"Yes. After I forbade her from doing so. She's embarrassing the family name." Himiko drank the remainder of her wine in a gulp.

It had been a month since Himiko's birthday, which meant that yesterday would have been Kuzunoha's. There would have been no fanfare, no party for her except for something Himiko may have planned or more likely, what Kuzunoha herself planned. She wasn't the oldest and didn't have Himiko's burden.

"When did she leave?"

Himiko stared at her glass as though its newfound emptiness was a personal affront. "Yesterday. I asked the sheriff and he was on-board until I said it was for Kuzunoha. He's insisting that if I'm that worried I should start the paperwork with Mayor Dieter to take away her autonomy first. But if I do that…" She paused, swirling her drink in her cup.

Isashi knew how she felt about the mayor. She avoided him whenever she could. Also, if she started the paperwork, Himiko would be responsible for Kuzunoha essentially the rest of her life. She wanted her sister safe, not underfoot for the rest of her life.

Himiko slammed her cup onto the table. "They all know that this Richard character is bad news. They just won't do anything about it. 'She's an adult now, able to make her own decisions' is what Deckard said. Can you believe it? That man she left with is a smooth-tongued demon. Kuzunoha was perfectly happy before he showed up."

Isashi thought 'happy' was a step too far. Kuzunoha had never seemed particularly happy, even as a child. Her hand went into her pocket, her fingers brushing the torn note again.

"Keep the gift…" she muttered. That phrasing bothered her more and more as she thought about it. What sort of person offered other humans as gifts? A sudden chill ran down Isashi's spine.

What had Himiko called him? A smooth-tongued demon? What if after killing the men who had come to take him back, he'd decided to pay off his debt to the person who'd owned him…by offering someone of equal value? Kuzunoha probably didn't have any of the skills that had made Richard valuable, but like her sister, she was beautiful. Had her personality not been so prickly she would have had her choice of men in Hidan for life, rather than just her choice for a night. Yet, for beauty like that, someone just might conclude that as a debt covered.

"Isashi?"

"Huh?" She pulled her thoughts back to the table. "Sorry, what was that?"

"You looked like you were a million miles away."

"I was. I'm sorry. Do you know which direction they went?"

Himiko frowned. "They were searching for a boat, so they should be staying coastal. They left through the southern gate. Why, Isashi? Can you"—she lowered her voice —"can you bring her back?"

Isashi shook her head. "I don't have any authority to do something like that. There would be legal entanglements...basically the same reasons no one else will." Himiko's face fell and Isashi let out a breath. She lowered her own voice to a whisper. "What I can do as a hunter is go after her and keep an eye on her. If she gets into any danger out there, I'll be there to keep her safe."

Isashi hoped her interference wouldn't be necessary. She didn't know this man, after all. Himiko could just be painting him in a bad light. On the other hand, if that was his plan, she could stop it. Clearly, the people who wanted him back were nearby. Those bounty hunters wouldn't have hired the boy to deliver their letter otherwise. She needed to leave.

She glanced out the window and a cacophony of orange and blue silk assaulted her eyes. She blinked and looked past the bright outfit to the woman wearing it. Hana was tall and had the blondest hair of anyone in the village, keeping it cut to the nape of her neck in defiance of the local fashion. She had been a hunter since she was ten and was even older than Isashi herself. Her clothes were always brightly coloured and she preferred the thinnest silks a hunter could afford.

Hana sashayed over to the table. With a toe, she pushed out the chair and fell into it, leaning towards Isashi.

Himiko's lip was curled in disdain. "Who…?"

"I'm Hana, dear, one of the hunters," Hana said, dismissively. She may have been talking to Himiko, but her eyes were locked on Isashi. "You're back in town early, Isashi."

Nobody in the bar had been paying them much heed, but with Hana's precipitous entrance, they all were now. Isashi realized that she'd tensed up. So long as she didn't bring Kuzunoha back kicking and screaming against her will, no one would care what she did outside the walls.

"Hana, this is my best friend, Himiko. If you don't know who she is already, you should. And don't be rude. I came back because I found something the Revered would be interested in and had to cut my trip short. I'll be heading back out tomorrow."

Hana smiled. "You haven't stopped off at your home yet, I presume?"

Isashi shook her head. "Not yet. Why?"

"Hunter business. I was going to head out and find you tomorrow, but here you are, as though it were fated."

"Oh?" Himiko said. "What sort of business?"

Hana raised an eyebrow at Himiko, but then shrugged. "Samuel found tracks of something bigger while he was out there. He's suggested that we all go out in pairs."

Samuel's suggestions may as well be law for the hunters. He'd been doing this longer than anyone else. Still, going out in pairs was a pain. Necessary at times, but a pain. Hana wasn't a great team player, either. The part of the job she enjoyed most was when she got to hunt the monsters, rather than just making sure that the area was safe.

Samuel's command also meant that citizens shouldn't be out either. An even better reason to find Kuzunoha and Richard.

"Isashi?" Himiko hissed.

"She's right, Himiko. This is hunter business. Hana, if we're going to do this, we need to stay near the shore. A few innocents headed up that way."

Hana wrinkled her nose. "Babysitting? Do we have to?"

"It's part of the job and you know it."

"Who?"

"The younger Tanaka and a traveler."

"If we must," Hana said, pushing herself up. "What gate will you be at tomorrow morning?"

She nearly cursed, looking out the window. Full night had fallen while she'd been here. A hunter could leave after they'd locked the gates at night, but leaving without resupplying or sleeping would be stupid and panic wouldn't get her to Himiko's sister any faster. Fortunately, she had everything she would need to resupply herself at home already.

"Can you supply yourself for this journey? We can meet in the square at Second Light," Isashi said. Second light was just an hour or so past dawn, when the sun rose high enough to be seen over the walls and buildings of Hidan.

"Of course," Hana said, her eyes glittering with eagerness as she stood. It was standard procedure for a hunter to have extra supplies for times like this. "We can leave via the South Gate."

Himiko waited just long enough for Hana to leave the Koi. "Isashi… this sounds dangerous."

"It is." Hunting monsters was never safe. Still, Isashi was a good hunter. She knew the signs and she was a survivor.

"Will you be able to take care of my sister out there?"

"It's my job, Himiko."

"What about her?" She gestured towards the door Hana had left by.

Isashi winced. "It's her job, too, now, no matter what she thinks otherwise. And in this case, I now have the authority to insist she return to town immediately, or stay with me, whichever will be safest."

Himiko set her mouth in a line. "Fair warning, Kuzunoha does not do well with authority. But…thank you. Please, bring her home safely."

Chapter 27

Kuzunoha ran through the forms her training master had drilled into her for the three years her father had kept him on retainer. Richard was not being particularly kind to Master Chivek's work.

"Did your father tell this man to make you useless in any sort of combat? You can only use that attack on people smaller than yourself. Trust me when I say there aren't many."

She flushed. Her height was a weak spot for her. "Why not? Master Chivek said I was as well trained as any youth."

He pulled out one of his own blades. "It's an issue of reach, not training. Let me show you."

Kuzunoha moved toward Richard. Lazily, he caught the tip of her blade near the hilt of his. He flicked his wrist and Kuzunoha almost lost hold of her dagger. She looked disgusted. "He said he taught us all the formal forms."

Richard nodded. "Formally, you're very well trained. But he didn't teach you how to fight. If you were just trying to dance with it, play fighting with other nobles, you wouldn't have an issue. You would look very pretty while meeting blades and not hurting each other." She growled and he gestured for her to attack him. “Let’s get to work making you efficient. Come at me. Full speed.”

“Are you sure?”

“I don’t think you could hurt me unless you got lucky. I’ve been working with blades a long time. You learn best by doing.”

With trepidation, she held her blade in her hand and took a fighting stance. Her lunge was slow and faltering. His blade caught hers and he pushed back harder. She came at him a few more times, feeling her way. He looked bored, annoyed at her ineffectuality.

“I told you to come at me full speed, not a snail’s pace.”

“You took a bolt to the side just over a month ago.”

“Thank you for your concern, but it’s not necessary. Stop trying to hit me and hit me.”

She let go of herself and lunged forward. Richard adjusted to match, finally grinning. Her attacks hit closer and she pressed, wanting to take the advantage.

“You’re fast and agile,” Richard said, “but you can see that all the forms you’ve been taught all end with my blade meeting yours. That’s what they’re supposed to do in fake combat. In a real battle, never. You need to learn to hide your movements, hit harder, and know where to strike.”

Somehow between one breath and the next, he’d pushed her back. Kuzunoha’s breathing hitched, trying to keep up with him. She backed up, trying to anticipate his next strike, working hard to regain the ground she'd lost.

"Better," he said, "but this is what you need to be able to do. The dagger is an extension of your arm. Be aware of all your weapons and all your opponent's weapons."

His left fist came at her. She leapt back, dodging the blow but falling on her ass. She grunted at the impact on tired muscles.

"Not bad. Even if you weren't trained to use those skills instinctively." With a fluid motion, he put his dagger away and reached a hand out to help her up.

She took it. "So, I'm not completely useless? Good to know."

The falling sunlight flashed in her eyes as she looked to the ocean. She hadn't thought they'd reach the bluffs past Nordstrom on the second day, but they had. Seen from the ground, the bluffs were beautiful, black and white stone with no clinging ivy to distract the eye, over a hundred feet tall. Tiny purple and red flowers stuck out of tiny cracks on the cliff face they stood on and the dimming light made it feel like the world ended there, dropping into an abyss in the encroaching gloom. To the west and south of them lay a swamp that would soon be buzzing with life, but, for now, was still blessedly quiet.

Richard smiled at her. "For a noble, you're decent. The problem is your master trained you, never imagining that you would need to use it in a life or death situation. You might dance with other nobles but he didn't think you would need to know how to kill someone."

Kuzunoha felt blood pouring over her hand again and swallowed tightly. She distracted herself by wondering if her father had demanded that she and Himiko only learn the formal forms, effectively preventing them taking drastic measures against him, or perhaps if he had believed fighting with a blade was too barbaric a pastime for his daughters and had curtailed their teachings. Either way, she cursed his intrusive hand on her life again. "While I don't want to get comfortable with—"

"Defending yourself is something else entirely. I understand. Come on. Let's clean up." He gestured for her to walk with him.

In the copse of trees that backed their camp, Richard had tied up a blanket to offer some privacy. He proudly opened the blanket and she saw a black sack up in the tree with an attached tube hanging a mere foot or so above her head. She'd expected to see a collapsible tub, if they were going to have a chance to bathe.

"The water has been heating since I set it up. When you twist this"—he tapped a small lever attached to the hose—"the water will flow. I put sand down too, so the ground won't get muddy."

"How hot does it get?" she asked.

Richard shrugged. "If we'd left it out in the sun over the noon hour, very. Right now, it's only sun-warmed, like a swimming pond, midday."

"It'll be safe?" She asked.

The check they'd done on the area had come back clean of monster tracks or any of their leavings. From what she or Richard could tell, nothing but regular animals had been by this way in quite a while. Still, she had to ask. Perhaps it had to do with her never being this far out of Hidan, on her own essentially, but starting about midday she'd felt as if she were being followed though neither of them had seen anything.

"We've checked. There are no tracks, no sounds of monsters, no leavings, offal, or even anything left to show that the area has been recently cleaned. We'll sleep lightly, but so long as we stay somewhat alert, we should have plenty of time to respond to any threats. I'll go first though, so you can stay on watch."

"I can do that," Kuzunoha said. Somehow, she felt better knowing he trusted her to be on watch.

He smiled. "Why don't you get dinner started? We'll trade when I'm done."

"Sounds fair. Have fun." She gave a little wave.

He grinned and stepped behind the sheet.

Walking back into the camp, she grabbed the pot that Richard had used the day before. How hard could cooking be? Vegetables, meat and water, the pot on the fire. It would be easy.

When Richard was done, he came out dry, wearing nothing but pants and boots. He looked good with his hair and skin wet. His dark skin gleamed in the fading sun. Most that lived in Hidan were Sian Ku or the descendants of the Corvidae who had given up their wandering ways, like

Tieni. A few were like Deckard, with his skin and hair so pale it seemed like a glass drained of ink. None of them were like Richard, a dark almond-caramel mix. He smiled and she looked away. She hadn't been staring...had she?

"The rest of the water is yours. Don't use it all if you don't have to. We can use what's left to wash the dishes and save us another trip to the water."

She nodded and stood, handing him the spoon she'd been mixing the pot with.

"Kuzu, what were you making?" he asked as she left. His voice was tense.

"My name is Kuzunoha," she reminded him. "I was making soup. Is something wrong?"

She turned back to see him frowning over the pot, spoon in hand. With a dismissive wave, he shooed her away. Kuzunoha left him to it, shrugged out of her clothes and stepped onto the sand.

She had to reach to twist the valve, but Richard had been right about the water. It was still warm and soothed her muscles. She sighed, glad to finally wash off the two days of sweat. Still, she washed quickly and toweled the rest of the water from her body. Only the faint sounds of crackling flame and boiling pot permeated the night air.

A heavy thud broke the calm. Kuzunoha dropped her towel, grabbing her dagger with her other hand. "Richard?"

There was some grunting before he responded. It sounded forced, as if through clenched teeth. "Kuzu, I could use some assistance."

She didn't even take the time to dress. Richard was lying on the ground, a few feet from the campfire. A cockatrice was poised above him. His sides were bloody, caught by the creature's flechette-like wing tips. They would hurt but weren't usually deadly. Its beak, on the other hand, could tear children's arms from their bodies and was only inches away from Richard's neck.

Neither Richard nor the cockatrice moved, locked together in a frozen tableau. Richard's dagger had driven just behind its beak towards its brain. Unfortunately, Richard couldn't make good on the blow. If he pulled it out to try again, the creature would be at his throat.

Neither wanted to die to succeed.

Kuzunoha ran at the creature, aiming with the metal hilt. She hit its head and the cockatrice stumbled to the side, off Richard. She followed up her attack with another, forcing the creature to back away further, though it was already shaking off any disorientation from her first blow. Behind her, Richard swore and ran to the fire.

The cockatrice's head came up. Richard's knife was still in it, dripping black blood and gore down the handle.

The cockatrice opened its jaw and hissed at her, cutting off midway as it focused on the blade in her hands. Its eyes, shades of piss and summer grass, blinked. Slowly, it lowered its head, never dropping eye contact, and lifted one of its legs, a black scaly stick with three talons nearly an inch long. It grasped the dagger handle and ripped it out, dropping the pitted blade with an insectoid *click.*

Kuzunoha brandished her dagger and the cockatrice tilted its head to the side, an almost human gesture of confusion. Blackish blood dripped steadily from the hole in its neck, making red mud on the ground.

From her right, a black blade whisked by, catching the cockatrice in the head. The creature slumped down, the light leaving its eyes in a rush.

Kuzunoha felt shaky and she wondered if her legs would hold her up. The creature jerked and she flung herself back, its wing tips missing her by inches. She hadn't realized that she'd been that close. She breathed a sigh of relief when the creature stopped spasming, as if even in death it wanted to claim their lives. From behind it and to the right, Richard stepped out of the shadows.

"Richard… what happened? Where did it come from?"

Richard was covered in sticky, black blood and his eyes were wide, focused on the creature in front of them. When he looked up at her to answer, his jaw dropped.

"I'm not— Wow."

She blinked at him and then looked down at herself. Her skin was wet, luminescent in the dying sun rays. She'd forgotten she was naked. She turned, and Richard coughed into his hand. She glanced his way and was relieved to see that he had turned partially from her as well. She ran for her clothes, dodging back behind the curtain.

"Ahem, no. I have no idea where it was hiding or why it waited until now to come out. Are they usually this silent?" Richard called.

Kuzunoha shook her head, forgetting he couldn't see her behind the curtain. "Sorry, I don't know...I'm not a hunter."

"Don't apologize. Despite your training, you're an asset and lucky to boot. We'll both know to keep a better eye out from now on. Thank you."

She smiled with pleasure. "There's water left. You can wash off and then we can see if any of those injuries need stitching."

"Give me five minutes to sort things first. In the meantime, finish getting dressed."

She had just finished when Richard came to rinse off. Most of his wounds were thin slits, but two needed stitches to stop bleeding. She had a steady hand, even if she hadn't stitched a wound before.

When they returned to the fire, her soup was gone, replaced by cut vegetable and meat cubes on skewers. Richard sat down and coaxed red hot coals to flame again.

"What happened to the soup?" Kuzunoha asked.

He looked at her. "Have you ever cooked before?"

"No," she said. "I figured soup would be the easiest to make. Did I do it wrong?"

He was silent. "It got knocked over during the battle. I saved what I could." He pulled a skewer from the fire and handed it to her. "This one should be ready. Eat."

Chapter 28

Another two days of travel and Kuzunoha felt like they were getting somewhere. She didn't think she'd ever been this far outside of Hidan before. Flat patches of drying mud and dirt covered everything Kuzunoha could see to the north and east. The whole area, including their camp, stank faintly of sulfur, and the ocean air did nothing to clear it.

There had been one other dry spot that hadn't stunk like this. An old streambed. Though it was currently dry, there was evidence that mountain water still ran through it every spring. Despite her protests, Richard had insisted that this campsite would be safer. Less of a chance of waking up to water filling their tent while they slept.

While she wasn't very impressed with the stink, she could hardly contain her excitement at being out in the world. She was glad to see that camp was nearly set up. If she was lucky, they'd be done and could try to move someplace that smelled better.

They were a little more than half a hundred feet up from the ocean and it looked gorgeous from above—orange and yellow rippling on uneven blue. The ocean was always at its loveliest during late spring.

"So, what do we work on now?" she asked Richard.

Richard caught her gaze and shuddered. “While we still have sunlight, I want to inspect that cliff face and see if we can get down to the water. If we need to do some exploring that is seaside, rather than shoreside, I’ll want to know it’s safe. Plus, we may be able to add to our food stores by setting up a trap. There are lobsters around here, are there not?”

Work, but good work, and it would get her closer to the clear ocean air. She nodded. “The lobsters are further out, I think. We might find crabs, though.”

The cliffs were nearly straight up and down in most places, but with Richard’s help they managed to find some steps carved into the stone; uneven and eroding away. It was a treacherous path, but they took their time, making sure that the steps would hold their weight. The beach was beautiful. Grey-brown sand, a shade lighter than the cliff walls, covered the distance between the water’s edge and the cliff. A few shells and other flotsam showed that during full tide the water would climb up the cliff wall a short way.

“It should be safe enough down here for now,” Kuzunoha said, looking back out towards the water. The water was rising, but they would have an hour or more before the beach was lost beneath the waves, “We’ll lose the beach at dawn and dusk, but we should be fine the rest of the day.”

Richard didn’t answer, having walked to a bulbous mass of rock protruding from the cliff face a couple dozen steps away. It looked like bubbles of dried sludge and mud. There was a crack or two near the ground above the cliff, where darker stone peeked through.

“Hey Kuzunoha, what do you make of this?”

"I think this is the Fall. The stream bed that we saw above used to end here in the ocean. The elders say that years ago, a distant earthquake diverted the water to a lake further south."

"That riverbed is still getting water," Richard pointed out. "It's still moist in some places."

Kuzunoha shrugged. "Clearly it isn't getting enough to be a waterfall anymore. If anything, that moisture might make some of the mud overflow. Maybe that's what's coating it?"

"Might be. Still weird," Richard said, staring up at it. He was grinning like a kid with a silver piece, told to buy as much candy as he wanted. Tired as she was, his pleasure was infectious.

"Don't you have landmarks like this where you come from?" she said with a laugh.

He shook his head. "Jisa is flat, bound by a tropical forest on one side and the sea on the other. Neither tends to change much. Not really. The plants grow bigger, longer, and cover shit again, but that's it." There was a note of sadness in his tone.

"How long has it been since you left home?" she asked.

He grimaced, shaking himself free from the mood. "Too long and the odds of ever going back again are slim." He silenced her with a wave of his hand. "It would take months, even if I could. I may as well keep moving forward."

Kuzunoha touched his shoulder, but he moved away, picking up a tiny rock at his feet. With a well-placed throw, he chipped off some of the dried mud. The chunk crumbled, landing in a pile on the ground. Kuzunoha picked up the largest chunk and dropped it when it wriggled in her grasp.

Richard gleefully grabbed the rock that had trundled away from her. Chipping away the mud around the edges, he revealed a large crab, nearly the width of a small plate. Its pincers were sharp but they looked more for digging than snapping. Eyes on stalks stared them down and it clipped its claws menacingly.

"Did you bring a bag?" Richard asked.

"Why? Are we collecting crabs now?" she asked, a cautious grin in her voice.

"Yes. Honestly, it will be good to get some that we can keep alive at the camp. It's only been five days but I'd love to add some fresh food to our supplies. Also, if they're anything like the ones we had in Jisa, they'll sell well, even if we don't end up eating them."

Richard rinsed the creature off in the ocean water, revealing a mottled brown shell before he threw it into the bag she produced. A claw snapped, catching some of the fabric. "If we can catch enough we'll have made a good profit when we head back, even if we don't find treasure. At least, if we return quickly enough."

Kuzunoha smiled. "That's what I like to hear."

The sun was only a sliver in the sky now. "That mud doesn't look strong enough to support us. We'll try to mine it for a few days, using a knife and a rock to knock off the outer layers. For now, though, we'll head back to camp and see if these guys taste as good as the ones back home. I don't want us trying to climb those steps in darkness."

Kuzunoha smiled and looked up to the cliff. Her heart caught in her throat when she saw a shadow overhanging the cliff's edge.

"Richard? Do you see that?" She turned to him pointing.

He looked up from the bag, frowning. "What did you see?"

She looked back up, blinking. Whatever she'd seen was gone. "I thought I saw a shadow up there."

"I don't see anything now. Could you tell what it was?"

She swallowed and shook her head. "No… maybe I'm still just worried about being out of town?"

Richard turned to her. "If it is a monster, and wasn't just some sort of animal, we'll be prepared for it and we can search the area again before we try to sleep. If something was up there it has to have left tracks. We can move the camp if we need to. Come on, we'd better get up there as quickly as we can."

He leaned over and kissed her. Kuzunoha tried to ignore the flutter of her heart as Richard grabbed her hand and pulled her towards the darkening cliff face.

Chapter 29

Isashi looked at the carcass of the cockatrice. The creature only had two wounds on its body, which was odd. They were alert creatures that regularly dodged arrows. This one had a gash, nearly healed, near the base of its beak, and the strike that had killed it, a blow with a blade to the side of the creature's head.

The first had been done by a regular steel weapon, she could tell that by the way it had healed. Cockatrices were some of the more dangerous creatures because of their immunities. It was why Isashi carried around stone and cold iron-tipped arrows, as well as regular steel. An acidic substance had followed the blade in on the second wound, which was a typical reaction from weapons it was vulnerable to—cold iron in this case. Even after the blade had been removed, the damage continued, eating away at the creature's brain and head.

She waved away the flies and turned from the body to the destroyed cairn she'd found the creature under. Smaller pebbles filled in the bigger holes left by the fist-sized rocks that had comprised most of the cairn, but soon after the burial, something big had been drawn to the smell and unearthed the kill, feeding upon it. The confusing thing was that there were no tracks. She couldn't tell if it had been done by one creature or many.

She didn't understand why anyone would have cairned the bird in the first place either. The ground was wet enough here that whoever had killed it should have been able to bury it, though burning would have been even better. The stench of death wouldn't have hung around the area. A pall for the mood instead of the eyes.

Why wouldn't they have burned or buried the thing instead of just piling rocks on it? Townships didn't pay individually for creature deaths. Some monsters had useful parts, though the birds weren't one of them. Something to mislead Kuzunoha?

"He hasn't been proven guilty yet, girl," Isashi reminded herself. Somehow, even after saying it, she didn't know if she believed it.

Hana's voice broke the silence. "Isashi, I've found blood, quite a bit of it. Two areas, here and here. Both mixed with the dirt until it was nearly dry."

Isashi walked over to where Hana was pointing. Trying to puzzle out what the marks in the ground meant. One scuffle, a human laying on the ground with something heavy on top of it, weighing it down. Perhaps the cockatrice? If it had been, the beast's claws had dug into the ground, pausing, if the change in weight on its feet was an indication. There were more claw marks, as if the creature had been digging its talons into the ground for purchase, too. Perhaps it had been hiding from a larger enemy? She'd never seen such odd behavior for a cockatrice before. Usually they charged headfirst, killing with claws until there were no more enemies or they fell from their wounds.

"Have you tested either of them?"

"From what I can tell, though, this is mostly human and this"—she pointed to a nearby mound of dirt—"is only cockatrice blood."

Isashi crouched on the balls of her feet. "The bugs?" It was the most unscientific way of telling, but if you had nothing else, it worked.

Hana nodded. "There are regular flies and their maggot spawn on this one with one or two death flies. That one"—she gestured to the pile Isashi was standing over—"only has death flies."

Isashi batted away the flies and pulled up a clod of the dirt. The flies buzzed around her angrily, but she ignored them. Death flies preferred monster blood to human and were double the size, but they weren't dangerous. She'd never found out which her own blood would be preferred by. She hoped never to have to.

"No death maggots," Isashi said. The regular flies had been breeding for a day or so already, by the looks of it. Regular maggots were teeming in the dirt. Her eye caught on a soft looking pebble. She picked it up and saw another a little further away.

"No, but there are eggs," Hana said as one of the pebbles wiggled. Isashi grimaced and squished it. Bug eggs. "Two and a half days? Maybe three."

Isashi stood and walked away from the abandoned campsite.

"So?" Hana asked, following her out.

Isashi ignored the question, needing to be clean first. She drenched her towel with wood alcohol and breathed in until the stink chased away the scent of death. Then she cleaned her hands and all exposed skin with the cloth. The second time in less than a week. She would usually go months without finding dead bodies.

Hana cleaned herself as well. "You can't avoid the question forever. Do you think it was them?"

Isashi clenched her fist. "I don't think it could have been anyone but them."

"How bad do think the attack was?" Hana asked.

"One of them was injured but there were death flies on both piles. It suggests that one got sliced by a wing or talon and bled before he could get it off her."

"He got it off her?" Hana repeated.

Isashi looked into the clear sky. "The stranger took out three guys wielding swords, Hana. Who do you think is the most likely one that got injured?"

"Himiko is going to be pissed," Hana said. "Hey, no one's died yet and if we're right about that sandy alcove being used for cleaning then they've less chance of getting sick." Slim hopes, but they were all Hana had to offer. "Do you think they were planning to come back for it?"

The sun was a few finger lengths down from where it had been before. She and Hana had been here almost an hour; they had maybe another three before darkness fell. How far could she and Hana travel in that time? Where was the next good campsite? It was bad practice to sleep in a place that already had the pall of death.

"I don't see any other reason they would cairn it when they could have buried it or burned it. I'm sure they would have had shovels with them. This would have kept the flies and maggots from getting at it for a few days longer."

"Do you know if this guy she's with had hunter training?"

Isashi frowned. "Rumor says he does, but I don't know for sure."

It was confusing behavior if Richard did. There was no reason to leave it to the elements. She supposed that if he wasn't, he could be one of those who believed that monster parts could be harvested for money. In reality, there was little further from the truth. You had a better chance of becoming rich if you signed on with a merchant wagon or traveling caravan than turning in a bounty from a kill like this. Isashi had no desire to leave Hidan, but she might just suggest those options to this Richard fellow when she found him. Himiko seemed to be right about him being a bad influence on Kuzunoha, if nothing else.

"You think we're catching up?" Isashi asked, settling her pack on her back again. Himiko would want to know that her sister had been hurt. There was no way Isashi was going to be the one to tell her that without any better news to soften the blow, or without having Kuzunoha there to take the blame.

"It took us a day and a half to get out here, they had two full days head start." Hana did some math in her head. "We're catching up, but they still have a decent lead on us."

Isashi clenched her fist again. She'd hoped they would have made more time already. Damn it, she didn't like her townsfolk getting hurt. She'd failed Himiko's family by letting her father die already. She'd only been a block or so away when he'd died during the attack two years ago. If she'd just been faster, she could have saved him. She wouldn't lose Kuzunoha, too.

"At least we know they're still alive," Hana said. "And we haven't found any tracks."

"What worries me is that there aren't any footprints near the cairn at all. I'm worried that the creature out here may be intelligent enough that its hiding its tracks."

Isashi fixed her bag more comfortably on her shoulders. "Let's do what we can to shorten their lead then."

Chapter 30

It was nice to wake up and not have to pack up their entire camp. As well, she finally didn't feel like anything was watching her this morning.

"Are we really going crab hunting this morning?" Kuzunoha asked, washing the pan that he'd cooked breakfast in.

"Yes, I've been thinking about the best way to go about it," Richard said, packing both pots onto his pack. "We'll use the big pot to hold the crabs. We can start our search after getting a full pot of the things back to camp."

"Sounds good to me," Kuzunoha said.

Crab hunting wasn't what she'd come up here to do, but she had to admit, it did sound fun. And the crab last night had been tasty, if not succulent.

They grabbed their packs and headed towards the cliff stairs. It felt odd not to be wearing her armor, but Richard had agreed that if the armor got wet enough when the tide rose, it would destroy it. Since they still hadn't found any sign of any monsters around, Kuzunoha hadn't argued. She preferred the way the breeze danced over her as they clambered down the steps to the ocean and to the mud bubbles.

Richard smiled at her and took out his dagger. "Let's get started."

He dug his knife into the mud and levered it until the caked layer dropped off, revealing a few crabs, scuttling away from the sudden light. He grabbed one before it ran too far and used his knife to knock the dried mud off of it.

“If it’s smaller than a double sentine copper, you can let them go. They don’t even taste good,” he said, dropping that mud clod. “If they’re bigger, wash ‘em and drop ‘em in the pot.”

“Alive?” she said, surprised.

“They’ll stay fresher that way. Ready?”

When she’d caught five or six of the larger ones and he’d caught seven, he stretched.

“It’s near midday, what do you say about a break? I can make a fire here on the sand and we can cook up some of this right away.”

She mopped at her brow. She’d just pushed her dagger in the mud again. No point in wasting the thrust. “Sure. Just let me check this clod.”

He nodded and opened one of his fuel packs to start the fire. She’d found out they were made of animal dung, cotton and straw, which was slightly disgusting. She paused as a slim breeze blew over her, drying some of her sweat and cooling her down. It was glorious. She grabbed her knife with renewed vigor and started working the blade back and forth.

“How long will you be staying?” she asked Richard.

“What do you mean?” He had some sticks on top of the flaming bag.

Kuzunoha heard a pop as some sap expanded in the heating wood. She worked the knife more.

"After we find this treasure and get back to town? Do you plan on staying long afterward?"

He stared into the growing flame. The mud clod shook loose. She caught the rock and heard a squelching sound. Suddenly her hands itched. With a grunt, she tossed it back onto the mud bubble.

Small white tentacles whipped back and forth as an octopus the size of her fist shook off a layer of half-dried mud. She scratched at her hand, surprised.

Richard's laughter startled her. "Never seen a mud octopus before? They aren't dangerous. It's too bad you let it get away. They're tastier than crab."

"I haven't let it get away," she muttered, clambering after it.

"Hey," Richard said as she heard a crack in the mud beneath her.

She was proud that she didn't shriek as the hillock of mud beneath her gave way, plunging her into dark ocean waters. The cold ripped away her breath. She shivered and popped up just long enough to suck in some air. It was late Blonimem and the water was still cold enough that she could freeze to death, if she didn't drown first.

She heard a loud crack. Without waiting, she ducked back under the water. A cacophony of vibrations shook the pool, sending chunks of dried mud and crabs into the water around her. She covered her head and caught sight of the octopus, fleeing to the sand below.

That seemed like a smarter idea than staying near the surface while the rocks came down. Besides, she still wanted to prove herself by catching the critter. She dove towards the many-limbed creature as it caught the wall and slipped under a crevice she hadn't seen from above. She reached for it, feeling the rubbery skin squeeze out of her grasp. Her hand felt hot and she fought to hold her breath as her lungs burned. Her toes tingled painfully.

She bared her teeth and let out a small burst of air, shoving both hands under the rock. She pulled herself down. The water down there was becoming murky, but Kuzunoha caught sight of a tentacle changing color from white to brown. She grabbed at where she thought the body might be and managed to pull the creature toward her along with a hard pile of dirt from the sea floor.

With the air in her lungs gone, she pushed upwards and gulped fresh air she broke the surface. In her hands, the octopus, desperate to be free, stung her with its tentacles. Her hands and lungs burned.

"Kuzunoha? Kuzunoha...you were supposed to be careful, are you hurt?"

"I'm fin-blff-" Her mouth sank under the water and she kicked up again, making certain she stayed above the waterline. "I'm fine. Take this and then get me-OUCH..."

Richard reached down and grabbed the octopus. The pain blinded her as he pulled the suckers, like tiny hooks, from her. She sank her hands under the water and realized that there was something in the dirt she'd grabbed. She let it go, but a flash caught her eye. She grabbed at it, wincing as something hard as rock dug into her palm.

Then Richard was there, reaching down for her. It took him a while, but he was able to help her out. They collapsed on the sand, breathing heavily until a rattle startled them. The cooking pot had fallen over and the octopus was flailing towards the ocean.

Kuzunoha groaned and tried to get up, shivering with pain when her hands protested her putting any weight on them.

"Let the gods-damned thing go," Richard told her, pulling her back down. "It's fought long and hard for its freedom. By the light, you're cold."

She tried to nod but Richard pulled her to him, grimacing. His body was pleasantly warm on hers. He looked at her hands.

"We're going to have to wash them until that muck is gone, let alone the sand. It will take days to heal, it looks like quite a bit of your skin is…"

She kissed him. It was what she'd wanted for weeks. Richard seemed paralyzed and then kissed her back softly and then harder, more insistently, his hands caressing her everywhere. She moaned, desperately trying to contain a yelp when her hands touched him.

He pulled away. She could read his eyes. Want, tinged with frustration. Then he looked at her hands. "I'm sorry, but we have to see to these first. Then we'll warm you up. You don't look well."

Kuzunoha felt woozy and her hands were throbbing and burning. "I can hardly feel my toes... What did I do to my hand?"

"Later," he said. "Help first."

He stood and helped her stand without touching her hands. He was gentle with her, rinsing her hands with clean warm water, though his shoulders were tense. An almost palpable anger emanated from him as he finished. She stayed quiet; every breath was a benediction. Richard threw a few more logs on the fire and his coat over her. Then he reached for the medical kit and pulled out bandages and cream. He opened her clenched fingers, pausing when a small lump fell out.

"What is this?" he said, grabbing it. It was a ring. "It's covered with barnacles."

She'd forgotten that she'd picked it up. "It was in the sand with the octopus."

He slipped the lump into a pocket and opened a jar of cream that smelled dizzily of pine and some sort of cinnamon-like spice. It warmed her skin and she gasped, expecting pain. Instead, her hands went numb. She blinked and tried to move her fingers. Her hands didn't want to work, but she was able to force them.

Richard tapped her wrist. "Stop that."

She did, realizing that she was giddy with relief. She wriggled her toes instead, warming them in the sand near the fire.

"Why did you go after that octopus?" he asked her as he bound her hands. "I told you to be careful."

"You also said it was tasty and I felt annoyed at losing it in the first place."

He finished the other hand and leaned in to kiss her. Her breath came short and she shuddered as he touched her breast.

"We need to talk, Kuzunoha," he said.

She didn't want to talk. She wanted him to push her to the sand and kiss him again. She shivered and regretfully acknowledged that now wasn't the time. She scooted closer to the fire, feeling the heat finally starting to wash over her. Richard slipped down to her right, just out of reach. Despite saying they would talk, he just sat there. Richard played with the ring she'd found, picking at it. He refused to look at her.

"Richard, why did the octopus burn me?"

He let out an annoyed breath. "They do it when monsters catch them, but usually just ink to get away from humans."

"Then why...?"

"You haven't bathed yet since the cockatrice battle."

"You think it smelled it on me? It's been over twenty-four hours."

"They don't have much of a nose, but sharks can smell blood over a mile away, so you never know. I'll help you wash tonight to make sure it doesn't happen again."

He stood abruptly, striding to the other side of the fire. He put another stick on and set up the pot again, and used some of their water to refill it.

"Why are you angry?" she asked, annoyed for asking the obvious.

His voice caught in his throat. "I thought I'd lost you. Then there you were, coming up towards the surface."

Her heart skipped a beat. "I'm sorry."

"It's nothing."

"And the kiss?"

There was pain in his eyes, along with desire. There was something else there too, but before she could identify it, he looked away. "That wasn't nothing."

"Richard, I don't want this to be a solely professional relationship," she said. Her cheeks were warm and her stomach danced with nerves. She'd never been the one pushing for more. She didn't know what to do with herself.

"Me neither," he admitted. "But…Kuzunoha, I'm a follower of Kristinel."

She smirked and he made a frustrated noise.

"No. Forget what you've heard. Those are rumors. Kristinel is a goddess of lust. Her followers don't have relationships like you do. Everything is a professional relationship."

"Can you explain that? Her followers don't fall in love?" She wanted to ask about marriage, but that would have been too forward. Not that she knew if she loved him yet, but she would have to know eventually.

"Not in the way you do. Sex is not the same thing as having a relationship. Sex is fun, a release. There are no strings attached. Sex does not mean that you are in a relationship. There is respect, yes, and desire, but there doesn't have to be more. A loving relationship can include sex…but usually won't. It is something…more. I am not looking for that second one right now. Just the first."

According to the custom in Hidan, sex was only done with somebody you cared for greatly. In practice, it was treated more casually. You could have a single night with somebody and people would overlook it. Still, people would not overlook multiple nights without letting you know that you were breaking societal norms. As a rule, after Deckard, she hadn't wanted anything that might be considered permanent.

"Richard, I understand that…and I would still like to enjoy you."

He shook his head. "You don't understand… this is—"

She put her finger to his lips. "This isn't something else. This is only going to be for fun. One time is just fun, even for us here. Any more than that, and we'll have to talk again, first. All right?"

"Kuzunoha…" he said.

She moved her lips near his. "I know what I want. I trust you."

He shivered and ran a finger down the side of her face. She waited for him to decide.

"That is a terrible idea..." he whispered.

This time, when she moved in to kiss him, he didn't pull away. She wrapped her arms around him, playing with his back gently; light feathery touches that were as easy on her hands as they were effective for him. He gasped, yanking her onto his lap. She pushed him to the sand.

"My mistake to make." She whispered, lowering herself onto him.

Chapter 31

The sun had set by the time she'd finished washing. Richard leveled a scowl at her.

"Sit. I'm going to get that fire going before I come over there. Octopus aren't dangerous, but you're having a worse reaction than I've ever seen."

Kuzunoha nodded. Her hands were puffy, crisscrossed with red welts. They stung but she had full movement and no numb spots.

Richard was frowning, though. "You are going to let those hands rest tomorrow. Right now, soak your hands in this."

He slid a pot in front of her. She put her fingers in and felt cool water. Her flesh tingled but didn't hurt. She let out a delighted breath.

"It's ocean water and some of the herbs we have. Mostly, the cold water will do the work, taking down the swelling. The herbs are in case this wasn't a regular octopus. It could be poison." He paused. "If they aren't better tomorrow, we'll pack up and head back to town for Deckard's expertise. I can do field kit, but I'm not a healer."

Looking at the angry welts, she had to admit he was right, even if she didn't want him to be. "Is there anything I can do?"

He gave her a stern look and she rolled her eyes.

"Just something to keep me busy."

He relented. "How is your eyesight?"

"Probably better than yours." She'd never had a problem seeing in the dark and had always been better at it than anyone else she knew.

"Let's put that to the test."

Within a few minutes, he had her set up near the fire with the ring and a thin book of notes using a thick tree trunk for a table.

"This is what you pulled up from the bottom of that grotto. I cleaned it up and found this sigil. I came across a description of a similar ring that the captain supposedly wore during my research. See if it matches the one in my book. I'll start cooking."

"You don't think…"

He shrugged. "Small items like this get pulled in with the tide. It would let us know if we were near the right area."

Her hands tingled pins and needles while she flipped the pages, and she soaked them whenever they started hurting. The third time she put her right hand back in the water, she wished Deckard were there. She didn't think her hands were that bad, but he always knew how to make the pain disappear and stay gone.

She turned another page in the book and stopped, her hands forgotten. A picture of a ring dominated the top corner of the page. She dried off her hands and picked up the ring for comparison. The ring she held was thicker by a few millimeters and the sigil wasn't quite right—a shaft of wheat crossed by a trout rather than a pussy willow—but they looked close. She picked at the ring, trying to see if she could clean it up more. Giving up, she read the notes scribbled in the book.

The words were cramped and tight. Most of them seemed to be about the ring's owner, The Captain of *Sight to Sea*. He'd never been seen without it tied on a black cord around his neck. Kuzunoha looked at the different sigils. They could have been different rings. On the other hand, the fellow's memory could have been bad. It was an extremely easy mistake to make and whoever had given this account (had it been the first mate?) wouldn't have seen it since their childhood.

Richard moved the dinner pot off the fire to a nearby rock. "Did you find anything?"

"I did, but there are some differences. The sigils are close but don't match. Even so, I'd say we're looking at the same ring. He makes a point of saying that the man wore it around his neck rather than on a finger. Why would you do that?"

She untied a small ribbon from her hair and tied it around the ring, using the long end to mark the picture in the book before she closed it.

"When you work on a boat, you don't wear things on your hands. It might catch on something and cost you the finger or the item itself."

Richard poured her a bowl of the stew and set it down on the stump.

He grabbed the book on the way, smiling at the ring. Her hands throbbed uncomfortably when she touched the warm bowl and Kuzunoha decided against picking it up yet.

"You said the ring was just lying there on the ground?" Richard asked, sitting down with a bowl himself.

Kuzunoha put down her spoon and recounted her underwater adventure. "The seabed wasn't too deep, only eight or nine feet. That ring was in the sand I picked up."

"Was there a lot down there?"

Kuzunoha tried to recall. "The sand was everywhere. Even the ring was covered originally." She'd expected a floor of rock or shale, not sand. Even the beach was closer to gray-brown dirt than proper sand like they used at the glassworks.

Richard gestured at her hands. "You're not holding your bowl? Are your hands too sensitive?"

She tried touching the bowl again. It was cooler to the touch but it still hurt. She picked up the spoon. She could still eat on her own. "They're sensitive to heat."

"Do they actually hurt? Or have they gone numb?"

She put the spoon down and stretched them, wincing. "They hurt. The spoon isn't too heavy, though."

"I was more worried that the poison may have done damage to your nerves. If it's still hurting, there isn't a chance of that. I'll use more of the numbing cream on you tonight and tomorrow we'll go with just the healing stuff. It's only a few layers of skin, but we'll want them healed enough to not hurt before we continue."

"What will you be doing tomorrow while I sit around camp?" she asked, refusing to add, 'while I growl at everything.'

Richard smiled as if he'd heard it anyway. "I'm thinking that you need to rest, but you can watch just fine. I want to see if there's anything more in that sandy seabed."

"You did say the ship may have sunk near land…"

She shook her head. No, there was nowhere for a whole ship to hide there. Even if the mast had been broken, that seabed would have had to be more than forty feet deep. There were few places that deep this close to shore.

Richard turned towards his stew whole-heartedly. "What I know is that you found us something today. If nothing else, we should make sure that we got all of it that's there."

Chapter 32

The vivid red welts on Kuzunoha's hand weakened to a dull orange-red shade by the next morning. Richard never heard of someone reacting that way to an octopus. He was just glad they looked better. He didn't relish the thought of taking her back to Hidan without finding the ship first. He was certain they'd never get back out again if they did.

"Your hands are looking better," Richard said, dropping their sacks on the sand, below them. She was clenching her fingers again. He gestured for her to leap to the sand from the cliff step she was on.

"Are you sure? I would have thought that they'd be better by now. I mean, the cold is glorious on them, but any heat and I flinch."

He caught her as she leapt, and took the opportunity to run his hand up her back. As he'd expected her to do, she arced towards him.

"Nothing heals in a day," he whispered before kissing her. He loved the way she tasted. Her mouth was sweet like she'd been eating honey.

"It should," she grumbled breathlessly.

He smiled. He hadn't always cared about his partner's pleasure but somewhere along the way it had become a point of pride.

"Come on, I want to check out this pool of yours. How cold was it?" His hand had gone numb just from grabbing her yesterday.

"It's warming up, but that's an ocean-fed inlet. It won't be livable till late Flinomem, or even Quinomem."

Months then. He'd have to be quick. "Do you have any tips?"

Kuzunoha pursed her lips in thought. "Move quickly and don't stop. The cold will take longer to settle in if you're moving. No matter what, come out after five minutes and warm up by the fire. I'll keep it stoked high."

He nodded, and glanced up as they reached the little inlet…and stopped in his tracks.

The wall had been a solid sheet yesterday with the uneven mud making it appear as though slime had slid down its surface for years. About twelve feet up from where Kuzunoha had scrambled up to, there was a crack in the mud. It looked deep and didn't lead to more shale like the walls around it. Instead, it looked dark, as if it didn't have shale at all underneath it.

"Kuzunoha, do you see that?" A stupid question, since it was clearly there, but the question he wanted to ask, *why*, seemed too outlandish still.

"There's a crack. It looks deep," she said. Her head was tilting like a confused pup when you only pretended to throw a ball. "You can't think it goes all the way in…?"

He grinned, glad that one of them had gotten the words out. "Let's see."

That was easier said than done. The mud scaled, bits and pieces chipping off whenever they tried to climb.

"This isn't working!" Kuzunoha complained, about twenty minutes later.

"It's chipping…not enough to be useful either," Richard mused.

"And we'd be lucky to have the wall not collapse on us," Kuzunoha gripped.

Richard smiled at her. "Now that might be exactly what we want to happen, if it could be done safely or quickly. For now, let's try putting you on my shoulders. You can stand there, and see if you can see anything inside."

Kuzunoha shrugged. "I don't know how well I'll do, but we can try."

She didn't weigh much, but it was enough to nearly overbalance. "Hurry, if you could."

She put her hands up against the wall, still wrapped, and leaned out as far as she could reach, trying to reach the crack. Richard moved with her, trying to use the wall to keep his balance as well. He couldn't see anything though, couldn't even look up due to the angle.

"Wait. There, I've got it… I can just see. It's dark inside, and it looks mostly filled with water. It smells of more sulphur. There's something in the back. I can't tell what. Its all in shadow."

She used her hands to move back along the wall and he helped her get down.

"So, it's filled with water. Do you think we can just knock the wall down? How large is it inside?"

Kuzunoha bit her lower lip. "It's really thick. Even if we were willing to take the time to batter it down, I think it would take more time and supplies than we have here."

"It might also draw some of the nearby monsters too," He said. "So far, we haven't really made a lot of noise. But pulling the whole wall down would probably be enough to do it."

"What can we do then?" she asked.

Richard thought about it and then glared at the pool of water. When the mud had crashed down on Kuzunoha, it had shattered into fist-sized chunks. She'd been lucky that none of the pieces had hit her. It had taken time, but the water was mostly clear now, a deep shade of blue. It reminded him of danger, since the only time the clear waters of Jisa darkened that much had been during her yearly violent storms. He couldn't see much of the mud though. If they could dig their way under it, they could completely ignore the wall.

He started unbuttoning his shirt.

"Richard, what are you doing?"

Kuzunoha was flushing and her wandering gaze stopped near the remnants of yesterday's fire and the small dunes they'd made. She'd been an eager partner, wet and imaginative in all the right ways. He still wasn't sure it had been the best idea, but he couldn't deny that he'd loved the way her body had felt, molded to his.

"We expected to do some swimming. I'm going to see just how far this mud goes."

He tossed his shirt away, shucked his pants, and tied one of his knives around his thigh. Grabbing the edge, he swung in.

The instant his feet touched the water, his breath came out of him in a rush and his stomach cramped as if he'd been sucker-punched. The only reason he didn't go under was because his fingers dug into the stone hard enough that he thought they may have left an imprint. His muscles locked. For a moment, he wondered if he could move at all. He clawed in a ragged breath, feeling like ice was settling inside his body.

"Would you rather I look?" Kuzunoha asked him.

With an act of will, Richard unclenched his fingers and forced his lungs to take another deep breath. He would accept her help, but not her pity. He kicked off the stone and dove under.

The water around him was nothing but shadows and light. He kicked his feet swiftly, heading down. She'd been wrong about the depth. It was closer to double his height than hers. As he neared the bottom, he saw the ocean floor undulating. Richard blinked and grabbed up some of it.

Thick mud slid from his hands, more slime than wet dirt. He let go of it and a large crab caught it in a claw, dragging it down. The floor was teeming with movement and he lowered himself to make sure it was just crabs. It was, but they were acting oddly, wrapping up the slime into balls. If these crabs used it to make their homes, it would build up year after year until it collapsed. At that point, they would need to build anew; collecting what they could to aid in rebuilding only made sense.

Such intelligence wasn't usually found in animals, but monsters weren't usually so innocuous. He considered catching one but put it aside as a bad idea. He didn't want to know that he'd been eating monster meat all this time. Besides, his fingers were cold and he could feel his chest tightening.

He blew out a bit of air and swung his arms and legs harder than he would have back home, forcing blood to run faster through his veins. The ship had been a caravel with a low draft. It only would have needed two or three meters of clearance with the cargo it was carrying.

The edge of the rock wall was thick with barnacles. He ignored it, scooping away slime until he could see the sandy bottom. When he cleared enough, he thrust his hands under the overhang. Shivering, he blew out more air. He'd only been under a minute, but he already knew he wouldn't be able to stay in much longer.

He pushed his hand in further, trying to see where the overhang stopped. It didn't.

Ducking his head under the overhang, he could see that the rock was only five or six feet long. If he could clear out the sand, he would be able to get under completely.

Smiling, he felt his chest tighten painfully. He wasn't going to finish this in one trip. He pushed forward to clear as much space as he could. The crabs seemed angry at him but moved further away to do their work. His fingers felt like they'd frozen into claws by the time he'd finished clearing about a foot of the sand out. It would be enough, so long as the sand was loose the whole way in. He pushed back and propelled himself towards the surface.

"Richard, did you get caught on something? How are you?" Kuzunoha asked him before he had even cleared his eyes of water.

Cold was the answer, but his teeth were chattering too much to be flippant. He shook his head and raised a hand. Kuzunoha apparently hadn't expected a response anyway and continued.

"I didn't mean that you should try to do all five minutes in a single breath. I've never seen anyone stay under water that long."

"It… it wasn't five…" Maybe three at the most, but he couldn't stop his teeth from chattering enough to finish.

She grabbed his hand and helped him out. She winced and he remembered her hands. He would have to check to make sure her wounds hadn't opened. Kuzunoha set him in front of the fire and he groaned when she wrapped a warm cover around him.

"It isn't as warm as it could be, but it will help," she said, still fussing. "Now, what did you find?"

The heat helped immensely, even if he was still shivering. "We can dig ourselves a way in."

Kuzunoha let out a breath. "What can I do?"

"If we empty out two bags to cover your hands, do you think you can help me clear out the sand underneath?"

She nodded. "I'll do what I can."

Chapter 33

It had taken the rest of the prior day to clear enough sand to safely move under the rock. Two and a half feet deep and nearly five feet across, plus additional space at both ends. Even if they had to turn around underneath the gods-damned thing, they wouldn't get stuck.

It would have taken maybe an hour back in the warm waters of Jisa. The water was too cold to work for long, though there was some sort of current bringing warmer water their way on occasion. Even with that touch of warmth, they'd had to take longer and longer breaks warming up by the fire afterward.

It was morning now, and they were nearly ready to go.

"Done," Kuzunoha said, stretching.

Her body was toned, with just enough plumpness around her hips and breasts to make things interesting. She grabbed their bags, sealed with their clothes, tools, and the other sealable bags she'd had the presence of mind to pick up.

"Here, you'll need this," Richard said, opening the jar of algae mix.

She wrinkled her nose at the scent of fish and gagged a bit as he rubbed it on her palms, her collarbone, down the sides of her breasts, her arms and the outside of her legs. He finished off by putting a little bit on her cheeks and forehead.

"It smells like rotting fish. What exactly is this stuff supposed to do?" Kuzunoha asked, dipping a finger in one of the streaks on herself.

"It's a type of slime made from algae that glow, quite brilliantly. When it gets wet, it will start glowing blue. It should give us a light source while we're in there since I don't think that crack will be enough for detail work. We'll have to reapply it in about an hour if we're still swimming."

"Let's get going, then," she said, jumping into the water.

Richard didn't wait to see if she came back up. It would be easier to get underneath the rock if he had the advantage of speed. Diving in beside her, he shouldered his way past her and under the overhang. As always, the rock above him felt like it was pushing him down, as though it wanted to feel him squirming.

His chest tightened but the algae on his hands started glowing. Seeing the light helped ease the sensation that he was trapped.

Then he was clear. The water beyond was dark, filled with tiny floating bits of dust. He swam up, feeling the barnacles along the side of the wall. They stopped and he felt dried stone. A moment later, his head was above the water.

He took a breath and almost gagged. The air was stale and he could almost taste the scent of sulfur and fish that hung so thick it was like breathing smoke near a fire. Despite that, it was still breathable. He lifted his arms. The cavern roof was higher than he could see, but when he turned back, he could just see the crack. It was much smaller on this side, only a few centimeters at its widest spot. The light it let in did more to create shadows than it made anything else.

A flash of light swam underneath him and about twenty feet further than he had gone. Kuzunoha popped out of the water like a dolphin, straight up. She gagged on the air and slid back under the water, looking like she was about to retch. She left her mouth and nose below the surface when she came up again.

His heart skipped a beat. Her hair was wet and floating behind her. Her face, arms, and legs glowed. The effect was disconcerting, like she was some terror from the deep. He covered the sudden clench in his stomach with an uncomfortable smile. If a woman like her looked unworldly in this darkness, how must he?

"Kuzunoha, are you all right?" he asked, swimming towards her.

She lifted her head out of the water. Her voice was strained. "Have you not smelled this air? It's fouled! It wasn't that bad when I was looking in."

The water was warmer where she was and the scent of sulfur in the air was even stronger. "It isn't that bad. A bit stale, I'll give you that. We should be grateful for the sulfur. I think there's a hot spring somewhere in here."

She glowered again so he grabbed her, lifting her out of the water.

She yelped and giggled as he twirled her back down, slipping under the water himself.

When he rose to the surface again, she kissed him lightly and pointed behind him. "Hey, I thought I saw something over there."

He turned, but all he could see was shadows on shadow, obscuring everything. "You're sure?"

She pushed out of his hands and started swimming that direction. "I am. I don't know what it was, though. It was big. That was all I could really tell."

He hadn't questioned her eyesight before, but after swimming for forty or fifty feet towards the shadow she'd seen he was starting to wonder. This cavern was immense. How far could inland could it go? The water was warming up too. There had to be a natural fissure pumping out the heat. Concerningly, he still couldn't see this object that she'd claimed to.

"Are you sure you saw it this way?" he asked.

While she could swim, she was loud and her movements were huge and wasteful. She wasn't graceless, but it was clear that she hadn't been taught to swim like he had been. She stopped. "I can almost make it out now. It's huge and almost certainly a ship. Can't you see it?"

He growled, glaring into the darkness and she pushed herself forward again. He watched her for a few moments, following the light on her arms, and stared ahead of her. Then he saw it, a shadow, darker than the others. Her eyes weren't just good; they must be amazing to have seen anything from back near the cave's entrance.

He swam forward, shaking his head. It was a ship, just about twenty feet wide with an even taller mast. It looked like the ass-end of a cog, which was the type of ship they were looking for.

"Well, we found a boat, even if it isn't the right boat," Kuzunoha said, swimming into his arms.

He would have kept her there all day if he could. The water was warm, like the water in Jisa on a cool day. "Let's see if we can find a way on board."

From his limited light, he could tell that there had been a dry dock set up here that the ship had crashed through when it arrived. Despite the crack, at this distance, the light provided no help and his own lights, though bright, were a bit harsh. The cave was silent other than the sounds of Kuzunoha's splashing. He smacked the water twice, just to break the oppressive quiet.

On the nearest side, he found a small part of the hull peeling away from the ship's ribs. It wasn't much, but it was enough to let him climb up. Even on the main deck, he couldn't tell how high the ceiling of the cavern was. It couldn't be too thin. The dried riverbed and mud flats were up there and they would need a solid base to be on.

The boat didn't rock or creak. It must have settled as deep as it could go. Perfectly natural, but it was unsettling. Leaning over the side, he helped Kuzunoha get the packs and herself to the top of the deck. She swayed at the top, her foot not wanting to grip the deck.

“Careful there, some of the boards are unstable.”

She rolled her eyes and shook him off. “I’ve never had trouble being on the water before—”

As she stepped past him, the floor creaked dangerously, and she yipped as her foot started breaking through the floor.

“Kuzunoha!” he yelled, turning around to grab her. She had half turned towards him and scrambled up his body, yanking herself practically into his arms.

He grunted and took a few steps back, banging against the side of the ship. He felt the dagger he kept tied to his upper arm fall out of its sheath. He tried to drop Kuzunoha in his movement to save the blade, but she was holding tight, her legs wrapped around his waist and her head on his shoulder.

He couldn’t see the blade, but he heard it bump to the deck and then a few moments heard it splosh into the water.

“Titopi take it, Kuzunoha, let go of me. You’re not in any danger.”

She pulled away from him, her cheeks burning. “Sorry. I thought I was going to go all the way through.”

He sighed. She was lucky she was so adorable.

Chapter 34

"It was right here," Hana said. She was crouching, her hand in one of the biggest footprints Isashi had ever seen. "Not too long ago, either. The mud hasn't had a chance to harden yet."

Isashi grunted her displeasure. Unlike Hana, she kept her gaze up. The creature was close and clearly a meat eater. The pile of its excrement they'd found gave it away. It had the fur and hair tuffs found in most predators shit, but as if that wasn't enough, this one also had stringy black hair and tiny bits of bird skulls in it.

It had been eating goblins. It had probably been eating their birds and other small things it could catch as well. The creature had to be stopped and killed.

Small creatures weren't too difficult to deal with. They tended to have numbers on their side more than anything else. Twenty small creatures could take you down, even if you were a good fighter. Superior armor and weapons helped and could turn the situation around. It was how people survived.

The big creatures were much more difficult. They tended to have supernaturally thick hides that turned all but the best blades. They also hit a lot harder. Their superior size led to an increase in strength as well, making them masters at taking down prey. They were more difficult to kill, but speed and using their size against them, as well as knowing their vulnerabilities, could turn the tide. The real issue was that littler monsters tended to follow them. Even seeing their friends get eaten didn't stop the creatures from sensing that their loyalty would be rewarded with safety and sustenance.

The only time they fought amongst themselves was when they were too similar in ability and power. This one wouldn't have anything in the area to fight against. They might need all five hunters working together to take on it on, depending on its strength. With superior numbers and perhaps even some of Hidan's guardsmen to help pepper it with arrows, they could kill it and send the goblins packing again.

First things first, though. They had to save Himiko's sister. Before she had been focused on getting the girl away from the man until she could put her fears to rest. But with this creature circling the area, Isashi knew they had to get the civilians back to safety as quickly as they could and then find the other hunters to help them take out the threat.

"Isashi," Hana said, "I think we need to discuss what we're doing out here."

Isashi bristled. "What do you mean by that?"

"I don't think we can keep going after Kuzunoha and her boy-toy."

"It's not under discussion. That's why we're out here, Hana."

"We came out here to track it."

"And save the civilians."

"You can tell it's close just as easily as I can, Isashi. Don't play dumb. You know what that means."

Isashi narrowed her eyes. "True, but it isn't heading towards town. Its circling something and sooner or later it will come across those two. We need to get them back to town and grab the other hunters."

Hana turned back to her glaring. "Stop the attitude. This is more serious than either of us thought it was. Your thoughts may be on that girl back home, but I need you here, not daydreaming. Not with the creature this close. I need your head in the game."

Isashi bit back her first response and reworded it. "I don't know what you're talking about. My thoughts are on getting Kuzunoha safe and sound back home, that is true. But my mind is not on Himiko or anyone back in town. This problem is way bigger than that."

"Then you agree we need to change our priorities. This monster needs to be destroyed."

"I don't disagree at all. I am disagreeing with your method. We can't kill it alone. Unless you can tell me you've learned about its weaknesses so that we can have a chance at killing it on our own."

"I know this monster is skilled and it's hunting in our territory. The fact that it left this here and part of a second"—Hana pointed at a second track, visible only because a small amount of water had sloshed into it as the creature made it—"means that we might be gaining on it. If we can get closer, we can start harrying it. It will start making more mistakes—"

"Having it make more mistakes won't help us. Not enough," Isashi told her. She couldn't believe that they were even having this discussion. "We need the other hunters. If its already gotten to the goblins…by the gods, Hana, those goblins killed nearly a hundred people five years ago when they snuck into the city. The five of us were hardly enough to defeat them. We can't take it and the goblins ourselves. Maybe with the other hunters, with some of the better bowmen in the city as backup. Maybe then. What we don't need is to back it into a corner before we're ready for it."

Hana snorted and stood, brushing her hands off on her pants. "I don't think it's got the goblins under it yet. Their home is over a day and a half to the south. It may have found a few goblins that have left the main tribe, maybe on a nest collecting mission. It hasn't found the rest though. If we go after it now, the little creatures won't get involved. If we wait a day or weeks like you're suggesting, it will have the entire goblin town under it and then yes, we will need additional archers. It will put everyone in danger, rather than just us."

"You're talking about leaving Himiko's sister out here, on her own, while we hunt something that we need the other hunters to take on. I can tell that this creature is stalking something and it clearly isn't us. What if it's them?"

Hana stood up. "The girl got herself out here. She can take herself back and send the other hunters out here. Besides, she had that guy with her, didn't she? She'll have protection. Not a hunter himself, but certainly he's travelled enough to know some of the tricks. She'll be fine. It's us that you should be worried about, not some townies."

"How do we know we can even trust this guy?" Isashi growled.

"How do we know we can't? I figure if he hasn't done anything yet, he isn't going to. Give the man a little leeway to at least make the mistake before you skewer him."

Isashi let out a harsh breath. She didn't want to bring up the note she found, though she couldn't say why. That was a lie. She knew exactly why. Hana would assume some slavers had gotten through or she would argue that the letter had no connection to him or that the slavers would have left after hearing about all the trouble caused. She'd thought of those arguments herself.

While true, it was the thought of how Himiko would look if Isashi had to be the bearer of bad news that made her desperate to rescue the girl. Kuzunoha was Himiko's only family member. Despite their differences, Himiko would never want something bad to happen to her. She'd been there for Himiko when she'd lost her father. She didn't want Himiko to have to go through that again. Ever. "Can we track it to its lair?"

Hana stood up and kicked at the print. "If we hurry, I think we can."

"Let's go and see what the situation is. Then we can decide what we need to do," Isashi suggested.

Hana nodded and started tracking the creature again.

Chapter 35

Richard gave the bottle one final, violent shake before handing it to Kuzunoha.

Kuzunoha was glad to be dressed again. Even with the warmth of the water in the cavern, she'd been starting to feel quite cold. She was glad that the waterproof bags had held, allowing them to bring an outfit each. She took hold of the bottle and her extraneous thoughts stopped.

The bottle was cheaply made, the glass opaque, lumpy and thick. She could tell by the uneven weight that the bottle had been blown in haste by an apprentice, too new to their craft to know any better. Worse, the unfortunate child hadn't even tried to hide the faults. Had it been from her family's glassworks, the offending thing wouldn't have made it to the child's master, let alone been marked. This bottle proudly bore half a stamp, probably as hard as they had been able to stamp it, in blue and red on the bottom.

She wasn't surprised that she didn't recognize the name. Her father would have never dealt with a craft master who'd cared so little for his apprentice's work.

Richard didn't seem to understand her hesitation. "It's caused by a chemical reaction by the borneo fungus. It causes light, but almost no heat. It's more than safe to hold."

"How much did you pay for this?" she asked.

"The fungus? It's common back in—"

"No, I mean the glass. This is terrible workmanship."

He blinked at her levelly and then rolled his eyes. "Look, Princess, just hold it over the side of the ship so I can read the name."

Kuzunoha growled at the idea of being called a princess but held the light over the side while Richard crawled over the decking.

"Well?"

"I can't read it," he admitted. "I think it's written in Pania."

Kuzunoha pursed her lips. That was a good sign, though she would have expected the name to be in Cantouk, since most ships that ran through this area named their ships that way. "Let me take a look."

Richard crawled back onto the deck and took the bottle from her. Kuzunoha took a deep breath and climbed onto the hull. The wood was rotting, but not enough to do more than crumble at the edges. She dug her nails in. It would hurt if she fell, but she did feel steadier traversing the outside.

The name was mostly legible, though the paint was chipped and thoroughly cracked. "*Li Sant...* no, *Senta... Talrit..* no, *Talriet. Li Senta Talriet...*" She started climbing back onto the ship. Richard grabbed her hand and helped her. "It means *Sight to Sea*, I think. Translating is much easier when I have paper to work from."

Richard took a second look at her. "I don't remember you saying you spoke Pania?"

Kuzunoha smiled. "My father believed we should be able to speak to all our business associates and read their contracts. So in addition to those, I can read some Pania, though I can't speak it at all. My first language is Siangu."

"Siangu? Not Cantouk?"

Richard's surprise was understandable. It was the language they spoke to each other, the most common language in the area. "Siangu was the only language spoken in the house until we were five. We were only allowed to use Cantouk outside of it. What was your first language? I doubt Cantouk is the usual language spoken in Jisa."

He moved his lips over a language she'd never heard before, though it had a musical tonal quality. She raised an eyebrow, but he waved away her question.

"Dorrani is the main language in Jisa, actually. I learned Cantouk from a friend. Since it and Pania share a base alphabet, I can sometimes decipher it as well." He looked rueful. "Though not here, obviously."

"I never thought about trying to use languages that way," she said, considering. She noticed Richard shivering. "What was that other language?"

"It's not important. Those are the only words I know in it." He bowled past his words as if he were embarrassed. "*Sight to Sea* is the ship we were looking for. Congratulations, Kuzunoha. If any of the original shipment remains, you and I will have made a lot of money."

"So, how do we go about exploring this thing? Together or apart?" She trusted him, but she didn't want to be walking around on her own.

"You have amazing vision, but don't know much about ships or reading the danger spots. I think it would safer if we were to go together."

"I only slipped..." She nearly bit her tongue. It was embarrassing. She didn't want special treatment. Richard's face darkened.

"I hadn't made that decision because of your fall, Kuzunoha. After so many years, this place is a death trap of rotten wood and rigging. I would prefer to have someone watching my back while we go through it as well."

"At least, I kept my dagger," she grumbled.

He bristled. "Yes, and should we find mine while we explore the lower decks, I want it back. It was a good dagger, made of Karnesian metal. They have some of the best iron and silver mines on the continent, you know."

"The Karnesian forest is on the other side of the Great Bowl," Kuzunoha said, staring at him.

The Great Bowl was a lake set in the center of a huge ring of mountains. According to the myths, the area had been a plain until the first monsters ripped and tore their way out of the earth. Kuzunoha had seen the maps. Now the bowl was nothing but water surrounded by huge mountains and rolling hillsides. Kuzunoha had always held a natural wariness about the place, mostly because Himiko's mother had always told her that the Great Bowl was where bastards were sent if they didn't know their place. She knew better than to reiterate that to Richard. He'd probably laugh himself silly.

"You can't be suggesting that you traveled here through there," she said.

"Not through it. The forest is near Kentar. They have a harbor there that almost rivals Jisa's. It was how I reached the mainland." He looked up. "Hey, can you see the ceiling from here?"

She glanced up. "Of course. There are stones that almost look like teeth. Sharp pointy teeth."

"Stag stones? Can you tell how large they are? How high?"

"The closest ones look pretty big. Bigger than me, not as tall as you? I'd say they're a good forty feet up, though. Is that a bad thing? You look...concerned."

He shook his head. "Stags form when water runs down from the ceiling of a cavern. Normally I'd attribute it to this—" he gestured to the water around them—"but I'm worried it may be due to the river."

"The river that's been gone for years? Richard, even if it had been caused by that, it wouldn't be a problem now."

"Still... I'd feel better if I could get up there and look for cracks. Can you tell if the mast is close enough to the roof for me to take a look?"

"It is. It looks like it may have carved a path through them, actually."

"We definitely want to check it, then. I'll climb it and make sure that's safe."

The mast was covered in some sort of fuzzy black growth. It smelled sour, like old socks without the sweat scent. Richard put on some gloves and tapped the mold. Where he touched, the growth stuck to his glove. What he didn't, pulled back into the rest of the mass of fur-like mold. He swore.

"Black mold. It can be deadly. I won't be climbing that unless there's no other choice." He pulled off his gloves in disgust and wrapped them in a small bag that he sealed and tugged on a replacement pair.

Kuzunoha turned back to the mast. "That bad?"

He sighed. "If you were to just touch it, no. However, if it gets in you, it can be very dangerous. It doesn't send out spores, though. So at least we won't have that to worry about. We'd better put cloth over our mouths and throw on the thick gloves, though, just in case."

A search of the top deck revealed only one room. The door was caked with slime, not mold, and they were able to wedge it open without too much trouble. The room inside would have been opulent before the shipwreck. The curtains, though half-rotted, were a dark green velvet and the walls were covered with flecked gold leaf molding and rotting cream-colored paint. There was a dresser with greenish handles, perhaps from patina. Strewn around a table and chair in the center of the room were clothes and bones. A destroyed painting, that may have been of mermaids or just a watery scene, covered one large area on the western wall across from the door.

Richard moved away from her side, but Kuzunoha's gaze was locked on the bones. In the books, skeletons remained preserved long after the flesh had rotted away. This one had fallen apart, leaving a terrifyingly gruesome mess of once-living caltrops in the center of the floor. The skull had rolled on the table, complete with an unkempt Sian Ku-style bun. She moved closer, horrified to see that all the bones had been scratched, as if by hundreds of tiny teeth.

"Have you never seen a dead body before, Kuzunoha?" Richard asked.

"Of course, I have… even from our first meeting."

He shook his head. "I mean the long dead. Something like this."

He'd moved to the other side of the room and was inspecting the dresser now.

She looked away, swallowing hard. "No. This is my first time for one dead… long enough for the flesh to have…" she frowned, "Richard, there are marks on these bones. Maybe some sort of insect horde?"

Richard glanced at her rather than the bones while he tried to pry open one of the drawers. "On the water?"

"They are underground now."

She had the feeling he was rolling his eyes internally as he turned back to the drawer. "It could be crabs and the like. They would have been drawn to the smell of death."

Kuzunoha took a deep breath and tried to shrug away her concerns and look for what they'd come for. The captain's hat had fallen to the floor but had weathered the trip better than the curtains, even if it was still a disaster. She turned the cap up and looked on the inside. Most captains sewed their journey records into their caps. She could see some of the fine stitching but didn't even try to read it. Most captains used a code and this one had rotten skin and hair to be removed before they even tried.

The man had a blade in a half-destroyed scabbard amongst the bones. She took a deep breath and reached down for it. The handle was moist, but the blade seemed to have weathered its time well, aside from a bit of rust. She packed it away in her bag, tying it in tightly hoping that the crossguard would keep the weapon in her bag. She made a mental note to ask Richard if it could be saved later.

A quick search of the rest of the room provided very little. She found an ivory-handled brush with a matching grooming kit near in a cupboard below the polished metal the man would have used as a mirror. In the drawers, Richard found a rotten bag of coins and two small music boxes. Both were rusted but Richard thought he might be able to clear them out enough to make them work. They put all the items into one of the bags to take with them.

"Are we continuing on?" She asked.

Richard shook his head. "It's nearly midday, Kuzunoha. We'll eat lunch first and then check the lower level."

Chapter 36

"Are you sure you don't need any help, Kuzu?"

"Kuzunoha." She didn't stop trying to open the door.

There had only been one other door on the main deck and the damned thing had taken on water, enough to warp it shut. Kuzunoha seemed determined to open this one herself. She'd been working on it for nearly five minutes now.

She gave a yell and the door popped open. As he'd expected, she wasn't ready for it and fell back into his arms. He loved the feel of her body. She was soft everywhere he liked his partners to be, while still having enough muscle to be a challenge.

"Oof. Thank you," she said.

His fingers squeezed her and she flashed him an exasperated look. He shrugged, chagrinned, and helped her to stand. Before they left, he was going to find time to push her against the hull and have his way with her. He would have done it already, but she'd been distracted since they'd found the ship.

Kuzunoha didn't let him pull completely away. She caught his hand and put it on her belly while she looked into the stairway. It was black as pitch down there and Richard stepped beside her, shaking his bottle of light again. It would only last a couple more hours, less if he kept shaking it to keep it bright. Considering the expense, he wanted to get as much use out of the thing as possible.

The stairs were steep, even for the ships he'd been on before. They were about three feet long and four feet wide and only went down six feet. It also smelled of old fish and stale water. Nothing dangerous, if unpleasant. He handed her the bottle and started down the stairs. They were moist and bowed under his weight. He bounced on the last one, just to be sure it would hold him. The floor sagged but held.

"We'll have to be careful. No sudden moves or jumping around if we can help it."

The roof didn't open below the hull and was only an inch or so above his head. The boat he'd fled Jisa on had been much larger. He tried to take a deep breath and felt his chest constrict. He shivered and shook his light again. He wouldn't let a shadow and tiny space set him off.

"It smells...salty. I thought it would be mustier," Kuzunoha said. The roof was over a hand span above her head and she looked completely at ease. For just a moment, he envied Kuzunoha's diminutive stature. She didn't seem to notice him as she slipped around him, never looking at one area for longer than a moment. "A Kostas design. This will be easy."

Richard hadn't expected Kuzunoha to know anything about ships. Personally, he had never seen a layout like this, but she was right, it would be easy to navigate. There were eight rooms, three to each side, one door leading to the bow and another to the stern. He was pretty sure the one behind them had been a galley if the rusted pot sitting just inside the circle of light meant anything.

"You've seen this type of ship before?"

"Of course. It's a junk, like you said it would be. Why?"

He seemed a little confused. "I said it would be a caravel."

She shrugged. "It's the same thing, essentially. There are a few differences, but they're the same size, just made in different parts of the world. These are the types they make in Sian Ku. My father thought we should at least know our way around one. They have higher ceilings usually but only the one level below deck. Each room is designed to be watertight; if one gets a hole blown through it, they can still sail with ease. It makes them near unsinkable."

"Watertight? How do they stay in these rooms when they're traveling?"

She shrugged. "They don't. Kostas usually take on cargo rather than passengers. The crew would stay on deck, even in storms."

Richard thought about that. "Watertight should mean that there will be less water damage overall."

"It is one of the good things about the design."

"Which should we open first?"

She looked around. All the doors looked the same: simple unpainted wood. They would have been smooth, but the years had left them looking pitted and raw. One of them, the door at the bow, had been left partially open.

"How about the one at the end of the hallway?" she suggested, pointing at the open one. "We can work our way back around."

Richard shrugged. "It's as good a place as any other."

The door opened easily, revealing a floor swarming with small blackish-blue crabs. The creatures' eyes glittered, shiny and alien, but they fled the light, running down a hole in the floor as quickly as they could. The only other thing in the room was two skeletons and a pile of ratty clothes that had probably belonged to the men once but were now being used as nesting material. Kuzunoha drew a breath at the sight of the crabs fleeing en masse, but didn't say anything as she stepped in the room gingerly behind him.

Richard wondered if she would go to the bodies again, even though it was clear they had nothing of value on them.

He walked over to the hole the creatures had gone through. It was only about just big enough for a ground adult to step through and led to a pit filled with water. He grinned. A hidden compartment. That would be where the expensive contraband items were. With his light, he could just make out some boxes, bloated and covered with barnacles and other deposits. He pulled up the closest one, a two-and-a-half-foot crate, while the crabs made the seabed below appear to move as they scuttled out of its way.

"There's nothing of value over here. Anything down there?" Kuzunoha said. She'd been looking through the clothes. The bodies hadn't been moved, but he knew that Kuzunoha was still unnerved having them so close.

He gestured to the crate. "I found something. I think it might be contraband items."

It only took a few minutes to open. Inside, there were pale red, blue, and green packages. They had probably been vividly colored, before sixty-some years of soaking had removed all but the most stubborn of the color. Kuzunoha helped him drain the water without disturbing the other sacks inside and then Richard pulled one out gingerly. The sack had no cohesion and almost fell apart in his hands.

"Put down one of the bags, Kuzunoha. This is going to fall apart quickly. I think it's some sort of paper, not cloth at all."

She put a small bag down and Richard dumped the disintegrating bag into it. It was filled with blackish-grey sand, tightly packed. The mixture was gritty and odorous.

"Oh, fireworks. I wonder if they still work," Kuzunoha said brightly.

Richard wondered just what in the Consort's name a firework was. He hazarded a guess. "The sand burns then? Are they worth much?"

If they weren't, he'd leave them in an instant. The grit stuck to his hands where he'd touched the sand and even soaked, it stank of sulfur and some other harsh chemicals. He would have attributed the caves stink to the strange powder, but with the water's warmth, he was certain that even if they hadn't seen it yet, there had to be a vein of hot springs water pouring in from somewhere.

She shrugged. "There are some in Hidan who would pay for them, but only the wealthiest. They're quite rare. My father would have to order them in for the Shuntanbun in Digomem."

He didn't even bother to ask what a Shuntanbun was. Most likely it was some sort of festival for the dead. Most cultures had one and Digomem, the month of fading fire, was known to be when ghosts and creatures of the dead returned to cause mischief. "So, they may be worth quite a bit...if they still work. Is there a way to test it?"

Kuzunoha gave another shrug. "I'm not an expert. We can dry some out and see if it still burns."

The idea of lighting something on fire to see if it still worked when he had no idea what it did in the first place seemed like a bad idea. A favourite phrase of an old friend came back to him. *Just enough knowledge to be dangerous.*

"We'll take this box with us to test then. If it…burns, we can come back for the rest."

She nodded and together they carried the box up to their packs.

Chapter 37

"Ship supplies in this one, too, mostly rotted. Did you find anything in yours, Kuzunoha?"

Putting her back into it, she pushed down on the crowbar. Her hands hurt, even through the soft gloves Richard had given her to wear.

"It's all well and good to think about finding treasure in a warm tavern with some mulled wine and another thought entirely to be without the wine and actually have a crowbar in my hands," she growled.

They were in the second room and had been for nearly an hour. They'd found nothing of value but old ship supplies. Somehow, she didn't think eight hammers and a crate of nails, rusted or not, was the treasure Richard had been hoping to find.

"Kuzunoha?" he asked again.

She heard a satisfying creak as the nails squeaked out of the crate.

"Good job. All the nails were still good in that one, too. We might be able to pry them loose and mix them in with the crate. That should cut a few more coppers out for us."

She looked at Richard to see if he was laughing at her. He didn't seem to be, so she let it go in favor of seeing what was in the box.

"It looks like...metal hooks? No, wait…rigging?"

She picked one up. It was heavy and solid. She rubbed a finger on it. The rust crumbled at her touch, marking her hand with red-brown dust. She set it back in the box.

Richard knocked on one with a tiny hammer and then rubbed it with a cloth. "Shackles," he corrected her. "We might be able to get something for them. They were quality at one point. Heavy, though. We'll put them on the maybe list."

"We could try selling the location to Jack. If we could knock out that mud crab front, we might be able to get one of his ships in and get everything out." Richard grunted as if he didn't like her solution. "Do we want to try the next room?"

He nodded and leaned in to kiss her again. All the men she'd had since Deckard had treated her lips as if they were nothing but a gateway to getting the rest of her clothes off. Richard liked seeing her without them too, but he always took the time to make her breathless first.

"We could bring a horse and cart up here when we come back," he suggested as he let her go.

The next door was the same as the rest, though, on closer inspection, it didn't seem to have warped as badly. The air that rushed out when Richard pushed it open was dusty and thick. She coughed. The air tasted stale. Kuzunoha pulled out the cloth fan they'd made and waved it around, holding her breath against the tickle in her throat.

Richard's eyes were watering as he yanked out his water bottle. "Holy hells, that air is dry."

He splashed some water on his face before handing it to Kuzunoha. She drank until the tickle subsided. They looked in the room, holding the lantern high.

Unlike the other three, this one had taken no water damage. There was a single bed with a dead body on it, a chest, and tucked into the furthest corner from the door, a chair, and a broken portable desk. There was also a small oil lamp hanging from the ceiling. Richard removed the old lamp and hung his.

Kuzunoha smiled at him and went, as she always did, to the bodies first. In her mind, she repeated her family's prayer for the dead as she had for every other body they'd found today. A man that was not honored when he died returned to stalk the living. She would have said it out loud, but Richard would have laughed at her.

The man's clothes were like her own, a Sian Ku men's design, a black-blue robe over pleated black pants. The clothes were bug eaten and worn, but the man's bones didn't have any tooth or claw marks on them that she could see.

Richard had gone to the chest at the end of the bed. He looked at it like it was a particularly interesting puzzle. He crooned softly to it while he rubbed at the greasy dust on top. Kuzunoha kept herself from snorting amusement.

“I wonder who he was...” she mused, touching the man’s sleeve as gingerly as she could.

A patch of the sleeve, the size of her outstretched palm, puffed to dust at the touch. The skeleton’s hand showed no rings or jewelry. She was about to turn away when she noticed something hidden beneath his fingers—a slim blade wrapped in the Sian Ku style.

The sword was heavy and was wrapped in black and red cloth that flaked away where she touched it. She could tell by its size that it was a short sword, most likely a wakizashi. They were carried by a noble’s most trusted retainers. Tied to the hilt wrappings was a signet ring, covered with a blue-black patina. She tugged at the reddish string, expecting it to puff to dust like the sleeve had, but it held fast. The symbol on it looked like a knot of some sort, but she’d have to clean it to be sure.

She quelled an almost insurmountable urge to unsheathe it. Richard would want to see it as well and the material was already falling to shambles. She bit her lip. Praying over the bodies just made good sense. She wanted to take his sword, though, and this felt like theft more than anything else here had. She let out a breath and straightened her back. Then she clapped her hands together and bowed over the body, reciting the goddess Ameterri’s words in Siangu. It wouldn’t feel right to take it without asking first.

“By the death above, as all below, all will return to the path, following her golden coils. They will search unending until she takes them in her claws to be judged, following the precepts set down by the book of

Just Sight. Those worthy will serve, in death, as they did in life. Those who did not will suffer her disappointment and return to the well of all."

She touched the dead man's head and whispered to him. "I know you are serving her now. If you wish me to leave the blade, send a sign. But with your permission, I would see it brought to beauty again."

If the man's soul disapproved, she saw no sign. Tentatively, she picked up the blade, surprised by how light it felt in her hands. Richard coughed quietly.

"If you're done, do you mind checking if he has a key on him? That chest is beautiful and I can break into it, but I may have to destroy the lock. I'd rather not if I don't have to."

She nodded and lifted the dead man's other sleeve. Sifting through the cloth dust, she found a tiny key ring with a few old blacked keys in it. She handed them to Richard. He took them and gestured at the sword. "Nice find. Is the ring silver?"

"I think so," she said, touching it gently. The ring swung around, catching the light in the room. "The knot is still rather tight and hasn't fallen apart at all."

When he gestured for her to unsheathe the blade, she held her breath and did so. It felt right in her hands, a beautiful weight. As if it had been meant for someone her size.

"Nice. That will get us a good price. It's held up extremely well." He glanced at the swinging object. "A signet. Have you ever seen the symbol before?"

She shook her head. "It looks like a knot, but I can't tell more than that yet. We'll have to clean it. I should be able to check my family's library at home when we return to Hidan as well." If her sister let her. She felt the pain as a physical thing in her chest. Himiko would understand, and if she wouldn't… well, then Kuzunoha could figure out what she could do then.

"Wonderful. Would you carry it for now?"

She smiled, holding it as if she were going to use it as a weapon. Richard laughed, and she flushed, sheathing and tucking the blade into her belt. More of the cloth flaked off, but the hilt itself held. It must have been made of good leather underneath the cloth. "It wasn't that funny."

"I'm sorry. It's just that you were holding it like you would a dagger. It's closer to a short sword's length."

He turned the key in the lock. The chest was beautiful: dark lacquered wood and matching metals under the smeared dust. The large key fit and clicked satisfyingly open with just a bit of pressure. Kuzunoha saw books, papers, ink, and quills. Richard took out the top book and opened it. The paper was fragile but it had held up better than the man's clothes had. He gestured her closer.

"I don't recognize the language. Do you?"

The script was in a messy hand and the ink was faded in places, but she did. "Its Siangu...though an old version of it. *Koin* hasn't meant *illustrious* in ages."

"Oh, what does it mean now?" Richard said while he pulled out the rest of the books and items.

She paused, trying to translate it. Normally she would have said *pretentious*, but with that specific character, it also could have meant *leader of the way*, which changed slightly as well depending on the context. She shook her head. Simpler was better. "Something closer to pretentious. What are you looking for?"

Richard had put the book down and was tapping the bottom of the chest. "There's over an inch missing here. I think there's a false bottom."

She closed the book and set it down on top of the others. Richard made a pleased sound and lifted out a thin wooden slat and a black lacquered box. There was no dust on it and carved dragons coiled on the lid. She blinked. Those looked familiar. She ran her fingers over the design in the ring. Perhaps they were the same.

Richard flipped through the key ring again. He settled on a tiny scratched key and put it into the lock. It turned, but not all the way. He frowned and chose a slightly larger one. This one clicked through.

The lamp's light flickered off four thin ropes strung with gleaming coins. Richard pulled one of the strings out. Nearly half a foot long, there were dozens of coins strung on it. The coins had a hole through the center and had been strung on a red cord with huge knots at either end to keep the coins tied on. Richard held it as if worried that the thick cord wouldn't hold the weight. He put the bottom down and tugged at it. As the knot became unbound, he pulled off a coin and handed it to her.

"Can you read this as well?"

His tone was hard but she couldn't begrudge him the reaction. These were Sian Compa, Sian Ku's most valuable coin. She hadn't been keeping up with their worth since her father had died, but they had been worth a pretty penny. Lower than the gold Sempa coins, but not by much, and a gold-copper mix that made them difficult to counterfeit. It was also one reason that they were valued lower than the bright garish gold colour they preferred here. For Kuzunoha, their gorgeous shade had made them her favourite type of coin to handle.

"They're the most valuable coins of the Sian Ku Empire, Compas. These symbols around the innermost circle"—she pointed them out—"are connected to the four celestial animals that guard the Sian people. On the other side are the four names of heaven. This symbol around the edge is always the current ruler's name, with this symbol being their predecessor's name and the left side their ruling grandparent's. The bottom name is always the same, Ameterri, the goddess that first ordained the Emperor's family with the right to rule."

"You know a lot about them," Richard said, taking the coin from her.

She sat up straighter. "One thing my father made sure I could do was recognize all the common, and some uncommon, currencies. How else would I be able to tell their value?"

"That's useful. What about general appraisal?" he asked, putting the coin back onto the cord and retying it. The knot he used was different, but would suffice, though tighter than she would have made it.

"Cloth mostly...some glass, but it's too valuable to be judged in the same way."

"You could tell me what type of glass was used to make a window, but not how much a statuette would be worth?" he clarified.

She nodded.

"Good to know. So, how much are these worth?"

Strings had usually one hundred coins each on them and they were worth about three-quarters of a gold Sempa each. She worked it out. "I don't know the exact rates, but they should be worth six to seven hundred gold sentine."

He blinked and she got the feeling he was glad he was sitting down. She wished she was too. "Gold?"

Most people lived their day to day lives in coppers and even she tended to live her life only in silver. Gold was something that royals lived on. It hit her that with her percentage, at least one of those strings would be hers. She suddenly wished she were sitting beside him.

Her hand closed on the hilt at her waist. She could claim it. The money left over from her share would pay for her to live quite well and away from her family's household. Long enough to have a home built?

Richard closed the money chest, patted the case, and arranged the books and papers on top again. She was surprised to see that his hand shaking as he closed the lid again. “Let’s take this up and see what else we can find.”

“Sounds good.” She took a calming breath. “How long until sundown?”

He touched her jaw suggestively and his eyes had a wild lust to them. “Another few hours. But we can always stay the night if we need to.”

Her breath caught and she followed him upstairs.

Chapter 38

The final door was stuck solid but Kuzunoha was relieved that water hadn't come pouring out when Richard wedged the crowbar between the door and the frame. That had happened with the room before this one. Richard cracked his neck and grinned.

"We'll go back to it after. The ship most likely ran aground and that was the room that took the most damage. I don't want us to fill the ship with water until we've done all we can first."

"And have what we were able to find off the ship?"

"That too. If it's going to sink, I want everything of value off it first."

They'd only found six vials of dye in the other rooms, it had hardly been enough worth exploring. All the dolls, clothing...all the actual treasure had been destroyed by water and mold. There may be some in with the contraband items since they hadn't cleaned all of it out yet, but neither of them were confident that the treasure would have survived sitting in water all this time.

She touched the hilt of the sword again. "So, ah, Richard..." Kuzunoha said. "I... the sword... do you mind if I keep it?"

He glanced down at it. “I thought you might. You haven’t been willing to let go of it.”

“It was that obvious?” She took hold of her side of the door and he grabbed hold of his.

“I don’t mind. I prefer daggers to swords. We can discuss what we both would feel is a fair price for it and—”

The door cracked open and a wave rushed out. Kuzunoha grabbed for the stairway and narrowly missed being knocked over. Within moments, the water slid to a trickle, leaving a thin layer of water covering the floor. Richard growled and smacked at his pants. He’d grabbed the doorway to avoid being knocked over, but his pants all the way up to his waist were soaked.

Kuzunoha’s clothes were also soaked through. It was a small blessing that the water was warm.

Richard grumbled but gestured her to come near with the light. “At least the light didn’t go out.”

He gagged and a second later, the thick scent of fishy rot assailed her nose. A hole big enough for a horse to walk through had ripped through the hull on the far side. Things floated in the water. The scent made every hair on her arms stand straight up.

“Go back upstairs, Kuzunoha,” Richard whispered.

She hadn’t even had time to move when he stepped backward, bumping into her.

"Richard, what's wrong? Why...?"

Richard leapt around her, dragging her towards the stairs. Her right leg burned with pain and she shrieked, catching sight of blue-green pincher claw, crab-like other than its immense size. She stared, dumbfounded, while the creature moved towards the door.

The thick-shelled creature was taller than she was and appeared to hover, its four legs almost invisible in the gloom. It had two large pinchers and near its mouth, dozens of smaller legs flapped. They were like fingerless hands, grabbing things in the water. Its mouth was tiny, filled with sharp teeth and purple flesh. She quivered, her stomach trying to empty itself. Its eyes were tiny and black, squinting at her from deep underneath its shell.

It couldn't fit through the doorway but that didn't stop the creature from striking out at her again. Richard pulled her away as the claw connected with the stairs instead of her and nearly disintegrated the wood under its force.

"Move that ass. Upstairs now!" Richard shouted.

She nearly tripped, he was pushing her so forcefully. As soon as they were upstairs he slammed the door shut. Her ankle was burning and red with blood, dripping from a thin cut longer than her hand. She shivered and put some pressure on the wound, winding a length of cloth around it. The cloth sagged when she was done but it would hold for now.

"What can I do?"

"It's not coming up through the door. Stay quiet, move towards the center of the boat," he whispered.

Kuzunoha moved but heard a discordant hum and scraping coming from over the side. One of her tutors had dragged his nails across a chalkboard once. This was worse. She put her hands over her ears and bent over, trying to block out the noise.

"Kuzunoha, what are you doing?"

"That noise...it hurts," she said, shaking her head.

"What noise...?"

Richard suddenly went stiff and pointed with one of his daggers. A claw had silently reached over the boat. It hung in the air like the incessant hum before the guardrail cracked as the creature yanked itself onto the deck.

She didn't remember pulling out her dagger, but it was in her hand.

"Hit anything fleshy that you can," Richard snarled, darting into the fray.

Kuzunoha's blade scored the creature's shell once and clattered against its thick armor covering the long legs. It seemed to ignore Richard, reaching out pinchers the length of her arms to snip her in half.

The creature reared, the undulating hum turning to a shriek. Richard yanked his knife from the creature's flesh between two plates on its underbelly.

It turned, hissing threats at Richard and she tried to catch one of its deep-set eyes. Her blade skittered off the shell and dug into one of the little scuttling arms near its jaws. It tore off when she ripped her blade out and sprayed her with a thick blue-grey mucus. It stank like rotten fish and iron.

Bile rose in her throat and the creature lowered itself, hiding its soft underbelly from them. It aimed a claw at Kuzunoha again and the undulating hum lowered to a hiss. She leapt back, but the creature caught her shirt. It sliced open and Kuzunoha fell just out of its reach, her blade skittering across the rotten deck of the ship. The creature scuttled to her, forcing her to clamber after her weapon until she could grab it again with numb fingers.

It had the reach to be dangerous here. She didn't.

It clubbed her instead of spearing her. The force spun her around and blinked dumbly as she saw her blade fall over the side of the ship. She hadn't even felt it come out of her hand.

She swore under her breath and scampered back, catching the next claw that came for her. If she wanted to survive, she'd have to be faster and stronger than it was.

Richard landed on its shell, throwing off one of the creature's attacks. His daggers came down on it and she heard a thick crunch. Then Richard rolled away and the creature hissed, rearing in pain.

She needed another weapon. She hesitated to draw the wakizashi. Think. She was no hunter. She didn't know where its weak spots were. Obviously, its underbelly had less armor, but it would be luck, not skill to get in a killing shot with it hiding so low to the ground. There had to be something she could do that wasn't just taking her weapon to it.

Richard's voice rang out. "Move."

She jumped away from his voice as flames spread across the deck. She looked for the source and saw Richard's lamp shattered across the wooden floor. The broken glass sparkled like red diamonds in the firelight. The creature roared, nearly deafening her again. Unfortunately, the flame wasn't killing it, just slowing down.

"We can make it to the water," Richard yelled at her. "Come on."

"Fight it in the water? Are you mad?" she yelled back.

"Got a better plan?"

She looked up again. "Yes. Get it over to the main mast after I'm up."

The mast was tall enough that she thought she could see where it scraped the roof. She hoped that the small metal bars sunk into the wood weren't too damaged. Climbing had never been her forte. She grabbed the pillar and tried to pull herself up, hoping the creature wasn't too close to her yet. The gloves slid, unable to give her the traction she needed.

Swearing, she threw them to the deck and grabbed the mast again, her spine tingling in disgust at the feeling of moist fungus under her hands. It felt like wet fur that melted under the pressure from her hand. She nearly let go but reminded herself that the mold couldn't kill her just from touching it. She would worry about how it could kill her when she wasn't fighting something that could.

She grabbed the first metal bar and pulled herself up, grabbing for the next as soon as she was high enough. She missed it and had to steady herself before she could reach again. All she could think was that she had to climb faster, be faster. It was so dark. How long could the fire below burn?

Her heart skipped a beat when her foot slipped before her hand had caught the next rung. She hissed as her leg caught on the metal bar, ripping down its length. She grabbed the metal bar under her hand. Her shoulder ripped and she knew she'd pay for the fall later, but for now, her hand held.

She looked down, her heart beating so fast and hard that it might burst from her chest. She was nearly thirty feet up. She took a deep breath, wincing at the pain in her shoulder. Her hands screamed with the abuse she was putting them through and her leg itched as it had never itched before. She shivered, imagining the fungus moving towards her leg, creeping towards the bloody gash.

Kuzunoha bit her lip and took a deep breath, setting herself to climbing again. Richard was depending on her. She'd just reached the top when the last of the light from the deck flickered out. The next few moments as her eyes adjusted were brutal. Nothing but that undulating hum, getting higher and higher in pitch.

Just as she started to make out the stalactite directly in front of her, Richard swore. "Kuzunoha, I'm blind. What are you doing?"

"Climb the pole. I can see enough to do what I need to."

Richard swore again and she heard him start to climb. She needed to hurry. It took too long to find the crab in the dark and she couldn't see the deck, she was so high up. Twisting so that she was on the same side as the creature, she reached out for the nearest stalactite. Her fingers didn't do enough and she took out the sword, not caring if she destroyed it. She had to save Richard.

The sword bit into the rock, better than she thought it would have. The stone above was weak, more like hard earth. She sliced and stabbed, determined to make it fall, ignoring the feel of dirt falling into her hair. She heard Richard yell and looked down. Even she could hardly see him in the gloom, but he kicked and climbed higher. He had to be ten feet or more off the ground and it could still reach him.

She slammed the stone once more. It sunk it, tearing out chunks as she thrust, but as soon as she pulled it back, she could feel the hilt of the weapon disintegrating under her hand. She thought it was only staying attached because of the material wrapped around it. Swearing, she sheathed the weapon and attempted to kick the stone the rest of the way off. The mast shuddered under her and she almost slipped again. Her heart pounded, but she felt the stone move. She braced herself on the mast and kicked with both legs. The stone snapped and fell, strangely silent, until a moist cracking sound reverberated through her skull.

The creature below shrieked and the mast shuddered again. Her heart hit her stomach and she heard the stone above her shriek, matching the creature below. The mast began toppling and she saw the deck come up to meet her. She wound her arms and legs tightly around it. When the mast hit, it threw her loose like an angry storm would a sailor She bounced off the floor and back into the mast. The floor cracked under her when she landed on it again, dropping her into the water. She coughed fluid and suddenly there was light and sound all around her. She screamed as the world went frighteningly dark.

"Richard!"

Chapter 39

"What in the hell was that?"

Hana's eyes were wide with a terror that mirrored Isashi's. She took a deeper breath to answer and the stitch in her side lanced her chest.

The ground had started shaking under their feet. Land shakes weren't uncommon, but then the ground forty or so feet away had started falling away. Whatever was pulling the ground down was coming towards them. They didn't stop running until Isashi nearly doubled over from the pain.

Behind them, the ground had finally stopped falling. Or that was what Isashi assumed, as the clouds of pale grey dust floating into the air looked less like mini explosions of dirt. A faint breeze brought a faint scent of rotting fish to her nose.

Hana's breath was still coming loud and strained. Isashi opened her water bottle and drank some, almost coughing as she wheezed it down. The water helped her throat, but was a bad idea for her stomach, which apparently thought the ground was still tossing them around. She took a deep breath. It would take time to recover, and she wasn't moving yet. She lifted the skin tiredly towards Hana. The other hunter nodded gratefully and lifted it to her lips. She stopped, swearing.

"Screw it all to hell…the tracks were in that mess. How the hell are we supposed to track it now?"

Isashi took another deep breath. This time, she didn't feel like her lungs or side were going to explode. "The monster isn't going to be our concern. If it has any intelligence, it will get the hell out of here for the next few days."

Hana snorted. "Yeah, but every one of the little ones will start running over here to find out what happened."

It was true. The little monsters tended towards stupidity. Running towards something that made the ground cave in wasn't intelligent. Isashi's lips strained to a flat line. If it was stupid for the monsters, what did that say about her? "We need to go back there."

"Go where?" Hana said. "The entire area is gone."

"What if Kuzunoha is there? We can't take it for granted that she wasn't."

Hana stared at her, looked back at the camp and swore again. "Isashi, I can understand your need to look for…survivors, but…"

"Something caused the ground to fall, Hana."

"And you think it's that slip of a girl? Next you'll be telling me she's also a mage."

The thought of Kuzunoha as a mage, one of the few people able to command the spirits, was a ludicrous idea. They were rare and were astounding people to begin with. They tended to be the sort of people that got stories told about them, even before they became one.

"We need to at least see if they were nearby. If they're out here alone without any of their supplies—"

Hana sighed. "What are the odds of that? If they were that close to it, we would have seen them."

"What if they got caught in it?"

Hana looked at her seriously. "If they were, then they're probably dead."

Isashi's jaw locked. She wouldn't believe that. Couldn't believe that. At least not yet. When she had some proof, or saw firsthand the damage…maybe. She wouldn't allow herself to let Himiko down, Her friend was counting on her to make everything right. She shook her head, trying to relax. "Not yet. If they were caught in it, then we might be able to help. If we can't help, then the least we can do is to assess the damage."

Hana sighed. "That is something we can do. We won't make it back before dark, though."

"But if they're hurt—"

"Then they'll either survive until morning or they won't," Hana bit out. She looked away. "I want them to be alive too, but there is no way to get there and look around before night falls. And if other monsters came up from it that hole…"

Even Isashi had to admit that fighting creatures in their native dark environment would be a death wish. And Hana was right. They wouldn't be able to search, certainly not safely. It wasn't as though walking around calling for her would work.

"I agree, heading back in the dark won't be useful, but it isn't as though this hole leads to the world of the dead, Hana. There will only be regular creatures for us to deal with."

"The dead light the way for others," Hana whispered, touching at a small wooden pendant at her neck. She sighed. "First things first. We'll need some dry tinder for a fire and fresh water. Do you want to set up the camp or find water?"

"Water and tinder. It isn't a good season for leaves, but I should be able to find some bark that's dried."

Hana nodded and turned, already opening her bag to unpack their tent. Isashi turned, hiding a frown. If Kuzunoha hadn't been tricked out here by the Richard fellow, Isashi wouldn't need to be out here worrying about them. She wouldn't be worried about how Himiko would react if her sister had been too close to the sinkhole and hadn't made it.

Sinkhole was entirely insufficient to describe the destruction she'd seen. She'd seen a house fall into a sinkhole once as a child. The aftermath had been horrible: a destroyed house with half the family coughing horribly and the others lying dead on the ground, pulled out of a hole with half a house sticking out of it. The thing she remembered the most was the sickening scent that had hung in the air that night.

She took a deep breath in as she filled their canteens. There was a bit of that rank scent on the air, like rotten eggs or very stale air. Maybe it was a sinkhole…a large sinkhole.

Either way, it was too big to be ignored and the area would become dangerous for months. They also had to get the other hunters out here so they could decide how to deal with it.

First though, they had to make sure that Kuzunoha was safe and that Richard hadn't led her to her doom.

Chapter 40

Richard's breath came in short bursts. How long had it been since the last round of rocks had come crashing down? He couldn't remember and he was quivering. Part of him was certain that he had to run to escape the death from above. Unfortunately, the rest of him was convinced that if he left the thick table he was hiding under, more rocks would cave in on him.

He didn't know what had happened to Kuzunoha. He'd thought he heard her during the collapse, but not since. He had to find out if she was safe.

He'd run to the captain's quarters after the mast had fallen. Of all the rooms in the ship, it had taken the least damage. His gamble had paid off when he hadn't died. Light shone in through cracks in the roof, a sign of something wrong with the world. He was underground. The idea of sunlight underground was all wrong.

He was procrastinating and he knew it. If he were going to find out if Kuzunoha was safe, he'd have to leave the safety of his hiding spot.

The idea sent a wave of nausea through him. He forced himself to take a single slow, deep breath. He had a wet cloth wrapped over his mouth, but the air still tasted like dirt. He had to calm down, he had to focus. He forced his mind to Kuzunoha. Where could she have gone to escape the rocks?

Maybe she was dead and if she wasn't, she definitely wasn't worth putting himself in danger for. He ignored that. Kuzunoha was an asset, even if the list of things she couldn't do would fill a book. He liked her. She was a fighter, even if that meant that she was often fighting the wrong battles.

He'd lost track of her when the roof fell in. She'd still been high on the mast when it fell over. It had fallen towards the bow. Had she fallen on the deck or in the water?

He took a second deep breath and sprinted out from under the table to the thick doorframe that led the way outside.

Filtered sunlight and the scent of wet everything greeted him, but no more rocks fell and he relaxed, incrementally, while he looked around. Wet rocks, wet wood, wet dirt. The cave was gone. There was nothing but reddish sky with pink clouds above him. He squinted. The reddish sky must have been due to the dust hovering above the ship. Then he blinked again, noting where the sun was. It was nearly nightfall. Richard grimaced. If he didn't find Kuzunoha before the last of the daylight fled, he probably wouldn't find her at all.

The monster's corpse lay in the center of the ship, where the mast had been. The stalactite had done its job thoroughly, piercing thick shell by a good foot, perhaps a foot and a half. Blue-black ichor leaked and pooled from the wound. Despite the rockfall nearly killing him as well, Richard had to admit that bringing the stalactite down had been a good idea. When it had hunkered down, with nothing but claws and shell showing, he hadn't been able to hurt it with his daggers. He didn't think collapsing the cave had been part of Kuzu's plan.

"Kuzunoha?" he called out. His voice sounded out of place in the silence. Aside from the sound of lapping water, there was no noise anywhere.

He felt the boat rock slightly. The cavern was larger than he'd judged originally and the roof had completely fallen in. There was a good forty feet in every direction and the water was higher than it had been. The boat was no longer grounded. Richard grit his teeth. Depending on how much damage it had taken, the ship might be sinking and if he wasn't wrong, the tide would be rising already. He had to find Kuzunoha, grab whatever treasure hadn't been lost, and get out of there.

Richard ran towards the other end of the boat, where the mast had fallen, smashing its way through the hull. He ducked his head inside. Kuzunoha's body was there, floating face up. There was a chance she wasn't dead. The water was cooler than it had been, but not ocean cold yet. He swam in, grabbed her, and pulled her back to the hole. He left her floating and pulled himself onto the deck before he hoisted her up.

She was still breathing. He blew out a sigh of relief before he checked her for injuries. She was covered with scrapes, nicks, and bruises, but only one looked life-threatening. A long gash, nearly the length of her leg, was still bleeding. It was deep. She needed stitches, which meant he needed his kit. It wasn't on him. It should have been in his bag by the treasure. He sighed. Maybe he'd get lucky and it would still be there.

Most of their treasure was gone, bucked off the ship during the cave-in, but a few things were left: his bag, the chest of books and coins, and the fireworks. He picked up his bag, glad that they hadn't lost the healing supplies. He took everything with him. He wouldn't be able to carry them if he also had to carry Kuzunoha, but if she could handle herself some of the way, they could make sure the trip wasn't a total waste.

An earsplitting keen filled the air. Richard rushed back to Kuzunoha. She was sitting up, shivering and pale. Her eyes were wild, darting everywhere. Probably looking for the monster. He set down the chest and healing kit and tried to lay her back down. She swung at him and tried to creep away, still keening her hurt to the world. He forced her down and kept her there, one hand on her chest and another on her leg. She moaned, struggling, but seemed too weak to stop him.

"By Binahi's lost grace, stop it," he growled. "I know it hurts. Let me help. Kuzunoha, stop fighting me..."

She seemed to finally recognize him. She sucked in a ragged breath. "Richard, what's...?"

He didn't move. He couldn't until he could be sure she wouldn't. "You're hurt. You need stitches."

She took another ragged breath. Finally, she nodded. Tears ran from her eyes, but she seemed to have found her control.

Richard let out a breath. "I'm going to let you go. Stay still."

She nodded and sucked in a breath. He slathered her leg with numbing cream and strung the flesh needle for stitching. He wanted her distracted. Stitches were easier if you could focus on something else.

He smiled as he remembered her doing the same thing for him the first night they'd met. He wondered how long he could get away with jokingly saying her name wrong before she caught on that he was doing it deliberately. He shook his head. Nothing would have her laughing right now.

"What are you going to do with your share of the money when we get back?" he asked her.

"When we get back?"

He nodded. She let out another deep breath.

"A home, I guess. Somewhere away from my sister, maybe a job..."

She hissed in pain as Richard pushed the needle in. She cut off another scream and gasped. She grabbed Richard and he knocked her hand away.

"Stay still, Kuzunoha. Keep talking."

Her hand found her sword hilt. "My sword. I still have it? Richard...we never...figured out...how much my...sword is worth. One hundred gold? Is that...enough? I want a home too, but..."

He heard her jaw clink as she clenched her teeth. He pulled the string and then grabbed a bit of wood from the deck. Turning towards her, he pushed it between her teeth. He'd heard of men biting their own tongues off by accident. The first time you got stitches was the worst. This was probably the first time she'd ever been actually hurt. If she wanted to concentrate on the blade right now, he would talk about the blade. "Bite down and try not to move. It will help me to work faster."

She nodded, her eyes wide. Her hand was white and wrapped in a death grip around the sword hilt. She was quivering like a rabbit. He stuck the needle in again, running it under the skin and cinching the wound closed. She flinched and her teeth clamped down on the wood, but he could tell she was trying to stay still for him.

"One hundred gold is probably low. Despite the rust, that sword is still in damn good condition considering where it's been for the last sixty-some years."

He pulled the needle through her skin again, blood welling up and fountaining over his fingers.

"It isn't….rusty. So how much...?" she wheezed through the wood in her mouth.

How much was the sword worth? She had saved his life and nearly killed him. How would each of those figure in the equation? "You used it on the rocks, right? I don't think it's made of steel. Some other alloy maybe. The weapon itself is well made. It was almost certainly done by a master. I assume that's what the symbols on it mean. Maybe, one hundred fifty gold sentine?"

He silently cursed. That was probably still too low. Was his life worth that much? Was she?

"Names..." she confirmed, her voice difficult to understand through the wood. Her breathing hitched as he pulled the needle through again. "The name of the sword. It's called Blade of Four Feathers."

A named blade. It was probably worth double what he'd said. Kuzunoha's face was bone white and her gaze was wild.

If anyone else had wanted it, he would have insisted they'd find out the master's name, its age, and gotten it appraised before settling on a price. For her, he would take the hit.

"One hundred fifty gold, Kuzu. What do you think?" Remembering too late how much she hated the nickname. For now, it was fine. He was half done already. He just had to keep her talking.

"If that's what it's..." She stopped as he stuck the needle in again. "Fair. More than fair."

Kuzunoha was covered in a cold sweat by the time he was done. He poured some sea water over the wound, washing off the dried blood, but her leg swelled against the stitches. He had to get her back to camp before she couldn't walk at all.

"Kuzunoha? Come on, Kuzu…I know you're still with me."

She didn't respond to her nickname. That was bad. He kissed her and finally she focused on him.

"I'm done now, darling. You did really well there."

She forced a smile. This was the worst he'd ever seen her look, but the smile made him feel better about her chances.

"Let's get you back to the campsite, okay?"

She nodded, wincing.

It took longer than he would have liked getting her up the cliff to dry land, though he found a carved stair by the far end of the cavern. He supposed it wasn't a cavern anymore…a lagoon, maybe? Either way, he was sure now that the steps, leading up to small hole filled with dead tree limbs, had been a pirate cove at one point. A place to hide the ship, behind a waterfall.

Kuzunoha was shaking by the time they arrived at the campsite, which was still fully intact. He was doubly glad to have set it up so far away.

"Richard, what can I do?" she asked while he sat her down.

"Nothing. You need to rest."

Her voice was reed-thin and she was gray. She needed food and rest, in that order.

He started the fire again. He'd left the soup over top of it and though it had cooled, it would only take a few minutes to heat.

"Richard, let me help. I can cook..."

He glared at her.

"...or something else. I can't just sit here while you take care of me."

He sighed and made sure that the fire was burning steadily. Then he brought the fireworks box over to her. "You said you know a way to see if these things are still viable?" He waited for a nod to continue. "Good. See if they are. What do you need?"

"I'll need a tarp and a wooden stick or a fork. Where did we leave...?"

He'd be impressed if she was able to keep herself awake for another hour. He'd make tea for dinner. He'd brought chamomile. It should relax her enough to let her sleep. Maybe he should add some of the feverfew to it as well. She'd fall asleep easier if the pain was lessened.

"I'll get you those. Just give me a moment to put on some water. I need tea tonight, not wine. Would you like some?"

She nodded. "Tea would be wonderful. Not that our wine is particularly strong, but I'd rather avoid it all the same."

He set the water up and got her the items. Just before dinner was ready, she finished. She'd opened one of the smaller packages and dumped the contents onto the tarp. It looked like some sort of black crumbly sand. She was poking at it with a forked stick. She was having trouble keeping her eyes open, leaning to the side. He didn't think she'd last the meal.

"How hungry are you?" He set the steeping tea in front of her.

"I'm not."

That was bad. She's lost a lot of blood, too much, and she needed to eat to regain her strength. Her body wouldn't be able to heal or fight any sickness. He poured her a bowl of mostly broth, hoping that it would entice her to have more, the same way his stew had their first day out. She wrinkled her nose.

"It's been hours since lunch. At the very least, I expect you to drink that and finish your tea."

She grumbled but put the bowl to her mouth to drink up some of the broth. He was glad she'd started with the broth, as she'd be asleep within minutes of finishing her tea.

He ate as well, keeping his ears open. There was too much quiet here, which meant errant noises sounded louder and out of place. They'd have to leave tomorrow. Monsters would arrive to investigate what had happened far sooner than any hunters would, if the sound had carried as far as the town. He'd start packing the campsite tonight. They would leave by noon and get a few miles between them and this place before anything showed up.

Kuzunoha still looked ashen, even after eating. He hoped she would have her color back tomorrow. There was a lot to do and he didn't want to have to do all of it alone.

Then again, if he left while she slept...

Pain lanced his head, nearly doubling him over. He'd expected some pain to come with the thought, but apparently, it was a new low. He couldn't leave a convalescing person to defend themselves in a dangerous place. What if he went to town to get help? The pain eased, but still rumbled deep in his muscles.

Kuzunoha started bobbing her head and Richard helped her into the tent. It was the least he could do before he started packing up the camp.

Chapter 41

The hole was large, more than a couple hundred feet across, easily. Isashi could see that it went nearly all the way to the cliffside before moving inland. There had been blessedly few trees in the area, but those that had been were now sticking out of the water in the hole. If they hadn't been dead before, they would die of water rot before the summer passed.

No, she amended, they would be dead and not of water rot. She could still smell a faint sourness in the air, and the water was cloudy, not just with dust or displaced sand. It had a whiteish opaque shade, as though it was from a hot spring. Most likely these plants wouldn't be used to the sulfur in the water and would be poisoned within weeks.

"Holy hell," Hana growled. "What happened here? This ship couldn't have been sitting here for this long, could it? Under the ground…how would it even have gotten there?"

Isashi took a deep breath and rubbed her eyes again. She'd been trying to ignore the ship, hoping that it was some sort of illusion brought on by dust or ill-sleep. But it wasn't. Half-sunk, the ship was real. The left side of the deck was submerged, while the right was below the water. The mast had been snapped off, leaving an uneven hole in the middle of the deck. From fifteen or twenty feet back, it couldn't be seen, hiding perfectly in the new lagoon. Something about the way the ship bobbed bothered Isashi, as if it were unconcerned about their presence. As if the ship couldn't care less who had come to see it in its failing glory.

Near the center of the ship lay a blue cleris crab. It was thoroughly dead, which was a relief. They were difficult to kill, with thick armor covering most of their body. This one had been squished when the ceiling fell in.

Isashi shook her head. This entire situation was impossible. That ship was old. Even from the top of the cliff, she could see the water damage the starboard side had taken, as if it had been floating for decades.

"I'll kill him…" she muttered instead. It had to have been Richard's fault. Nothing like this had ever happened before he'd come to Hidan. What would Himiko even say about this? Were there enough words? She was a hunter, used to seeing weird things and she was still flabbergasted. "They're not here. Where could they be?"

Hana ignored her turmoil. "At least it doesn't look monster-infested. We'd be seeing the ones that couldn't get out if it was."

"No monsters? What about that one?" Isashi pointed to the dead cleris crab laying on the deck.

"Cleris crabs don't allow others to settle near them unless they're mating. Even then, they're only together for a week or two at the most. If we don't see the second one, then there wasn't a second one."

Isashi grumbled though she couldn't deny that Hana was right. If nothing else, there would be no need to go down into the hole. The breeze changed direction and a faint smell of dried ashes came to her. Isashi sniffed deeply. Yes, that was fire ash on the breeze.

"What have you got?" Hana asked.

Isashi put a finger in her mouth and then held it to the air. She pointed. "Remnants of a fire that way."

"You mean that someone survived this damage?! Good enough for me. Let's go see who it was."

It only took a few minutes to find what remained of the campsite. A small amount of garbage and a covered campfire. Isashi put her hand gingerly onto the sand and dirt smothering the fire. It was slightly warm and a small bit of greasy ash stuck to her fingers.

"We just missed them," she muttered.

"One of them was injured," Hana said.

Isashi turned and saw Hana crouching over a flattened patch of grass leading out of the area. It took Isashi a few moments to figure it out. There was only one set of footprints. "A makeshift litter?"

Hana nodded. "Heading back towards town."

"Could they be using it to carry treasure?"

"Not with only a single set of footprints."

Isashi bit her tongue to stop herself from swearing again. "At least, they're doing the smart thing and heading back to town. Let's go. We should see how bad off they are." She put her emphasis on 'they're'. She would not let

Himiko down.

Hana surprised her. “I agree. We’ll want to bring the other hunters to make sure that the area is clear afterward.”

It took another hour before Isashi caught sight of the pair. A man dragged a makeshift sled behind him. He wasn’t local; he was darker skinned and he wore weapons like a lord wore silk, as if he’d been born to it. The sled was a simple tarp and wood, piled with bags and... her heart sank. A delicate body.

Isashi took care aiming before she called out to him. “Stop right there, stranger. Move away from the girl.”

The man stopped and turned slowly. He matched Himiko’s description. He was also wearing all black. Strangely, he didn’t react like so many humans did whenever they encountered something more or less human than themselves. In fact, he didn’t seem to care that she wasn’t human. What he did react to was the weapon in her hands.

“Hello,” he said smoothly, he sounded exhausted. “I’m Richard. Are you friend or foe? From Hidan, hopefully?”

It didn’t look like he had a ranged weapon on him, but she counted at least three knives along with an odd sword at his waist. His hands twitched as if wanting his own weapons in hand.

Isashi drew back the string and his hands stopped moving. He would be good with his knives if she let him have them. Fast off the mark, and intelligent enough to know that he’d brought the wrong weapon to this party.

"That's not really necessary, is it?" Hana asked, jogging up beside her.

The man's eyes roamed her friend's body and Isashi wanted to let her arrow fly. He smiled. Isashi couldn't see any comfort in the expression. "Hello to you as well, Lady."

Hana smiled. "Always a woman but never a lady. I can see why you have everyone so up in arms, though. The name's Hana."

"We didn't come here to flirt," Isashi growled. The man was too dangerous to trust, especially if he was the one they'd come to find. "What did you do to the girl?"

"I'm fine…" The woman on the bed coughed and tried to sit up.

"Quiet, Kuzunoha. I've got this. Rest," he said.

So he did have her.

"Richard? I'm not that bad off."

Isashi gasped when Kuzunoha tried to sit up. She was covered with new scratches, dark bruises, and her eyes were sunken pits. She was sweating and her skin looked gray and pallid. Isashi's eyes narrowed. Kuzunoha had been in his care and she looked as though death would claim her at any moment.

"Kuzunoha, what happened?" Isashi said.

Better to find out what the stranger had done to her and then shoot him. It took Kuzunoha too long to focus. Every second scrapped at Isashi's patience.

"Isashi, is that you? Richard, help me up," she said.

Richard laid the litter on the ground. Isashi released her arrow, drawing a second before her first had finished flying. The feather brushed across his cheek landing far into the brush behind him. Richard understood the shot for what it was. A warning. If Kuzunoha died, so would he.

Richard narrowed his eyes in response and put up his hands. Hana went to Kuzunoha. Isashi fretted, wondering how she could tell Himiko about this. Her friend had trusted her with this duty. She hadn't been fast enough. Her hands clenched around her bow.

"I don't think that was necessary, Isashi. Her bandages aren't bloody, but the ones around her leg are…phew, infected, maybe? What happened?"

"Kuzunoha decided that it wasn't enough to get a fine sword and enough money to make our fortune. She had to change the very landscape to suit her whim," Richard said, a tired smile on his face.

Kuzunoha took a deep breath, "That creature had us beat. I had to do something."

Richard looked relieved and Isashi relaxed her weapon, reluctantly. "Sorry, Stranger. But I don't know you and this girl is…important. What happened?"

Richard didn't look mollified, but he nodded in a roguish form of assent.

"A crab monster, a giant one," Kuzunoha said.

She let go of Hana and grabbed onto Richard. Isashi cringed. He may not have caused her injury, but he wasn't safe.

"The cleris crab we saw back there?" Hana asked.

"Probably, I don't know what it was called," Richard confirmed. "The creature was two or three feet taller than us. It did look like a crab, somewhat. Blue, two big claws, four thin spider-like legs, dozens of tiny arms trying to eat you. It attacked us when we found what we were looking for."

"We saw its corpse. How did you two manage to defeat it?" Hana asked.

Kuzunoha blinked from the effort of standing. "I used a sword and dropped a staggy-stone on it."

Richard helped her back to the sled. He covered her in layers of blankets and boxed her in again. "You need to sleep now. I'm going to talk to these two fine ladies and find out what dangers are ahead of us, all right?"

Isashi heard Kuzunoha mumble a protest that was lost to sleep. He gestured, asking them to come closer. Isashi nodded, her hands clenched around the bow.

"What happened?" Isashi whispered harshly as she got near enough.

"We were near your mud flats when we found a cave with our ship in it. The last door we opened led into the creature's lair. When he attacked, Kuzunoha hit upon the idea of climbing the mast and dropping a stalactite onto the creature. When the mast came down, so did the entire roof. Fortunately, it didn't have a backup plan. The falling roof killed the thing."

"You don't look hurt," Isashi said while Hana replied, "Clever girl. That would do it."

"The creature scratched her up a bit, but the main wound is one she took climbing the mast. A bit of metal punctured her thigh and ripped its way back out. When the mast fell, she survived by falling through a patch of rotten wood and slipping into the water under a firmer overhang. She's damn lucky. I'm surprised she lived at all. To answer your question though, I've been in more fights and move faster on my feet. Also, I wasn't as high up when the mast went down, taking everything else with it."

"We saw that," Hana said. "The mud flats are now a scenic lagoon."

Richard ran a hand through his hair and looked back at Kuzunoha. "I'm worried. She didn't seem too bad last night, but when I tried to wake her this morning, she was like this. She can't walk and I couldn't leave her unprotected. I had to stitch up her leg, but I think something got in it, despite dumping some of my eighty-proof alcohol over it."

"We should get her back to Deckard. I can do field dressing, but nothing more," Hana said, glancing at Isashi.

Himiko would never forgive her if she brought Kuzunoha back like this. "Let me look at her."

Richard gestured. "Please. I'm out of my depth."

Isashi's worry increased as she checked over the girl. The cuts and bruises looked bad enough but they were light compared to the rip down her thigh. Her entire leg was puffy and red streaked from the wound like a bloodshot eye. She poked her thigh near one of the stitches and a foul-smelling yellow goo emerged.

"I can't help her. I would suggest draining it tonight and using the alcohol on it again, then re-stitching it. After that…we need to get her back to Hidan. A real healer needs to see her."

Richard looked around. "Could one of you run ahead and bring your healer back?"

She didn't trust him and didn't want to leave him alone with only Kuzunoha and one other hunter. "We'll make better time together. We'll do what we can on the road. Will you be good to go until dark?"

Richard was gray too and his eyes were dark with exhaustion. "I haven't slept for more than an hour or two in the last day," he said. "I'll survive though, especially if you guys can do the first watch tonight. I'll take the second instead."

Hana nodded. "Done. Let's go."

Chapter 42

Richard didn't know what he'd done to the silver-skinned hunter, but she didn't want him anywhere near Kuzunoha. Like she thought that just being in his presence was soiling the girl. He would have reminded her that Kuzunoha had been deflowered well before he'd arrived if he could have done it without sounding crude.

If nothing else, it made her companion that much more compelling. She wasn't as attractive as Kuzunoha, or even Isashi for that matter, but she was intelligent, friendly and not fever-ridden, making her better company than either of the other two at present.

"So, what did it look like over there?" he asked her. "I was a bit too busy carrying for Kuzunoha to really appreciate the damage."

"The mud flats are completely gone," Hana told him, sitting cross-legged on the dirt. She had short, toned legs that bulged against the fabric of her pants. "The cavern-lagoon that's there now is huge. By the end of summer, sand and silt will have started filling it up, I assume. We might have a little romantic waterfall there this time next year. 'Til it fills up and breaks loose into the sea again, that is. More noodles?"

"Yes, please," he said, passing her his bowl.

Isashi was still glaring at him, as if she'd already judged him for everything that had happened.

Richard shrugged and took the bowl back from Hana. It wasn't his fault, and he wasn't going to apologize as if it was. He'd be better served by finding out what Isashi had against him. "It is like I said. The mast fell and the whole roof fell in with it. What's the word when bridges do it? A capstone? Perhaps the mast area was that."

"It is amazing, really. That area would have been large enough for an entire underground dock. Can you imagine how much dockmaster Kurtz would have paid for that information? He was looking for an area to grow into just last year."

"He might still be able to," Richard said, tucking the information away. "They would just need to clear the mud off the cliffside and clear the wreckage."

"Not until the hunters have looked into it," Isashi said.

The eledar was definitely pissed. Richard was used to having women angry at him…but usually he knew why. Honestly, he wished he knew just so he could talk to her and get the issue aired out. He'd seen a few of her kind in Jisa but he had never gotten to talk to one, and he had been hoping to have some of his curiosity abated. It looked like that wasn't likely.

"We'd need more hunters to make it safe. Wooden walls could be constructed, reasonably quickly, but stone would be better. What monsters have you seen out here, Richard?" Hana asked.

"We were attacked by a massive bird a day or so out. I got sliced up here and here." He pointed to his chest and his side. "Those things have killer claws."

"Nothing else?" She asked disappointed.

"You saw the crab. The only other thing we saw out there that was even unusual was a white octopus. It stung Kuzunoha's hands."

Isashi slammed her plate down. "You didn't tell us that before."

Richard leaned away and then caught himself. He shrugged nonchalantly. "It didn't seem important, compared to her other injuries. Her hands are healing fine. They won't be a bother after another day or two."

"With her climbing the mast? What if some of that gunk got in her hands?" Isashi said.

Even Hana looked frustrated. "Lay off, Isashi. If it had, we would already be seeing the effect, considering how her leg looks."

"She will recover," Isashi said forcefully.

"Of course, she will," Hana said. "Deckard is the best healer Hidan's had in some time. If he can't fix her up then nobody can. Richard, you said you could take a shift watching tonight, right?"

He relaxed a little. She was overly worried about Kuzunoha. He could understand that worry, having it himself. Fortunately, he agreed with Hana's assessment of Deckard's skills. They would have to watch her, but the healer would know what to do as soon as they got her to him. She would be all right.

"If I could take the third shift, that would be best. I had to watch our camp by myself all last night."

"Poor boy. You need a full night's sleep before you can take one of the watches?"

They were right back where they started. Then he noticed Hana's inviting smile and her gaze running up and down his body.

"I would as well, Isashi," Hana said. "I'll settle this. Richard, you'll take the last watch, and I'll take the middle one. If you're up for it, we can have some private time before I tuck you in."

Tired as he was, he was always awake enough for a willing woman. The gods knew you slept better if you'd finished all your business before you crawled under the sheets.

Isashi flushed. "What? Are you going to…with him…? Now?"

Hana rolled her eyes. "It's just sex, Isashi. Relax."

"We know nothing about him," Isashi said, darkly glaring at him again.

"I know he's willing and that's enough for me."

"What if it isn't enough for me?"

Richard let them argue. It might help him figure out what Isashi had against him.

"Then you should be glad you won't be the one going."

"What about the monster?" Isashi growled.

Hana rolled her eyes. “We haven’t seen hide nor hair nor track since yesterday. I think it fled after the mud flats collapsed. It’s probably gorging itself on goblin flesh. It will be our problem when we come back. But not now.”

Richard stood up. “Isashi, what do you think will happen if we step out for a moment?”

Hana said, “Nothing that I couldn’t stop you from doing if I didn’t want you to do it.”

Isashi flushed. “At least, leave the camp first. We only have the one tent and I’m sure that, even sick as she is, Kuzunoha would wake up to that.”

Smiling, Richard took Hana’s hand, following closely behind her to the darkened forest. Before they’d gotten further than a few steps into the trees, Hana glanced at him. Hana wasn’t pretty—her hair was too short, her features too large. She was a hunter though, dangerous and coy. She didn’t smell like other people did, even after a hard day on the road in armor. Instead, she smelled of grass, night air, and wood smoke. He couldn’t help but notice she was damn near silent, almost moving like an animal herself. It was uncanny. Strangely, it made him like her more.

“Don’t be concerned that she doesn’t like you,” she said, surprising him.

Richard glanced back towards the camp. “I think it’s well beyond dislike at this point.”

“Unless I miss my guess, it isn’t you she’s thinking about at all.” Hana wrapped her arms around him, stroking his chest. “She’s sweet on somebody that doesn’t want her back.”

Richard pushed towards her until he could feel her chest against his back. He couldn’t see how her being sweet on somebody made her irritated at him. He hadn’t even been flirted with her.

“Well, it clearly isn’t me,” he said in an entreaty for more information.

“It’s your girl’s sister.” She nibbled his ear and started untucking his shirt.

“Her sister? She’s angry at me for bringing Kuzunoha’s sister grief over this?” He yanked on her shirt, searching for her skin to stroke.

“Hardly. She’s angry because she hasn’t admitted she’s attracted to the girl at all.”

“Oh.” Well, there wasn’t much more he could say to that. “And is the girl amenable?”

“How should I know? The lord’s daughter isn’t my cup of tea to talk with or screw. Why? Is she to your taste?”

Hana’s hands roamed back and touched the small of his back. He groaned, pushing against her, lowering his head to her breasts. The eledar’s suspicions could wait. His eyes fell on a small wooden pendant lay just above her breasts. A bit of wood carved into a symbol he knew well. A scarf, dancing in the wind.

“You worship Kristinel?” he said. She seemed blunt for a worshipper, but perhaps she had never been taught to properly worship her.

Hana pulled back in surprise. “You know of her?”

Richard grinned, willing to give her an answer that he wouldn’t have given a non-worshipper. “I have a green scarf in my bag for worship. From the church in Jisa.”

“It’s seen more than its share of travels?” she asked coyly.

He shivered, even if the play was simple by comparison to what he would have had with a fellow worshipper in his homeland. “It’s seen the Eyes at the center of the Great Bowl.”

Hana’s eyes widened in shock and then she touched her chest, her eyes filling with pleasure. “Worship with me, at the font of the Courtesan?”

Richard felt his heartbeat race. The ritual words spoken as they were meant to be. It had been long, too long since he’d worshipped Kristinel properly. You needed a partner, needed the interaction. Kristinel didn’t look down on self-worship, but it wasn’t preferred. It was to be pitied. One should never be lonely in her worship. He forced himself to move slowly, though he wanted to take her to the ground and taste her. He voice was husky as he answered her. “I see beyond your flesh to your core and I am intrigued. For our time together, I promise to see none but you.”

Hana leaned in close before she responded. Her eyes were beautiful, doe-brown with hazel edgings. They were her beauty. “I promise to be the one you lean upon and the one you dream with, for the moment.”

The air tasted different, sweeter. From the direction of the camp, someone screamed. Richard and Hana pulled back from each other. The last time he'd been to worship with the priestesses, or even another worshipper, had been back in Jisa. How long had that been? He couldn't remember.

The meaning of the scream penetrated him. Hana seemed to reach the conclusion at the same time and they both ran for the camp.

A ten-foot tall mountainous creature on the other side of the clearing snarled at them once before it spun around, running back out of the camp. As the thing fled, one of its arms hit a tree branch. The branch snapped, flipped in the air, and hit the ground. Three arrows hit the thing's shoulder in quick succession. It didn't even slow the creature. Within moments, it was lost in the trees.

"What in hells was that?" Richard said, trying to pull in more air.

Hana had strung her bow, but the creature was gone. Not even the sound of it moving through brush remained.

"I don't know. It came into the clearing after you both left," Isashi growled. She strode over to where they'd first seen the creature. She kicked at the dirt and picked up a shattered arrow. "I can tell you that it has a tough hide."

Hana narrowed her eyes and ran over to Isashi. "Cold iron, then?"

Isashi nodded but Hana was already moving towards the trees where the creature had gone. She bent low and swore.

"I was certain the creature was gone. We didn't see it following us today and I was looking."

Richard moved towards them, keeping his eyes on the forest. He touched his favourite blade, a long knife, closer to a machete than one of the thin daggers they preferred on this side of the Bowl. It was a comfort. She was looking over a massive footprint that seemed to waver and disappear before his eyes.

"Why would it come after us at all?" Richard asked.

"Damn good question. It seems to be hunting for humans, not just looking for new territory." Hana stood and stomped on the faded print.

"The situation is worse than that," Isashi broke in. "It came as soon as you two left. It was waiting for its chance."

"It's watching the camp, then." Hana looked annoyed. "I don't suppose you're actually a hunter in disguise, are you?"

There was safety in that distinction. People who fought the monsters were revered. On the other hand, they were also known, they were special. They were guardians of humanity. The lie would come so easily. His tongue prickled as if he'd sucked in a mouthful of confectionary powder by mistake and he knew he had only milliseconds before he coughed so hard his ancestor's throats would hurt. He swore.

"Not a hunter," he ground out. "I've fought before though, often enough that I know more than the basics." It was enough to satisfy them without telling them things that he didn't want to share.

"You'll be of help then…still, no less than two of us on watch at a time," Hana said.

Her nose crinkled as if she smelled something rotten and she looked at him apologetically. He nodded at her unspoken promise to continue where they'd left off back in town. It might be better anyway. He'd much rather complete her ritual in a comfortable bed than on an anthill or brambles.

"In that case, I'd better get some sleep. You'll need me a lot sooner than I'd hoped," he said. It was not going to be a fun trip back for anyone.

"Check on Kuzunoha before you go to sleep. She nearly woke up just before the creature rumbled into camp. If her wound is still leaking, we may need to clean it and wrap it again during the night."

Richard nodded, crawling into the low tent. If Kuzunoha had been waking up, she was sound asleep now. Her leg was warm, but the bandages still looked fresh. Good enough.

He tucked in on the other side of the tent. There was only enough room for two, but it didn't look like they would be having company, even if they had both been conscious enough to agree. It was going to be a long enough night without his libido making it longer.

Chapter 43

"Richard, I need to speak with you," Isashi told him stiffly.

Richard didn't look up from the cooking pot in front of him. Soup would be easiest for Kuzunoha to eat, but everyone else had to eat as well, and soup wasn't enough for people working as hard as they were. He had compromised by making the broth and then moving a portion to a smaller pot before thickening the rest to a stew. The wood was too warm and was burning hotter than he would have liked. It would make the bread nearly impossible to cook. Perhaps if he removed some of the coals and buried them, it would even out the heat?

"Richard, don't ignore me."

Isashi had been easily as unlikeable today as she had been the night before. A day of walking in her company hadn't helped. They had nothing to speak about; she'd made that plain enough. Every time he'd stepped near Kuzunoha or out of Isashi's sight, she had searched him out and snarled at him.

Her mouth twisted. "I suppose I don't need to ask you about who was following you and why you had to kill them to get away from it. I'll just ask the sheriff instead."

Richard's hand that was stirring the stew went still, thoughts of bread completely forgotten. He swore, took a breath, and forced himself to start stirring again.

"I thought that might catch your interest," she said, crouching down across from him.

Isashi was exotic and her hair burned like a corona around her silvery flesh. Right now, her blue eyes were trying to penetrate his soul. It wasn't her body or her race that interested him now. It was what she knew. Was she only fishing for information? Or did she have something on him that the sheriff and others had missed?

"Apparently, you have my attention. What do you want?"

"I want to talk about this," she said, pulling out a bit of paper.

The paper was plain, but of good quality. It was made of paper in the new way, rather than the more common animal-made vellum that was still common in most places. When he unfolded it, he saw a note written in fading ink.

Have tracked your lost property to Hidan. He is holed up in the inn, too busy to take him yet. We'll move as soon as he is able to be taken. Keep the messenger, if you like. A gift in return for your patience.

He froze. Who had sent this? When? How had she gotten it?

"What is there to talk about?" His voice was even, a feat considering his roiling mind.

"You're the lost property," she said.

He didn't dignify that with a response. It was clear. Too clear. It had to be from one of their human servants. That would explain the paper as well. Her type preferred vellum or parchment. If something had to die first, it would only serve their purposes better.

"I know you won't tell me why they were searching for you," she said. "What I do want to know is if you're a threat to us."

"A threat?" he said, surprised.

"Slavery may be outlawed in Hidan, but even we know that it's still practiced. Clearly, your master isn't a friendly one."

"Not a slave," he told her, cursing himself for saying it.

"Oh? Then please feel free to explain."

Richard sighed. "You clearly know nothing about slaves. Each one is marked with a symbol of the house they belong to. As you pay off your debt, the marks are filled in, finished. I don't have a mark."

She frowned. "I will admit to not knowing that. I thought the many tattoos that sailors have were just decorative."

She really didn't know. He started stirring the soup again. "In most cases, they are. Sailors aren't slaves. Even pirate captains don't generally mark you as a slave. They might tattoo you with their symbol to keep you loyal, but not to show ownership."

On the other hand, all of the rowers usually were slaves. They weren't marked either. Those poor souls knew that they would never step foot off the ship again. If they did, they were assumed lost to the captains. No need to make that distinction to her though, since it didn't apply to him either.

"As interesting as that is, that wasn't actually what I was referring to when I asked you to explain."

Richard clenched his fist with the paper in it. "She's a jilted lover. Or thinks that she is. Wealthy, noble…doesn't really understand how the real world works. She sent me on my way with her best wishes and decided afterward that she'd only done it because I was supposed to prove that I loved her by returning to her side like the lovesick puppy she thought I was." Richard uncrumpled the sheet of paper and looked at it again. "It works out about the same though. I never want to go back. Where did you find this?"

"I found a body a few days back. A monster that had been dead for weeks, but it had this on it. Is she a threat to us?"

He longed to lie. Couldn't. He met her gaze. "So long as she knows where I am, she'll send more people."

"No, I meant, what would you do to get away from her?" she asked. "Anything?"

He had to bite his tongue on the sharp *yes* that formed on his lips. He would do a lot.

"What do you mean?" he asked instead. "You sound like you have a specific question in mind."

He handed the sheet of paper back to Isashi. He should have burned it, but then she never would have trusted him. Her hands squeezed the sheet like he had, crumpling it into a tight ball. “Did you come out here to give them Kuzunoha?”

“What?” Of all the questions he’d expected, that hadn’t been one.

“Would you pay for your freedom with hers?” Isashi clarified.

The thought had never even occurred to him. If his mistress found her interesting…well, Kuzunoha did have all the hallmarks she would enjoy, except for those particular tastes that she shared with all her favourites, teaching you to like the depravity she offered, even if you didn’t start out that way. Would she accept her for him? Even if she would, could he live with himself if he did?

“No,” he said. “I don’t think she would accept that sort of a deal to begin with.”

And if she did, Richard was sure it would result in both of them being caught and taken back. That wasn’t something that he would ever want to force Kuzunoha into. It was something he didn’t want anyone else to have to suffer through.

“And if she would?” Isashi persisted.

“I wouldn’t give them Kuzunoha,” he said. “No one should have to serve in the way I did.”

Isashi didn’t say anything and Richard turned back to the stew, wondering if he’d said too much. He would have to flee Hidan as soon as they got back, most likely. He could leave now, but that would mean leaving Kuzunoha to be guarded by these two. They would do the best job they could, but Richard knew that the moment he left, the monster would probably make its move, either following him or moving in for the kill here.

He spared a thought, wondering if the beast was a creature of the woman who was no longer his mistress. After a moment, he discarded it. She used her own kind, not monsters, to do her bidding.

Isashi threw the crumpled sheet into the flames. Within moments, it burned to a crisp. The ash cracked and broke apart and Isashi smacked her hands, as if to clear them of dirt. She stood up. "I may not like you, Richard. But I believe that you wouldn't put Himiko's sister in danger to get yourself out of trouble. The body I found hadn't been touched, so most likely, no one knows you're here. If I find out that you have abused my trust"—her gaze bored into his—"then we will have more than words."

She walked to the other side of the camp. As soon as she was far enough away, Richard used his spoon to destroy the ash, all that was left of the message. He wished he could thank her properly. He turned towards the tent, where Kuzunoha and Hana currently slept, thinking about Isashi's last words.

"You'd be right to do so," he whispered, and returned to cooking.

Chapter 44

They'd been harried for three days straight and Richard was still exhausted. But it was nearly over. They were only a few hours outside of Hidan. Soon they would be out of the creature's reach. The creature had been a bother, taking out their food, destroying their fire and supplies. Anything left alone for more than a moment became a target. It seemed to want them awake, exhausted, and starved. The creature was blessed by some dark power, he was sure of it.

Kuzunoha was awake when Richard walked back into their camp. Not only awake, but she was clambering out of the tent. She'd lost weight and really hadn't had enough to begin with. She was gray-toned, soaked with sweat, and shivering, even though the air was warm this morning. She shook her head as if trying to clear it. She was holding the sword she'd claimed and yanked, trying to unsheathe it.

He ran forward and grabbed her, pulling her into his arms. She struggled and then collapsed against him. She shouldn't have been standing, let alone trying to wield her blade. Where in the seven skies was Hana? She'd been watching her this morning.

A moment later, Hana poked her head up from the other side of the tent. *Need me?* she mouthed at him. He shook his head and pulled Kuzunoha closer, wishing he could stop her from trembling.

"Richard, where did you go, was there something out there?" Kuzunoha mumbled at him.

"Kuzunoha, you shouldn't be up."

"Where were you?" she insisted.

Richard's mouth set into a line. "I thought I heard something out there, but it was nothing."

Which didn't mean that there wasn't anything out there. Since that first night after the monster had attacked, they hadn't found any other tracks. The creature was getting bolder and bolder in its attacks though. Hana thought that it had been hunting him and Kuzunoha for days and that something about Kuzunoha's sickness was making their party irresistible to resist.

Isashi flung the tent open, only half dressed and gloriously unembarrassed about it. She glared at Richard as she climbed out, reaching out for Kuzunoha. "I told you to wait. We need to get what we can out of that leg before we leave."

"I heards it," Kuzunoha mumbled. "I have to help."

"There's nothing out here, Kuzunoha. Come back inside." Isashi touched her arm but looked around. The creature wasn't able to appear out of thin air, but it had some ability to be ignored until it chose to attack. Isashi pulled her away from Richard as Hana stepped out from behind the tent, carrying three packed sacks. "Come on, Kuzunoha, we need to finish your leg now."

"I'm not in a city, but I'm ready," she mumbled at him.

For an instant, Richard didn't know what she was talking about and he let her go, turning and drawing his weapons, hearing his own voice chiding Kuzunoha, w*hy can't you treat these things as if we were in the city?*

"What are you—?" Hana began as the trees swayed and a shadow nearly as tall as the tree became the monster. Richard had seen glimpses over the past few days, but never the whole thing all at once.

The creature looked like a reddish-brown bear, larger than normal, which was scary enough. Its face was striped like a badger and its claws were similarly long. It was standing like a man, and it drew a sword taller than Richard from a belt at its hips, nearly lost among the great wooly fur.

Richard threw two knives before the creature had stepped more than a foot into the clearing. They hit the thing in the gut, but Richard couldn't even be sure that they had made it through the creature's dense fur. He yanked two more knives from their scabbards as two arrows sailed past his shoulder. They struck the beast in the chest. He would have been more confident if they hadn't just angered the creature more.

The monster roared, but the sound of his own mind screaming at him to run was louder. The beast snorted like a boar and charged him. Swearing, Richard sheathed his throwing daggers and drew his cold iron machete, better for hacking things than slicing them. It wouldn't be enough to get through the beast's fur. He hoped it would be enough to keep the thing distracted until Hana and Isashi finished it off with arrows.

Kuzunoha stepped up beside him. The blade with its broken hilt shook in her hands and she swayed on her feet. The creature's eyes focused on her with a horrifying glee.

"Kuzunoha, get out of here." He stepped in front of her. "You can't help."

She snarled at the creature, an almost inhuman sound coming out of her tiny lips. "I won't back down."

Stupid, Richard thought as he grabbed Kuzunoha's arm and pulled her away from the monster's charge. He had to get her someplace she could hide. Behind him, the thing screamed and Richard saw more arrows fly from Isashi's bow. Hana ran up to take his spot, drawing a longsword.

At the edge of their campsite, Richard pushed Kuzunoha to the ground behind a thick fallen log and wrenched the sword from her hand. Kuzunoha shook her head, reaching for the blade.

"Stay down," he hissed, throwing her weapon a few feet behind her. With its hilt cracked, it wouldn't even be effective. "We don't have the time to protect you." Kuzunoha turned toward the weapon and he snarled as he grabbed her shoulder tightly and forced her to look at him. "If you try to get up, I'll tell your sister you were a pain in the ass. That you didn't help at all."

She stared at him as if she couldn't comprehend the level of threat. She was sick enough that she probably couldn't anymore.

The monster pushed towards them. Hana's sword caught her opponent's with a deafening clang, five or maybe ten feet away from

Kuzunoha's hiding place. More of Isashi's black-quilled arrows peppered its shoulder.

"Stay here." His words came out like he was swearing and he moved towards the fray, having to trust she'd stay where it was safe."

"Get back!" Hana snarled at him. "Guard her. Your daggers won't work. It needs cold steel."

"I have it. Stay to the front, I'll move behind." He sheathed his machete and drew two long thin knives from his side. They would have a better chance of piercing deep than the heavier blade would of cutting more than the beast's hair.

Dodging to the left, the bear howled, but ignored him, intent on the prey in front of it. Two more arrows appeared in its back. The creature roared again and Richard stepped in behind, sending a smile Isashi's way, making sure she'd seen him. Then he dove his blades in and saw its hair curl, blacken, and become scorched. A thin scent of burnt fur tickled at his nose and nearly made him sneeze. He banished the urge and danced away from the creature as it turned to face him. Good. That meant that he must have gotten through to its flesh.

On the other side, Hana sliced at it again. It returned to her with a snarl for its next attack. If they could just keep it confused and turning towards both of them, they'd be able to defeat it.

A flash of blue from the edge of the clearing sent his next attack into the creature awry. Two greenish faces, so puckered they looked squished, who wore unbleached bird skulls and bright feathers, were watching the battle. The creatures grinned at each other, their mouths somehow too large for the rows of sharp teeth inside them. Palming one of his smaller blades, Richard embedded it in the left one's skull with a well-placed throw. Its buddy shrieked and ducked, running away. The last thing they needed was a horde of little monsters joining the fight.

The creature hadn't been slowed in his moment of distraction, despite two new arrows sticking out of the creature's back. One of the wounds bled viscous, black fluid. The creature slashed down at Hana and she tumbled back over the log, letting it take the hit for her. The trunk had easily been as thick around as Richard himself and he may have squeaked as it shattered into a fine mist of splinters and wooden stakes.

Hana blinked and then glanced down to her feet. Whatever she saw, her jaw dropped and her eyes widened. Richard snarled. Kuzunoha was there, probably dead now. Snarling, Richard drove his blades into the creature's spine. The bear roared, ignoring his daggers, though they singed and bled.

Instead, the creature drove its thick sword through Hana. Hana coughed and slammed her own blade into its wrist before she fell.

The creature howled, leaving his sword sticking in her. Richard's stomach roiled. Hana shivered and slid down the weapon. The thing threw back its head to roar and another two arrows plunged into it. Richard leapt onto the creatures back, climbing it like he once had a bison when he'd been working as a dockhand. Once he was near the base of its thick neck, he drove his daggers in and hung on.

He would kill this creature and set it aflame, an effigy to lead Hana's soul to Cardinte's realm, where it was always light. As a follower of Kristinel, Hana deserved that much.

The creature grabbed for him, but like a real bear, it couldn't reach him. It stumbled about, its hands thumping at him and it shook like a dog after it climbed out of the sea.

Suddenly, Kuzunoha was standing in front of it, her amber eyes gleaming in the early light. Richard sucked in a scream of relief that she wasn't dead. She took a stance he didn't recognize and drove her blade deep into the thing's chest, up through its ribs, towards where its black heart should have been.

The sword went in up to the hilt and the monster roared in a high-pitched whine. He couldn't tell if Kuzunoha screamed or just opened her mouth as the monster slapped her down. She hit the ground, bounced, and didn't move again while the monster stumbled towards her. Richard yanked another cold iron blade and sliced at the creature's throat. It had already killed Hana. He wouldn't let it take Kuzunoha as well.

Two more arrows bloomed from the creature's chest and it finally fell, burbling dark blood.

Isashi ran towards them, but Richard didn't wait for her. He stabbed the thing again, and again, making sure the monster was dead.

"Hana? Hana, don't die on me," Isashi cried, the first sound he'd heard since the creature had roared.

He shook his head and turned to see her holding Hana in her arms. The huntress shook, the monster's sword still running her through.

"Monster... have to stop it..." she burbled, her eyes wild. Isashi made calming noises through her tears.

Kuzunoha stumbled to Hana's other side. "You saved me. Thank you."

Hana shivered, even paler than Kuzunoha now. "Monster... watch out..." Hana's chest fell and her eyes became dull.

Richard grabbed Kuzunoha and held her. She was crying. "I'm sorry. I couldn't let anyone die. Even if you tell my sister..."

Kuzunoha's body spasmed and she started shaking. Richard grabbed her close. When she stopped, she let out a raspy breath as she collapsed in his arms, her eyes rolling up into her head.

Chapter 45

"Kuzunoha?"

She didn't move. Isashi leapt to them and bent, placing her hand over Kuzunoha's mouth. "She's not dead. I can feel her breath, faintly."

"We need to get her to the healer," Richard said.

Isashi nodded. "I think you're right."

"Can you run and bring him here?"

"There and back? Too long if she's already fading. We'll have to take her to him."

"The sled will take just as long," Richard said.

"Can you carry her?"

He stared at her.

She gave him an exasperated look. "I'm serious. We're a few hours away by the sled, but if you can carry her you could get her there sooner."

"I…Yes. I can. What about...?" He looked around their camp. He couldn't leave everything.

"I'll bring the rest with the sled. Go."

Leave his treasure? He would never... he looked at Kuzunoha. Did he care enough about her to ignore that part of himself? And to trust a woman who hated him to bring his treasure back for him?

He felt a twinge of pain, like a headache, the moment he thought it. Binahi's gravesite. A hero would trust the eledar, a life being more important than the gold.

"I'm going to grab my weapons and a few things. Make sure you keep an eye out. I saw some of your goblinoids over there while we were fighting."

The pressure released. Being a hero didn't mean being stupid.

Isashi didn't seem to notice his pause. "I'll get Hana's map"—Isashi paused and shook herself—"to show you the best way to get there."

Richard grabbed his weapons and was unsurprised to find that his knife and the dead goblin it had been in were gone. He also grabbed one string of coins and slipped it into his bag. If he lost everything else, at least he would still have that. Lastly, he flipped over the monster and pulled out Kuzunoha's sword. It was covered in blood and the silk on the handle was starting to dissolve. He wiped it off with the worst cloth he had and then used it on his other weapons before throwing the cloth away.

"The things blood is acidic. Wipe off anything you want to keep quickly," he told Isashi as he ran back over to Kuzunoha. Was she breathing slower and weaker, or was he just imagining it?

She nodded and rolled out a map. "Take this path here. It has the firmest ground, even if it isn't the smoothest trail. The only place you may run into trouble is this copse of wild woods. The land there is moist and if you're not careful you'll sink in a little with every step. Slow down and you should be fine. You should hit a path here, stone. You'll be able to follow it all the way to the city walls."

"I'll yell for Deckard at the first person I see," he said, memorizing the map.

Isashi looked towards town. "He'll probably be in the market. He usually shops for new herbs and bandages Solesti mornings. If he isn't there, that's where most people will be. They'll help you find him."

"Thanks," he said, standing and setting his stuff to carry. Isashi picked up Kuzunoha and put her in his arms then checked her breath once more. "Richard...try to avoid Himiko if you can. She will not be pleased to find Kuzunoha like this."

Richard nodded. He wasn't afraid of Himiko but could tell that Isashi wanted to cause him less trouble. He would take it. He started running.

Kuzunoha was light and had lost a lot of weight in the five days since their fight with the crab. Even so, by the time Hidan came into view, he was tired and thirsty, his arms and legs thrumming with use. His injury from the crossbow so many weeks ago did more than throb. He thanked his goddess and her avatar of dreams and fate, Firont, that the city gates were already open.

"Stop right there. Hold!" one called from the top of the walls.

"I have the lady, Kuzunoha," he called back, slowing to a walking pace, but not stopping. "She's been hurt. Where is your healer, Deckard?"

Richard heard the guard swear. One of the town men blanched as he got close enough to recognize Kuzunoha. "Healer Deckard? I don't know...his house is on the far side of town, but I don't...I mean..." The man looked around, not sure what to do.

Richard took pity on him, needing the man's aid more than he did intelligence. "Have one of your men find Deckard and bring him here. Lady Kuzunoha needs aid now. He may be at the market already."

The man snapped to attention and ran off, now that he had orders to fill. Sheep on a wall, Richard thought, despairingly. The man would be one of the first to die during an actual threat.

He laid Kuzunoha on the ground and dropped his bag before checking her over. Her breath came in painful gasps and even her lips had lost all color. Within minutes, a small crowd had formed, milling around. Sheep, all of them.

A few moments later, Deckard ran up with a bag over his shoulder. He pushed Richard away and took his place, face pale and drawn. He put a hand to her throat and checked her eyes. "By Janell's yellow ass, what happened to her?"

"We were attacked. She got some sort of infection but we returned as quickly as we could with another monster, some great bear, hunting us. She didn't listen when I told her to hide. She fell unconscious just after the battle."

"Infection? Where?"

"Her left leg. She was climbing a metal ladder and slipped. There was black mold on it. I cleaned it out as best I could..."

Deckard lifted the robe. Kuzunoha didn't react when he pressed on her flesh near the wound. Greenish-yellow pus oozed down her leg. Deckard sniffed it, swearing again.

Suddenly, Kuzunoha started shaking, her body convulsing on the pavement. She gave one last gasp and then fell back, still.

"No," Deckard breathed.

Richard slumped, waiting for her chest to rise again. It didn't. Deckard put his hands on her chest and then her face. He tried to breathe into her, but she didn't move, remaining as still as a corpse.

Richard corrected himself. Not as still as. She was—

"Dead."

Richard couldn't tell who in the crowd had said the word, but he fell back. He wanted to swear at Deckard, the crowd, the guard…somebody, anyone to blame.

"No," Deckard ground out between locked teeth. "She isn't gone yet. I won't let her die."

The change started in Deckard's blue eyes, filling them with sparkling power that leapt to the rest of him. It knotted around his arms in blips of light that looked like golden snake scales. Between his hands, the light became a glowing head, still scaled but stag-like, with gleaming fur floating around its head. The light thundered and bolted into Kuzunoha's chest.

Kuzunoha's eyes opened, glowing the same color as Deckard's, and she parted her lips. Instead of a scream, only a faint whine escaped while her body writhed under his magic. In the space between breaths, the light disappeared from both her eyes and Deckard's. The healer seemed wearier than Richard had ever seen him.

He'd never seen a blessed work before, but he was certain that was what he'd just witnessed. It was rumored that they could reverse death.

A blanket thrown over Kuzunoha startled both of them back into action. It took Richard a moment to recognize Tieni. He shot her a grateful look. Deckard smiled at his lover and put his hand to Kuzunoha's forehead, whispering that she could rest now.

Colour was rising in Kuzunoha cheeks, chasing away the gray. Her wide eyes finally closed and she lay still except for the steady movement of her chest as she breathed easily. Sweat poured off her.

"Blessed," someone in the crowd cried. "He's a blessed."

Deckard flinched, his eyes becoming haunted. Richard knew that feeling. He'd have no peace now that people knew. "Deckard, we should take her to your home so you can look her over."

Deckard jumped as if he'd forgotten Richard were there. Then he sucked in a deep breath. "Yes...you're right."

Richard picked her up, his arms and legs aching, his side burning. Despite that, he couldn't help but notice that Kuzunoha felt even lighter now than she had on his way here. Blood had pooled on the ground under her, filled with floating greenish-yellow pus; it looked like tiny malevolent flowers in the brackish mud. Kuzunoha mumbled but didn't move.

Deckard looked exhausted. "Tieni, thank you for getting the blanket for me. We have to get her back to the house. Kale, get them to clean this up without touching it."

The guard who had run to get Deckard shot up. "Yes, sir… Blessed, Sir."

Richard shook his head. As soon as she was safe within Deckard's home, he was going to find his rooms and sleep for a week.

Chapter 46

Richard looked up at the Tanaka house again. Unbidden, he caught himself thinking the same thing he'd thought the first time he saw this house: he may have gotten himself in over his head. He'd nearly gotten someone killed; Kuzunoha killed. It was true that going had been her choice and one he thought she'd make again given the chance… he sighed. Guilt was heavy, even when it was mostly unwarranted.

According to Isashi, the ones following him didn't know where he was. They would track him down soon enough, but he could take some time to finish healing before he left. Now that he knew Deckard was blessed, he wanted to make sure he was healed before he continued his travels.

He walked up to the door and knocked. A few moments later, the old, sour servant answered the door. She looked as if she hadn't even changed clothes since last he'd seen her. She was just as wide, just as snarly and glared at him just as much.

"Come in. Stand there. I know who you're here for, scoundrel."

She pointed to a spot by the window, notably away from every chair in the room. Her thick voice held dark threats if he moved. Silently, he dared her to carry them out and moved to the blue chair. She glared but he ignored it. She sniffed in distaste and took the stairs to the second floor.

The house was silent and felt less lived-in without Kuzunoha's presence. She hadn't been the heart of the household, but it felt less welcoming without her. He grunted and pushed that thought away. She'd be awake in another week or so and then she could return or not as she chose.

In the mirror on the opposite wall, he saw Miya step into the room, carrying a tray with two glasses and a bottle of wine. He smiled at her and stood up.

"Hello, Miya." His tone was soft with a cadence he used just for her.

Instead of swooning, she jumped back, her eyes wide. One of the glasses shook on the tray and he caught it before it could hit the ground. Even then she didn't seem pleased

"Richard! What are you doing here? Do you know what mistress Himiko will do to you if she finds out you're here?" She looked around as if she expected Himiko to step from around a corner, ready to punish her simply for being in the same room as him.

"Well, you weren't responding to my request for your company."

"I rather thought you and my lady Kuzunoha were…" She flushed and let the sentence hang.

"What me and your lady are is of no concern, just as I told her that what you and I were, was none of hers."

She flushed brighter and looked away. Apparently, she wasn't as willing to share as she had said she was.

He sighed. This was the problem with those who hadn't been brought up in Kristinel's religion. They could never just have a lover. They always wanted more. Richard wasn't going to push where she didn't want him to. Kristinel was also very strict on that and even if his Goddess hadn't been, he was.

"I see how it is," he said, taking a step back. "In that case, I was wondering if we still might work together."

He drew a book from his bag. It was the only one he'd brought, the one with the black cover that Kuzunoha had said was a journal. "Can you read this?" She took it hesitantly, thumbing through it. "I am in need of a translator and I don't know when Kuzun... your lady, may be well enough to."

She shook her head after no more than a glance at the pages. "I am sorry, but I don't read Siangu well and I don't read this dialect, at all. It's more the Tanaka's than mine."

"You don't speak the dialect?" Dialects were local slang, but he'd thought that couldn't affect a written language. He was considering how to answer her when someone answered him with a seething tone.

"Yes. There were seventeen different dialects spoken in Sian Ku when my family left the country. I am certain there are even more now. Ours is one of the lesser used ones from the Kinpo region."

He and Miya spun around. Himiko was at the top of the stairs.

Miya squeaked, banged her tray onto the nearest table, and fled the room. He reached for her as she fled, but put his hand down. She had already said that she wanted nothing more to do with him. To go after her would only make her more uncomfortable.

"So, you're saying you could translate it?" he said to Himiko as she walked down the stairs.

She looked good today, wearing a pair of silk pants, black with a red shirt in the style of Hidan rather than the traditional vest the Siangu wore. Her clothes hugged her in a way Richard would have liked to. Her hair was shorter than he liked on a woman, sitting above her shoulder, but she made the style work. Her beauty was less refined than Kuzunoha's but was no less arresting for that difference. Kuzunoha was the one that would act out, be wild, and make decisions on a whim. Yet her appearance was always immaculate, like the dolls they'd hoped to find on the ship. Her sister was more dependable, but her beauty was untamed.

"Of course, I could. Even Kuzunoha could do it, though it would take longer." She reached the bottom step and frowned. "Speaking of which, I want to talk with you about my sister."

"Oh?" he said, sounding bored. It was a complete affectation. Her frown looked more like a pout, and it made her red-tipped lips even more kissable. He remembered seeing her on the stage that first night. Had he not had a woman already on his arm he would have gone to introduce himself the moment she stepped down. Instead, things had turned out much differently.

"You nearly got her killed," she said. "I could have you locked away if I chose."

Her attractiveness ebbed as he bristled. He held his own guilt for Kuzunoha's injuries. He wouldn't add Himiko's to it. "For what?"

"Kidnapping."

He leaned against the nearest wall as if he couldn't care less. "Your sister was old enough to go. It was her decision. It would be a spurious charge and your sister would protest it every step of the way."

"She can't protest my claim if she's dead," Himiko growled.

Richard froze, wondering what she'd meant by that. He squeezed the book's cover and heard the paper in it crack. With an act of will, he loosened his grip.

"It almost sounds as if you're threatening to make sure she couldn't dispute you." His tone was even and cold.

Himiko's eyes flashed, her hands clenching to fists. Her jaw snapped shut, while her eyes showed a battle to regain her control. She turned away from him, her shoulders shaking. When she did speak, her voice was harsh. "I didn't mean it that way…I want her better. I don't want her to have gotten injured at all." Himiko slammed her hands onto the wooden end table. "Gods damn it, she should have come to me first. It isn't right for her to go off without my consent. I am the head of this family—"

Richard softened. "Have you taken that up with her yet?"

"How could I have? She isn't even awake yet. Richard, understand me. I have to protect her…while she can't or won't." Her voice dropped at the end as if she'd meant to only say it in her mind.

"Deckard says she will wake when it is safe for her to do so," he told her.

At the mention of Deckard, she looked her younger than her twenty-one years and uncertain. "He told me that as well. I…I need to ask. Are the rumors true?"

Richard nodded, envious for a moment. If he had to be a hero, having the power to save those waylaid due to threats from being in his presence would have been more than helpful. Still, he understood why Deckard hadn't advertised. "I haven't seen one before, but yes. He is blessed."

"I wonder if Kuzunoha knew."

"She didn't." Richard would have bet his entire treasure on it.

"Either way, it will cause plenty of trouble for Deckard. If it hasn't started yet, it will soon."

Richard looked away. He'd heard more than a few of the townsfolk speaking in awe of their healer. Only a few had worn less than pleased expressions; then again, it only took a few.

She sighed. "Richard, I don't want you around my family anymore. I'm not going to get what I want, am I?"

"That is entirely between me and your sister. Though I would like to point out that she and I still have a contract. Until that contract is fulfilled, I can't leave."

"I figured as much." She nodded at the book. "What is it you wanted my maid to translate?"

"We found some books written by one of the passengers. Some servant of a noble family. I was hoping to find out what was in it."

She held her hand out for it. Surprised, Richard handed it to her. She opened it with care and read through a few of the pages halfway through the book. Her breath caught. "You found this on the ship?"

"Yes. A passenger on the ship had it in his compartment."

"What else was with it?"

He was intrigued enough to answer. "There was this book, some money and a blade. Why?"

"I'll buy it from you," she said.

"What? The book?"

"Yes. And everything that was in that room."

"Sight unseen?" he said. Not that he had any intention of selling it to her. This change of heart was too dramatic, too obvious, even as a ploy to rush his time here.

"Yes." She closed the book gently, but her fingers continued to caress the leather cover.

"I can sell you the money if you like, but I was just going to divvy that without changing it if Kuzunoha will accept it."

"What type of money was it?"

"Kotsu gold. As for the sword, I cannot sell it. Kuzunoha has already claimed it."

"Kuzunoha would prefer the Sian Ku currency," Himiko muttered. "How can she have claimed the blade already? She's been unconscious."

He rolled his eyes. "Within a candle's span of finding it, she asked to keep it."

Himiko expression looked as if she had suddenly smelled a rotten egg. "The books, then?"

"I will sell you all of the books at a more than fair price, but only if you tell me what you saw that has you so entranced."

She paled but said nothing. Richard shrugged and walked over to her and carefully took his book back. Whatever it was that she had seen, Kuzunoha would find when she finished going through it.

Himiko stared at her empty hands and then at him. She wanted it badly. "If I tell you, will you sell it to me?"

"If you tell me, and provide a translation, I'll sell this one to you for ten sentine."

Books could be sold for quite a bit in a large city, but in a place like this, he would have to sell to her if he didn't want to carry it with him. On the other hand, a book like this could go for nearly a full gold piece in a bigger town. He was willing to take the hit to his profits, just to find out.

"I'll buy it for double that without the translation," she counter-offered.

He doubted the information pertained to more treasure, but if it was, would he be willing to forgo it? "Lady, what do you see in these pages that are so important to you? Fifteen sentine, without a translation, but I want to know why?"

She opened her mouth and he held the book out to her. She hesitantly touched the cover again. He almost missed her whispered response.

"He was family."

Family. Kuzunoha and her sister may have fought like cats in a sack, but to both, family came before all else. He could understand that.

She took the book from his hands and carefully opened it to the page she'd gotten excited about and pointed. "This line here. He's talking about why he was travelling. '*So to Hidan I go, with my master's birth gifts for his grandson, firstborn of the fourteenth generation. Even if Fumimaro has changed his name, he must see the grace and expense his father has put into these gifts. He must see that this rift must be repaired before his father falls to his illness*'." She swallowed hard and closed the book.

"We never met our grandfather, but one of his diaries speaks of the split between him and his father and how he changed his family name, but refused to say from what. This book should tell me."

"Thank you for your honesty," he said, stepping away.

Her voice was still unsteady. She had tears in her eyes. "Thank you. Let me get you your sentine."

He surprised himself. "There is no charge. The book is yours."

She looked at him, startled. “What?”

“I’m not a monster, Himiko, despite what you think. It was your family’s book. Kuzunoha has your ancestral sword; I see no reason why you should not have this book. It may help your ancestors find their rest. We can discuss the sale of the other three books later if you like.”

She shook her head. “I don’t understand you, Richard.”

He smiled and tipped an imaginary hat to her. “Sometimes, I don’t understand myself, Lady. And please, stop by to see your sister when she wakes up.”

He didn’t turn as he left the home, shaking his head. He had clearly been here too long if he was already going soft for pretty faces.

Chapter 47

Kuzunoha fought desperately to wake up. If she could, she would wash away the stench of blood, sweat, gore, and offal that choked her dreams.

"The Seven judge you, Kuzunoha, not yet," she heard Deckard snap at her.

She pushed towards that voice. Nothing could be wrong. Not when he was with her. No, that was wrong. He wasn't with her. She'd been young and stupid and he'd tossed her aside like the trash her father had always said she was.

"Deckard? I'm sorry," she mumbled.

It wasn't enough. She hadn't known how much she would hurt him, how much he could hurt her…

"Fine, wake up if you must. You've never listened to me before. I don't know why I would expect you to do so now." He sounded resigned.

Her mind cleared. Fog dissipated under the sun's light. Her muscles screamed in protest when she tried to raise her head. She heard a whimper, realizing too late that it was hers. She promised herself she'd never show pain in front of him again. It took almost everything she had to force her eyes open.

"Don't try to sit up. You aren't well," he told her.

The room was too bright, with yellow walls and a wooden roof. The light hurt and she squinted. It wasn't her room. Why wasn't she in her room? She couldn't be sick. She never got sick. "Deckard? Where am I?"

He moved away and the light dimmed. She opened her eyes again. Now that it wasn't so bright, she could see that she was in his healing room. Deckard looked lovely, as always, though his forehead was wrinkled and lined with worry.

"What do you remember?" Deckard asked, moving back to her bedside.

She reached up to touch his forehead and he forced her hand back to the bed.

"Answer the question."

The last few days had blurred. She couldn't figure out what had truly happened and what had only happened in her nightmares. She took a deep breath. The room didn't smell of blood. It smelled of cedar and sage. She relaxed, comforted, though she didn't know why.

"I remember leaving town with Richard and…we found the boat. There was some sort of crab-type monster on the ship. I…I think I got hurt."

She moved her hand under the sheets and touched her leg. Hadn't she had stitches running from her ankle to her thigh? Were her memories of Richard, Isashi, and Hana ripping her leg open and squeezing ooze from it her part of the nightmares? Did that mean that her need to kill the thing stalking her had been unreal as well?

Deckard grumbled. "Hurt is an understatement. You nearly died."

"You saved me?" She wasn't sure why it seemed outrageous. That was his job. He would never let his personal feelings come into it. His expression froze her thanks, unspoken.

"Oh yes. Though had you not gone out in the first place, I wouldn't have had to."

"But...we found the treasure." She remembered that. Strings of coins and books. She let out a breath. The sword. Her sword, if she remembered right. It meant that she hadn't failed. She'd done what she'd set out to do.

Deckard's eyes held nothing but contempt. "Oh, yes. You found money. You also found monsters. Apparently, everything outside the city finds you as frustrating as everyone inside. Don't try to deny it. I spoke to Richard. Speaking of which, that man is shady. Had I realized just how much, I would never have allowed you to go with him."

"He's not bad…"

She tried to sit up to defend Richard and pain rocked through her, making everything from her toes to her teeth spark with pain. She fell back to the pillows, her empty stomach warning her that dry heaving would make the sharp pain in the back of her skull much worse.

"How often do I have to tell you, Kuzunoha. Don't move. If you won't stay asleep, the least you can do is refrain from making my job harder. And he isn't bad… but he isn't good either. His morals… He's shady."

He put a cool hand on her forehead and she closed her eyes, drawing in a breath that was miraculously without pain. The morning she'd left, he told her that he expected to see something for all the trouble she'd put into this. How had it all gone wrong? Her eyes started closing and she felt heaviness overtake her. There was a scent in the air, not cedar, but something else.

She forced her eyes open and pushed Deckard away with all her strength. He fell back a step and his expression turned cold. He looked fuzzy. Just like that, she could see it. A dragon, like the ones drawn in her father's books, long and sinuous, golden like flames, coiling around him. The dragon stared at her, meeting her gaze with its own: inhuman and impersonal. The creature moved towards her, retreating when Deckard moved, vanishing into him as he crossed his hands over his chest.

"Deckard, what...?"

His face contorted in rage. "I hid it for years. Now…it's all I do to keep it inside when I'm in the same room as you. Do you know how everyone treats me now? Like I'm some god come to take them to task. And with everyone talking about it, how long will it be until the nobles hear? You know they won't let me live in peace even if the townsfolk would. I'd built myself a life here. Now it's gone."

"You're blessed?"

The look in his eyes was answer enough. Her eyes stung and she turned away.

She'd promised never to hurt him again. It hadn't been enough to break his heart…she'd ruined his life too by coming back as she had. How was she supposed to apologize for that? She opened her mouth but the words didn't come. She'd left town to find gold, and she had, but she'd found something more important than that, too. It hurt to realize that despite his pain, she would do it all over again if she had to.

"I can't apologize, Deckard. Even if I could take it back, I wouldn't. Though, if I'd known, I wouldn't have let them bring me to you."

He growled inarticulately and left the room, slamming it shut on his way out. His front door opened and she heard him snarl again. Richard walked into her room, looking confused.

"I've been told not to tire you out before Deckard… left. How do you feel?"

"I..." She didn't know how she felt. About any of this. "You'll have to excuse me. I only just woke up."

"You managed to anger Deckard that much in just a few minutes?" Richard raised an eyebrow.

"He didn't want me to wake up."

"I'm not surprised. You nearly died."

"I assume it was something bad," she said.

"Oh yes," he confirmed. "Speaking of which, did you know? That he was a blessed? People around town are saying that you must have since I went through so much to bring you to him."

She shook her head, not sure that she could say anything. She thought she'd known him.

Richard continued. "I've tried telling people that you weren't exactly giving orders at the time, but they aren't inclined to listen. It makes the story that much more dramatic, I suppose."

"No, I didn't know. If I had..."

Richard touched her arm. "There was nothing we could have done differently. If you hadn't climbed up there, one or both of us might have died. Besides, there are more pressing things to concern yourself over."

She frowned and he clasped his hands together. The sound reverberated through her skull. He winced in apology.

"Sorry about that. First things first, we made a killing. Four strings with one hundred coins each. The price has gone up, by the way. Something about Sian Ku buying back its old coinage so it can push ones with its current emperor. They were worth nearly a thousand, all told."

She blinked. "A thousand?"

"Not just for you. That's between us. And you said you wanted this."

He pulled out an item from behind his back and put it in her hand.

The sword. He'd replaced the hilt and had it recovered, exchanging the red and black for blue and green. The colours she preferred to the reds and blacks that Himiko and her father had always worn. Richard put it in her hands and she reveled in the silky smoothness under her fingers. Hers.

"You had the hilt fixed?"

He nodded. "And the blade sharpened and oiled as well. Your swordmaster said that we could have gotten nearly three hundred fifty gold for it in a big city. The blade is made of a strong alloy. He's not sure exactly what."

"Ah, thank you. That won't leave me with much, but for this, it was worth it."

He looked confused for a moment, then smiled.

"You are tired, aren't you? We agreed to a different price for the sword. Since we're not actually selling it, I'm good with that." He took out a sheet of paper. "Counting everything, the total came out to one thousand one hundred eighty-five gold and twenty silver pieces. Since you wanted the sword, that will make your cut three hundred twenty-four gold and four silver."

"Three hundred twenty-four gold…" she was rich. Her family's businesses didn't make that much in a quarter, let alone in a week of work. It wouldn't solve everything. But it would give her at half a year or more in a private room at the inn if she needed it. She might be able to pay to have a house built like she'd spoken to Deckard about. She looked at the sword. Did she want that? A house? A family?

Yes. With the right man, she did. Did she want Richard to be that man? She didn't know enough about him, about their relationship or even about what either of them wanted for the future to make that decision yet.

This money would give her time to make some decisions. She let out a breath, her eyes beginning to water. It was more than she could have hoped for.

"Richard… thank you."

He was smiling. "You are more than welcome. Oh, your money changer here doesn't have enough money on hand to change out all the Kotsu coins. Would you be willing to take the lion's share of your amount in Kotsu gold? I can have that brought whenever you'd like."

"The Kotsu is lovely. I'll take my entire share in it if you'd like." Then, she went cold. "Does that mean everything is settled between us?"

Richard smiled. "Well, not quite everything."

He leaned over to kiss her. His mouth was warm and soft, and she wanted him right there, right now. She followed him up when he pulled away and whimpered, falling back into the bed, nauseated. Flashes of pain broke out across her forehead and she thought she might faint.

He touched her. "Kuzunoha?"

"Nothing… it's just... I'm still…" She closed her eyes again. She had one chance before he left and she was going to waste it.

"Kuzunoha, I won't be going anywhere that quickly. You did say something about wanting me on a proper bed, did you not? I have to wait for that, at least."

"I thought you said you'd never settle down," she said, wondering at his change of heart.

She closed her eyes again and the headache wracking her brain subsided. She wished she could sleep. She caught a whiff of blood and squeezed the hilt tighter.

"For you, it wouldn't be settling. However, that is not what I meant. I'm not offering to be anything more than your eager lover. Any woman who wanted more would have to understand that I'm not one to stick to only one."

"Never first in your heart?" she said, confused. She opened her eyes to look at him. That hurt, more than she thought it would.

"Love isn't monogamy," he reminded her. "Love is trust, knowing that you are always in their heart, even when they're with another. And while I don't know if I am in love…I do know that I would like a chance to get to know you better. If you could abide by my goddess's rules."

Could she handle that? She'd lost Deckard because she hadn't realized what she'd had with him. Love without the possibility of making that mistake again sounded nice. "So, the position is open, then?"

He laughed, tousling her hair. She wished she had the energy to bat his hands away. "Yes, you little minx. I am more than eager to have you try."

Leaning down, he kissed her lips, softly and chastely. This time she didn't follow him back up and though she was still tired, no new pain flared in her body.

"I'll let you sleep now, but I'll come again tomorrow," he told her.

She nodded, asleep before he shut her door, the scent of cedar and her sword guarding her dreams.

Chapter 48

A week later, Kuzunoha still hurt. Her bruises were healing, but even Deckard's incredible powers couldn't fix her immediately or completely. Sometimes she felt a strange itch running down her entire body, as though the mold that had nearly killed her was still running through her. Deckard said that she would probably feel like that until she had completely recovered.

Despite their arguments, she was glad that Deckard still allowed her to stay. She couldn't stay awake for longer than an hour or two at a time and when she was awake, she was in pain. He may have hated his powers, but for Kuzunoha they were a comfort, easing her even more than the scent of cedar incense, used exclusively in her room since he'd noted her preference.

A knock at Deckard's front door got her attention. There was a chance that it was more company for her. Richard had been coming to visit her every day and even Isashi had stopped by to check in on her. Getting company was the only thing that pushed away the boredom. No matter how tired she was, she tried hard to be alert for them.

Deckard came to her door and peeked his head in. "Are you awake?"

She was sure that he didn't need to ask, making the question more of a confirmation of whether she felt up for company. If she didn't, he would send away the visitor until the next time. It also meant his dragons would come out, trying to heal her even faster. She could see his anger whenever they did, so no matter how she felt, she tried to smile and accept the company.

Fortunately, today she didn't need to lie. "Yes. Who's here?"

She tried to push herself into a sitting position. Deckard gestured her company forward and moved to the bed to help her. It was embarrassing, but she accepted the aid. It hurt less when he moved her than when she tried to do it herself.

Deckard's arms were around her and he was lifting her gently to the raised side of her pillows when her sister walked into the room. She tensed and Deckard did as well.

"Kuzunoha," Himiko crossed her arms. "Isashi wasn't lying, your skin is the same shade of yellow as your eyes."

Richard had mentioned that she'd looked pale, but Isashi had been more truthful and told her that her skin looked a jaundiced yellow, more so than even the golden tone of her normal skin tone could explain away. Combine that with unwashed, stringy hair and she probably looked like death warmed over.

Was that what she was? Deckard had said that she hadn't died. Not really. That her heart may have stopped, but her spirit hadn't left yet. It had given him the few seconds he'd needed to purge enough of the poison running through her body to keep her alive.

"She is healing, Himiko. In a few more days, the infection should be completely gone and her colour will improve then." Deckard raised a finger.

"She'll still be sick for quite a while though. A few weeks more, at least. Now both of you, play nice. I'll be in the kitchen if you need me."

Both sisters watched him leave. When the door was closed, Kuzunoha turned to Himiko. "Why are you here?"

Himiko frowned at her. "We need to talk. You left Hidan against my wishes."

"I'm an adult. It was my choice."

"You didn't come to see me for your majority." Her sister's gaze was intense.

"I didn't need to."

"It's tradition, not prerogative, Kuzunoha. The eldest family member alive takes you through the ceremony. They give you the title of adult."

"It's a stupid tradition when there are only two of us, Himiko. Especially since we don't know if you're actually older than I am." That was a bad argument. It was the same one they'd been having for over a month now.

Himiko looked down her nose at Kuzunoha. "According to every law in Hidan, I am the eldest. Even if I wasn't and we knew it, I am the heir, making me the matriarch of our family."

"A matriarch has to take care of her family while letting them grow up. You would have kept me at home, a child." Kuzunoha told her.

Himiko's mouth set in a line. "I would have because I am supposed to take care of you. You know how dangerous it is outside the village. The only reason you survived was due to Deckard's abilities. If we'd been waiting on your common sense to kick in, you'd be dead already."

"That is not how it—"

"Kuzunoha, every creature within a furlong came to attack you. Stupidity must taste better to monsters."

They had seen a lot more out there then they'd planned on. It had been bad luck, finding the cockatrice. Isashi had said that the bear-thing had been looking for humans to slaughter and anyone out would have been targeted. But the crab creature would have been inevitable since it had lived on the ship. Three dangerous monsters, but she had met them all and helped vanquish them. If only it hadn't been at such a heavy cost.

"Because I was there, Richard survived," Kuzunoha said in her own defense If Richard had gone without her, he would have run into the same creatures and been less equipped to take them on.

"And Hana is dead," Himiko pointed out. "You traded one of Hidan's best hunters lives for a stranger's."

Kuzunoha bared her teeth. "I did not trade anyone's life, Himiko. I was out there and we had a monster hunting us. If it hadn't been me out there then it would have been someone else. Maybe a farm hand or one of the other hunters."

"If you hadn't been out there then it would have left us alone."

"There's no proof of that. It was looking for something to attack."

"Which is all beside the point. You should have been at home!"

"No, Himiko. I shouldn't have been. I don't have a future there."

"Then where do you think you'll go if not home? What do you think you'll do?"

"I don't know. But I do know that I must find my own path. I can't follow yours anymore."

Himiko's eyes were narrowed.

"You will come home as soon as Deckard says you are well enough. We will discuss then what is to be done with you."

Her sister wasn't listening to her. She never did. Kuzunoha didn't think she ever would.

"Yes," Kuzunoha agreed. "I will come home. I have items there that I will want to take with me when I leave."

"Leave? And go where?" Malice poured off her sister in waves.

"I don't know yet. But I know I won't find it at home."

"You'll be back within a week," Himiko predicted. "Or when your money runs out."

"I don't plan on remaining jobless."

Her heart beat faster… All she had ever known, ever been taught was obedience and respect to her ancestors and her family. She had tried so hard to be the perfect daughter to them. For the first time in her life, she admitted to herself that she had failed.

Himiko's expression was stone; her posture, stiff and unmoving. "Not here. Nothing has changed in Hidan to make that happen."

"You're right," Kuzunoha said. Her stomach fell out. If she let that stop her, it would. "But I don't plan on staying in Hidan for the rest of my life."

Being nameless was worse than being the black sheep of the family. If that was what she had to do to find her path, then she would. She would search for a different way to seek her ancestor's approval.

Himiko walked stiffly to the bed. "May I see the sword?"

Kuzunoha hesitantly stroked it. It was hers, through right more than through blood. This was her life; her choice. Would Himiko understand that, by handing her the blade, she was putting herself one last time in her sister's hands?

She handed the blade to Himiko, unwilling to breathe.

Her sister touched the new banding around the hilt and unsheathed the blade. Though she was staring at it, Kuzunoha didn't think that her sister seeing it, not really. Himiko grimaced, sheathing it before she handed it back.

"If there were any justice in this world, it would be in the family's vault, not in the hands of one of its bastards." Kuzunoha shivered as her sister continued. "But you are a Tanaka bastard. I grant you your majority."

Kuzunoha swallowed. "I didn't need your approval, but… thank you."

Himiko eyes widened in outrage and she stalked out of the room. Deckard came in as the front door slammed.

“Kuzunoha, are you alright?” Deckard said.

“I’m fine, Deckard. Just fine.” She grabbed her sword hilt, ignoring the ache that burned through her muscles. She didn’t know what the future would bring. But she knew that she would have the strength to face whatever challenges this path threw her way.

Acknowledgements

I have always said that *'we'* are smarter than *'I'* will ever be. The first person to thank in my *we* is my husband. He's learned way more about story and plot and other writerly things than he ever wanted to and helps me figure things out when I'm stuck. More importantly, he still puts up with me spoiling movies we're watching when I blurt out things that destroy immersion. I promise, I'm just trying to figure out the structure and story they're playing with.

The next thanks go out to my family and friends. They have supported me and pushed me to publish even though the idea terrified me (and still does if I stop and think about it). They probably thought I would never get this out since I've been saying "it's nearly ready" for so long. In particular, I'd like to thank Breeana Putroff and Calvin Jim for being patient and answering all of the questions I sent their way. I couldn't have done it without you.

My final acknowledgement here goes to my editor, Clare Marshall. She's tough on my words, but in doing so, she helps me to become a better writer. Without her, this novel would not have been the best it could be.

About the Author

Brandy Ackerley is a creator of worlds with words. While primarily a fantasy writer of novel-length fiction, she also enjoys writing short stories and novelettes in a variety of genres. Hunter's Gambit is her first published novel. She adores anime, tabletop RPG's and finding out more about mythology and culture worldwide. Brandy lives in Calgary, Alberta with her husband, both of whom are owned by their cat.

If you'd like to read more from Brandy Ackerley, she has a dark short story, Fated, available everywhere ebooks are sold. Also, keep an eye out on Facebook or her blog, Musing About the Words, for more information on when Kitsune-Ken, book II, tentatively titled Lord's Curse will be available.

CPSIA information can be obtained
at www.ICGtesting.com
Printed in the USA
LVHW092031010819
626090LV00003B/8/P

9 781999 516529